Rock Spider

THE NEW HAMPSHIRE MYSTERIES
(BOOK TWO)

MIRA GIBSON

PROLOGUE

WARPED ASPHALT, marred with shallow potholes and buckled with frost heaves—the scars of harsh winters and brief sweltering summers—unfolded under a shock of headlights like a story Gertrude could recite. It didn't matter that a ghostly shroud of fog had crept in from the lake, clouding the road, or that the windshield was blurred with condensation. Gertrude knew every bump, its relationship to each bend, dip, and swell. Poor suspension on her old Audi had her anticipating the jolts and jerks. Her body was programmed to tense, to lean into the wheel, her chin to its clammy plastic, her hands in a white-knuckle grip.

A sharp bend in the road, hugging the south side of the lake, prompted her to downshift—a fast flick of the wrist, a precise stomp on the clutch, forcing the pedal to the sweet spot just shy of the carpet so the gears wouldn't grind. Then her hand was back on the steering wheel.

She wondered where summer went in the dead of night, why it chose to cripple the day then vanish as soon as the sun set, leaving the long dark hours chilly and dank, not typical of New Hampshire. Strange weather patterns were playing nightly practical jokes.

In the passenger seat sat Doris—cardigan wrapped tight but not buttoned, chipped polish over demurely rounded nails, eyes like a sun-startled raccoon. She used the hem of her sleeve to wipe away the condensation for Gertrude, but her effort only smeared the glass badly, leaving streaks too distracting to properly see through.

"Let's roll the windows down," she suggested, monotone, still rattled from their long, strange evening.

Doris was testing the vent, holding her hand above it and working the dial, as if it wasn't already blasting. Giving that up, she cranked her window down then turned and strained to reach into the backseat. Gertrude figured that Doris speaking to her at all was progress, so she cracked her window down by a good six inches.

As a result, damp air gusted through the car and kicked up a nest of junk at Doris' feet. She stomped on it, making an honest effort to brace down candy wrappers and old magazines, fluttering receipts and case files too hopeless to update, a graveyard of Gertrude's career and her sister's teenage deposits—every time they got home: *Could you take your trash?* A million excuses: *Next time? I'm tired. I have to get the grocery bag. I have to pee. It's not all mine.*

"Did it help?" She spoke up over the torrent, examining the windshield by sweeping her fingers over the glass and creating another smear Gertrude would have to strain to see through.

Doris' button-nose breath caused a feather of condensation to creep its way into her sightlines.

"We'll be home in five minutes," she said, implying there was no need to improve things.

"Are we going to talk about it when we get home?"

She was perched at the edge of her seat, forearm draped across the dash, as she rocked and bounced with the grain of the road like she was riding a wild animal.

A quick glimpse at Doris and Gertrude realized her younger sister wasn't wearing her seatbelt. Rather it flapped against the car door, the buckle rattling, metal against plastic.

"Put your seatbelt on."

"Why? We're at the bridge."

The glow of twin wrought-iron street lamps at the far end of the bridge cast just enough light to make Doris correct. They had reached the end of Messer Street, having navigated the jarring twists and hairpin turns which gave way to the smooth but rickety wooden bridge that would arch into Opechee Street, its fresh pavement, wind-kissed Maples, and the distinct scent of cut-grass mingling with the marshy breath of the lake where they lived.

Gertrude didn't nag her about her seatbelt as she hit the gas, accelerating across, popping the clutch and upshifting in rapid succession, old childhood fears that the bridge would give way and kill them, rumbling in the back of her mind as loudly as the wooden slats under her Audi's tires.

POW.

Gertrude was startled the second she heard it. The sound of a gunshot cut through her foggy thoughts—the fragments and images of their bizarrely rehearsed and even more bizarrely executed confrontation with their parents—had been distracting her, the entire drive home.

Doris didn't have to confirm it had been a firearm. They had lived in Laconia their whole lives, born and raised there, and the sounds of gunshots were unmistakable, though they usually heard the pops and bangs echoing in the afternoon and early evening; never at two in the morning, never a solitary shot, and never coming from the woods where homes were hidden away with mysterious characters inside—agoraphobic and tucked away until death, neighbors they didn't know existed until medics rolled them out in body bags.

Agitated by the disturbance and even more so by Doris' incessant guessing—*Hunters? No, not at this time of year. Maybe a car backfiring? Didn't sound like it. The Millers or Winona's dad, or that strange Chinese family that moved in last winter?*—all verbal blows both given and received during their volatile screaming match with Mom and Dad, now gone from her sister's skittering mind. Gertrude realized she had hit the gas, her nerves rolling around inside her, and the curve through Opechee would be a trick to control.

"Put your seat belt on now!" Not liking the fatal rawness of her tone, she repeated herself anyway, as the tires shrieked against the grain of the bend and the fog thickened. The road was disappearing—*It's a story and you know every word, rely on it, no need to see.* But Gertrude was wrestling down a sickening knot in her gut, a hot rush of bad tingles, an old reaction to weapons firing as though her body didn't know what age she was, didn't know she wasn't a child, didn't know the gun hadn't gone off in the next room, didn't know her sister was alive even though Doris was screaming at her from the passenger seat to slow down.

Her voice, shrill and desperate, cut through the noise of Gertrude's time warp, "Look out!"

Billows of fog slipped over the windshield then a figure appeared, a shadowy and unreal person in the middle of the road, the night telling a lie too complicated for her to make sense of. Were her eyes tricking her brain? White-hot panic disconnected her mind from her hands, and from her foot. Two seconds after she slammed on the brakes, cutting the wheel hard, vehicle careening sideways, she understood her reflexes had been fast but unfocused.

The next thing she knew, glass was shattering against her cheek—excruciating ringing in her ear, the Audi on its side, flying and scraping over asphalt. She was crushed—Doris: limbs loose, stretching, tucking, straining, the worst cry Gertrude had ever heard coming out of her like death clawing its way up her throat. And then she didn't feel Doris crushing her and then she did, and then she didn't, slamming and disappearing, over and over. When she finally understood the vehicle was rolling, the crashing splash that followed had her once again bogged in wooly confusion.

Ice water enveloped her. There was no air. Her skull was throbbing. Black water stung her eyes. She gasped then choked, coughing the lake water out of her mouth, as she frantically felt for her seatbelt, feeling, feeling, following the nylon strap down to where it met with a hard square of plastic. From the corner of her eye, Doris' chestnut brown hair waved at her. Her hand was lolling freely, loose and relaxed through the murk. Doris' body had a terrible ease to it, no fight, no tension as though her sister was no longer there.

Stiffly, muscling in slow motion, her hands quavering in the cold, fingers numbing, breath held and lungs burning, Gertrude pressed the seat belt release, yanking the nylon and when it gave, she drifted to the backseat, away from Doris. Strategies wouldn't formulate, her thoughts as devouring and jagged as the freezing depths of the lake. She pushed off hard, swimming downward, her hands tangling in Doris' cardigan, searching for something real to grasp, her arms, her waist, anything to push her through the window and free them.

She thought she saw the nasty gleam of eyes studying her beyond the windshield, swamp creatures lurking, but those were only white starbursts of pain flaring behind her eyes, complicating her effort.

Releasing Doris' sweater, she saw with her hands. Hard *cloth*? It was the ceiling of the car. *Plastic*? It was the door, yes a handle, higher a lip, the windowsill. She kicked through the car window.

The nose of the Audi was at the bottom of the lake. Looking up she gleaned ripples in the distance. The surface. She kicked downward, hauling herself deeper, and grasped Doris' arm through the open window.

Trusting that she had her sister well enough was a prayer at best, but her lungs were aching and her head was throbbing. Drowning was all too real.

She started kicking. Her legs felt like twigs ready to snap. Her hands were too numb to tell if she was still gripping Doris, but the weight of her sister told her that Gertrude had her. Half fighting, half surrendering to natural buoyancy, as lazy and gradual as it was, she rose to the surface and broke through with an exhilarated gasp, but got a mouth full of water, splashed up by her flailing arm. She coughed it out and got her bearings.

Stillness all around her—shimmering pinprick stars in timeless constellations, the lake as still as meditation, Balsam Firs and White Pines stately at the water's edge, the bloom of lights from the bridge in the distance, serenely oblivious to their dire straits. They were too far beyond civilization to be rescued.

Keeping her arm hooked firmly around her sister's chest and their heads above water—Gertrude paddling, Doris' limp and drifting, gurgles and splashes and monsters below—she came to the muddy shore.

Check for breathing, give mouth-to-mouth, pump her chest five times, check for breathing, give mouth-to-mouth, pump her chest five times.

But though Gertrude believed she was doing this, she had already collapsed unconscious beside her sister.

CHAPTER ONE

GERTRUDE COULDN'T place how long she had been sitting there. Even more daunting was trying to fathom how many days—*Weeks? Had it been months?*—she had been cooped up in this room where white tile floors, white walls, and a white hospital bed were holding her prisoner. She pressed the remote and her bed jutted upright, rigid in its mechanical ascent. The ward smelled like rubbing alcohol and death, if death was a musty, semi-organic, brain-stinging odor, the undercurrent of which seemed oddly familiar.

The staff's kindness was nightmarish. Their waning smiles beneath dead eyes reminded her of the old swing-set behind her parents house, frayed ropes that could snap, bolts too eroded to hold. *Better not trust it*, she had warned Doris, exercising teenage wisdom to keep her four-year old sister from bottoming out in the grass.

Orderlies provided her meals—white bread with luncheon meat and wilted lettuce inside, an apple too dimpled and waxy to eat, sweaty jello cups, milk and water and juice. They were always served on a plastic tray and placed beside a little white paper cup just like the ones her dentist used to hand her after fluoride treatments, *rinse your mouth and spit.* Then he would blot her lip with her own bib, the same gesture the orderlies used.

The little cups at the hospital didn't contain water, however, but rather pills that rattled around inside.

For your headaches, they had explained, for her anxiety, the tinnitus that would burst deep inside her ear when she felt too cold. Several times she had asked her nurse to raise the temperature in her room. It was freezing, the AC set too high, it chilled the surgical staples that arched in a haphazard semi-circle around her left ear, industrial stitches meant to hold her skull together, the side of her head that had cracked hard against glass when her Audi slammed on its side before tumbling into the lake. She argued that if it were warmer in here, then the staples wouldn't be cold and her headaches wouldn't be as bad. She wouldn't need the pills, see? The staples caused the headaches, which caused the anxiety, which caused the sleeplessness.

When that argument had failed, she explained how the pills bathed her in a vacant, zombie-like reticence, which prevented her from recovering, from excelling at retraining her cognition. Her physical therapy was suffering. Her explanation had been perfectly reasonable, but in response the morning nurse, Jefferson, had only feigned a smile that wavered badly. *I hear you*, her taut smile had said, but the nurse had been otherwise occupied, angrily stripping the bed sheets, grimacing at their smell, eyeing the bathroom then shuffling over, the bundled sheets under her arm.

She had turned on the shower faucet, ran the sink, tested the temperature, admonishing Gertrude with each action. *The sheets wouldn't smell if only she would shower,* had been what her pinched mouth told her.

The Evening Nurse, Salisbury, was no better, except rather than dismiss Gertrude and make passive-aggressive overtures, she had given Gertrude her undivided attention, leaning in close, eyes twitching, as she examined her like an insect, skeptical of a rotting piece of fruit.

As Gertrude listened to the melodic laughter of children too far beyond her window to spy, and as she studied the heat-heavy landscape outside, the Maples, their leaves green and lustrous, peat moss blanketing their trunks, and the blue sky, its popcorn clouds that looked solid enough to touch, Gertrude absentmindedly grazed her fingertips over the staples that arched around her ear like a train track, the flesh beneath still bubbling up and tender, the hair stubbly along the jagged track. The evidence of how long she had been here, she thought. A month's growth maybe, was that how long she had been here? A month?

Traumatic brain injury...

She knew that was what was wrong with her. The Medical Director, Dr. Hagstaff had been reminding her of the diagnosis every afternoon after her daily neuropsychological evaluations, and eventually the information had stuck.

She understood.

Her memory was jumbled up because of the accident. Her brain now organized events out of order. It fused memories together that had occurred years apart. Many life events she had probably cherished were now gone—birthdays and vacations, her first kiss, her graduation day. Things she felt certain had happened to her had in fact happened to Doris and vice versa, and realizing this was jarring. She thought nightmares were real and was convinced real things she had survived had only been nightmares.

She felt eyes on her, but didn't tear her gaze from the scenery outside to glance over her shoulder at the door, its narrow window where she sensed someone was watching her. She had been fidgeting with the frayed hem of her sleeves, poking her fingers through the loose chunky stitches, playing with the yarn, studying the gradient fade from purple to rosy brown when her gaze wasn't resting on the trees outside.

He was making her antsy. People always did. This wasn't a symptom stemming from the accident. She had always been this way, deeply anxious unless she was completely alone for miles and miles.

There came a faint knock at the door so she touched eyes with Dr. Hagstaff through the window then settled her gaze on his tuft of wispy brown hair, as he entered. He pushed his horned rim glasses up his nose and the angle magnified his dry blinking eyes. His skin was ruddy, though his face was boyish otherwise—down sloping nose and a taut, curling mouth. The mess of papers which were somehow always in his arms plus his worn out corduroy pants and rumpled button-down shirt gave him the appearance of a professor who had just lost tenure by way of scandal.

A sharp, nasality in his tone undermined his sincerity, as he asked, "How's it going today?"

He would have probably had a promising future after medical school, but social awkwardness must have narrowed his options. At least that was the story Gertrude had come up with. He was certainly old enough to have been rejected from a number of opportunities before winding up here, failing his way into the Lakes Region Brain Injury Rehabilitation Center.

When she met his question with a blank stare, he said, "Are the headaches easing up?"

"These windshields don't open," she complained in a far away voice that scared her. She must have slipped beyond her body again, detached from her mouth and tongue.

Placing his hand on the windowsill, Dr. Hagstaff winced a smile. "Windshields?" Then, encouragingly, he began mouthing the word as if prompting a toddler. "Wiiiinnndddoo-"

"Window," she said gloomily, embarrassment a hot flare in her chest. "That's what I said. My head is cold."

"It's very hot out, mid-nineties."

"I want real air."

Shifting her gaze out the window, she saw the children she had heard. They were waddling like a row of ducklings behind a woman wearing a floppy brimmed hat, long matronly skirt, and clogs. Gertrude wracked her brain for the name of the Montessori school nearby, but found only dark pockets in the hollows of her memory. They couldn't be in school, she realized, wasn't it July? Must be day care.

"Gertrude?"

"Yeah?" she asked, snapping back to the conversation,

"I wanted to hear about your headaches," he reminded her.

"I wouldn't have headaches if I got fresh air. Hot is fine," she explained, forming a cohesive sentence, her point finally meshing perfectly with her words.

"How about your anxiety?" Dr. Hagstaff seated himself on the bare windowsill, because, she gathered, the window was what interested her most.

The crinkling noises he was making with his papers felt like cuts on her eardrums.

"My anxiety wouldn't be so bad if I got fresh air," she said, then quickly revised her response. "Once I'm home I'll be fine. I'm sure of it."

He smiled, but it seemed brittle. "Well, I have some good news, Gertrude-"

Impatiently, she corrected him. "Gerty. Call me Gerty. I've told you that."

"Right." He took a moment to ride the swell of his incidental faux pas. "Well, the good news is that your motor skills are up to snuff, you've made wonderful progress in therapy, and the committee believes it's time to discharge you, or rather enroll you in our outpatient program."

"Really?"

Her heart felt strange, achy. What was that? Sadness? Happiness? It felt like doom.

When Dr. Hagstaff handed her a tissue, she realized she was crying.

"I have concerns, of course," he went on. "But at this point you're ready for a routine. We're confident you'll be able to acclimate to your old schedule and go to work, though I've spoken with your supervisor and advised that you should work less than forty hours a week. We would like to see you back here, as I mentioned, a few times a week."

His words turned garbled, consonants too round to discern, vowels too guttural to place like an ancient language she had once known in a past life, déjà vu washing through her as she tried to understand him, frustration building that she couldn't.

To anchor herself, she focused on a comforting thought: *Doris would help her.* No sooner than the notion had taken hold, her heart sank, pulling her into a cold daze.

Doris was dead.

"Did I go to the funeral?"

He startled, which told her she had interrupted him.

Gently, he reminded her. "Gerty, no." Taking her hand, which caused hers to go strangely limp, he explained, "You were in surgery. You don't remember that we've talked about this?"

Defenses rising, anger was strength, she said, "Of course I remember." She couldn't mask how jarred she felt, twofold in fact, she hadn't gone to her sister's funeral and she hadn't remembered asking. "What about my parents?" She hoped she hadn't already asked about them too.

Dr. Hagstaff frowned, releasing her hand in favor of pushing his glasses up his nose. "We notified them of your condition."

His statement immediately called to mind a string of memories. Though the details were fuzzy, the feeling behind them, the heartsick free-fall into oddly blissful resignation, came surging.

When she had been able to walk again, Gertrude had ventured down a darkened corridor to the hospital pay phone. After many rings, her mom had answered. She hadn't sounded concerned or alarmed or glad to hear Gertrude's voice, and soon her father wrestled the phone out of Marsha's grasp and hung up, leaving Gertrude confused. Attempts to contact them further had gone worse, her mother's curtly sighing into the receiver followed by a click, dial tone blaring in Gertrude's ear, as she stood in the hall, stunned. A certified letter from her parents had come next, which her therapist had read out loud: *It was you who said we had broken the family, it was you who blamed us, but now who's broken the family?*

In the whitewashed labyrinth of her memory, Gertrude knew her parents resented her, hated her even, for the accident, for surviving when her sister hadn't.

Outside, a child cackled.

Offering her a *buck up, kiddo* smile, Dr. Hagstaff jabbed her shoulder then said, "Let's not forget about your biggest fan," as if it were a consolation for her parents hating her. "Wendy Weisman?"

"Wendy," she said, trailing off.

"Got a bit of a promotion, I understand," he said with a nervous chuckle. "She's eager to have you back. But again, I told her it will have to be a very light caseload. Gerty, I wholeheartedly believe this will be the best thing for you. It's time. Once you immerse yourself in the day-to-day, your brain will adapt to organizing short-term information, which by the way, has been your strength. Your long-term memories are like a deck of cards strewn across a floor. It'll take time to find and organize them. But living day to day, forming memories as you go, will be easy, like being dealt a winning hand. You see?"

Gertrude suddenly remembered how useless his metaphors were.

"You think I'm fit to work?"

His expression loosened, causing him to look a bit ill, but he quickly launched into another forced smile.

"You may have some personality challenges. Word fumbles, of course, but..."

When he didn't finish his thought, she realized her savings had probably run out. The copay on her insurance was a joke and being discharged was likely the only option at this point.

"When do you want me out?"

More nervous chuckling ensued, as he assured her. "We don't want you *out*." He wasn't convincing. "Your paperwork will be in order tomorrow morning." He brightened as though he had forgotten a fun tidbit. "We have a very nice lady coming by this afternoon from Wonderful Wigs, a lovely charity who has donated-" off her narrowing gaze that must have looked appalled, he was quick with, "they're very tasteful, all kinds of styles and colors-"

"I don't want a wig."

Gertrude palmed the shaven side of her head, trying to visualize what she must look like—the buzz cut, the ghastly staples holding her skull together. The damaged side of her head was a stark contrast to the other side, where scraggly chocolate brown hair fell to her shoulder.

"A hat perhaps?"

Grumbling, she said, "I'll figure something out."

"The wig people also have makeup," he said, determined to sell her on the service. "Really neat brands. Movie star makeup."

Clearly, he had no idea what he was talking about, but the bruising on her face probably hadn't faded well enough or he wouldn't be suggesting makeup. She hadn't dared to look in a mirror since the accident and when she had felt her face to see if her cheekbone was still swollen, the bump seemed to have subsided, and she had figured she looked her usual self. But maybe that had been wishful thinking. At thirty, even a superficial scratch took time to heal and would often leave a lingering brown mark on her skin.

"Well," he announced as though concluding their time together, "you have options." Rising from the windowsill, he shuffled his papers, though as far as she could tell they were nothing more than a theatrical prop, and then he tucked them under his arm. "I asked Wendy to swing by at about three." Checking his wristwatch, directing the rest of his point there, he added, "I thought it would be helpful if she went over a few things with you before you return to work. Remember, anxiety is fear of the unknown, so the more you know, the less anxious you'll feel."

"How much time do I have?"

"Oh, just enough to get dressed properly. She'll meet you in the visitors center."

Properly? She thought she had, but giving her outfit the quick once-over—flip flops cracked at the soles, worn out sweats she had ripped at the knees, and her sweater, plagued with ratty pills—she had to admit she looked like a homeless person.

She went into the bathroom, which was a sterile cube lined with geriatric bars meant to assist patients in the tasks of getting on and off the toilet, in and out of the shower. She had hung a towel over the medicine cabinet so she would never have to see her reflection in the mirror, and had taped an index card on the wall. The card detailed a checklist written in her sloppy hand—*pick up toothbrush, put toothpaste on brush, brush teeth, rinse with tap water, floss, comb hair.*

With a child's lack of precision she accomplished all of these steps, but as she started for the hallway she suddenly got a nagging feeling like she was forgetting something. After a moment spent attempting to conjure it up, pausing then pacing around her room, she decided it was nothing, and made her way into the visitors center.

Wendy Weisman was a sigh-happy optimist, who looked as if she belonged mixing egg whites into cake batter in front of a live studio audience and not tethered to a dreary office desk, tucked deep in the annals of the Division for Children Youth & Families, typing Risk Assessment reports into her PC like a tireless squirrel.

Thrusting all two hundred pounds of herself up from a table when their eyes met, Wendy grunted to her feet and paid little mind to the chair she had knocked over then beamed her gummy smile at Gertrude, whose hands felt suddenly cold, though she ventured over using shallow steps.

She felt more comfortable watching Wendy's long skirt swish and sway with centrifugal force than holding her old friend's gaze. She hated anyone seeing her like this and as awkwardness took hold, Gertrude glanced around the room.

At one of the tables, a young blond girl—her arm as bent as a dying bird, her head wrapped in a turban that screamed cancer—was hopping a black checker piece over a line of red ones, while her mother smiled sadly as if this victory outweighed the siege on her daughter's health. Near the snack bar, a kid with an athlete's stature angrily snatched a carton of chocolate milk from a bookish, older man's hand, insisting, "On!" though it caused him to wobble on his crutches. Gertrude knew he had meant to say, *No.* She had felt the same way more times than she could count, the fury at being babied, the frustration of knowing it was necessary. The room smelled like mayonnaise, which she had come to associate with dashed hopes and outrage.

Arms open wide, ever eager to embrace her, Wendy sang, "Gerty!" inviting her into the pillow of her bosom. "Bring it in for the real thing! Make it count!"

The look on Wendy's face, the sinking smile and darkening eyes that indicated she was pained to see Gertrude bald and bruised, made Gertrude realize that whoever she used to be, the snappy personality, the witty retorts, the gung-ho flare for each moment, was no longer a part of her. Whoever that person had been never made it out of the lake that night, whoever she used to be had drowned in Winnipesaukee with her sister.

But when her cheek met with Wendy's chest as she accepted the hug and did what she could to reciprocate, Gertrude remembered she was still alive. She would go on. She had to.

Wendy relaxed her grip then placed her hot hands on Gertrude's shoulders, urging her back, as she angled her almond-brown eyes on her like an estranged grandparent marveling at her granddaughter's growth. "Let me get a good look at you. You look pale," she observed then screwed her face up with further examination. "Maybe not more than the last time I saw you. Are you eating enough?"

"Hard to tell." Gertrude wondered when she would release her.

"Sit, sit," she said jubilantly then uttered, "Oh." A guttural sigh came next, straining in her effort to pick up her chair that had toppled over. More wheezes escaped her as she got situated, face jiggling under skin as fine as rice paper. By contrast, Gertrude slid easily into a plastic chair across from her and stole a glimpse out the window to drink in the sight of rolling hills, the lake, white-capped mountains a whisper in the distance, the library's steeple jetting up from treetops, New England at its most picturesque. "Dr. Hagstaff says you'll be back with us tomorrow?"

Taken aback, though she tried not to seem so, Gertrude feigned a smile, but it must have looked worrisome, because Wendy dove in with, "Oh, no, no," reading Gertrude's apprehension all the while. "No, I've talked to Harry. You had way too many cases before. No, we've agreed what's best is to ease you back into the swing of things. Only one case for the rest of the summer."

Gertrude tried to mentally grasp for the date, but nothing came up. She wasn't even confident she knew what month it was. Her mind kept offering *October*, which couldn't be right. *August?* Then a worse obstacle, more than remembering what day it was, suddenly dawned on her.

"I don't have a car."

Wendy blinked and after a beat leaned in, cheeks lifting into a bewildered smile. "Gerty, we got you a car, remember? I told you as much on the phone."

Abashed chuckling followed. "It's a real clunker, but it'll do the trick."

"Right," she said, scrambling for an inkling of recollection.

"I dropped the keys off with the clerk out in the lobby," she said matter-of-factly, in the same friendly tone she generally reserved for staff meetings. She seemed to get a bit lost in brushing crumbs off the tabletop. "What happened that night?"

It was such a radical change of topic that she froze.

"You're such a careful driver."

There wasn't a hint of blame in her voice, only desperation to understand the unfathomable. The subtle anguish in Wendy's eyes mirrored the dark abyss that Gertrude had found herself falling into every night since she had arrived at the Lakes Region Brain Injury Rehabilitation Center, and the painful truth was that she didn't know. She couldn't remember a thing from that night, not even the smallest and most insignificant detail. Nothing.

"Well," said Wendy after letting out a resolute sigh, "the case Harry set aside for you is sure to get you back into the swing of things. A truly fascinating family." But her face contorted with a hint of bemused horror, which contradicted her statement. "Nothing too rocky," she added as if to convince herself. "I've got your back."

CHAPTER TWO

MONDAY MORNING, she dressed slowly and deliberately, one leg at a time into a pair of mint condition sweatpants that Nurse Jefferson assured her were tight and dark enough to pass for professional, one foot after another into a pair of black Keds, the laces of which took an indescribable amount of concentration to tie as Jefferson kept repeating *fine for the office*, though her tone revealed an edge of disdain for the shoes. Gertrude pulled a black sweater over her head, the nurse warning all the while that it would have her *sweaty as a pig*. Lastly, Gertrude gathered her belongings: the ratty purple sweater she had been living in day and night, her cracked flip flops with soles worn thin to the point of erosion at the heel, her comb and toothbrush, the toothpaste was theirs, the toilet paper was also, but she had put it in her box with the rest. She had signed the last pages of several forms that were so thick they could've been a graduate school thesis. And finally Dr. Hagstaff walked her out to the car that Wendy had dropped off for her the day before.

A clunker to say the least, the car looked older than Gertrude.

"She said you liked old Audis," he commented in an upbeat manner, juggling her box and his mess of papers, as they stared at the vehicle. Optimism faltering, he offered a few more comments then gave up, which sent her heart plummeting.

"Any car is better than none," she said, studying the Audi as though it was behind glass in a museum.

An Audi 80, muted blue, rusty halos eroding its wheel wells, and cloudy headlights flanking a dusty black grill, the car looked as though it had died in the early 70s, had a proper burial, and was somehow resurrected.

Peering through the passenger side window, he noted, "Manual," then swung his big face around to her and his thick glasses reflected sunlight into her eyes. "You okay with a stick shift?"

"I'll be fine."

As he stepped back, another glare bounced off the window, blinding her, and when she turned away from it she noticed her reflection in the glass. She didn't like what she saw.

"But have you driven a stick shift before?"

His concern was palpable and she had the urge to ask what it would matter. She'd had to relearn even the most basic tasks in the hospital. She would relearn how to drive. There was no way around it.

Dr. Hagstaff opened the passenger side door, which made an unhealthy snapping noise. Gasping, papers fluttering out of his hand, he caught it and laughed at his overreaction. The door was hanging on by a thread, but hadn't fallen off like he had expected. "Just a quirk," he explained once he understood its personality. He set her box inside then closed the door gingerly and backed away as though any sudden movement would have the vehicle collapsing like a house of cards. When it didn't, he let out a carefully measured breath.

Companionably, though their dynamic was anything but, he tossed the keys to her and they plunked against her chest and clanked to the gravel. It was then she realized he had meant for her to catch them. He looked perturbed.

She made slow work of picking up the keys, her left hip stiffening upon the forward bend, and when she straightened, she flicked away the small pieces of gravel that had come with the keys then rounded the driver's side door. Hagstaff followed, motioning to get the door for her, which revealed another quirk. The handle stuck a bit, clicking stubbornly, and it took him a few tries to get the inner latch to dislodge correctly. Then he reached for her, an awkward paternal urge to perhaps hug or assure her with a physical gesture.

Palm up to ward him off and a curt flick of her chin, asserting *that's not necessary*, she settled behind the wheel, then grazed her fingertips over the dash, the stick-shift, glancing around but too overwhelmed to get her bearings. When it occurred to her this was the grandfather of her faithful Audi, she felt slightly more at ease.

"You call me anytime, Gerty."

"Yes," she said, unfocused, sensing more than seeing him back away. Then he quickly shuffled near and gave the door a firm shove, helping her close it.

"Good luck out there," he shouted far too loudly. The glass wasn't that thick.

She shot him a brief smile then focused on the interior of the car, hoping he would go away.

Dangling from the rearview mirror was a rosary made of brown, weathered beads and a wooden cross she felt no connection to. Beside it hung a laminated prayer card of Saint Anthony. The saint's sorrowful, downcast eyes stared vacantly at her. His Mona Lisa smile and tipped halo that was too close to his bald head to look like anything other than a strange toupee, gave her a weird feeling. *St. Anthony, full of grace, please find me a parking space.* Her sister's singsong voice laced with impatience ran around Gertrude's head until she took her eyes off the saint. Wendy had probably meant well, but Gertrude wondered if she realized St. Anthony was the patron saint of lost causes.

She turned the key, but the Audi only whined and sputtered out. She felt lost without her index cards. She should make a few, detailing how to start the car. Angling her gaze down, she stared at the excess of pedals then remembered one of them was the clutch. She pressed it down with her left foot, remembered the left foot wasn't used for driving, pressed with the right, realized in fact the left foot *was* used for driving, shifted her feet and pressed again, feeling the prick she had forgotten something critical all the while.

Jefferson was right about her sweater. She was sweating like a pig.

Again, she turned the key and the engine started growling, but without her foot on the brake she rolled backwards, gasped and slammed on the brake, forgetting the clutch. The car stalled out.

Dr. Hagstaff caught her eye through the windshield from where he was standing at the entrance doors. He gave her two encouraging thumbs up that made her cringe.

Lost causes, indeed…

She tried again—clutch, brake, turn the key. It took some muscle and an air of intuition to find Reverse—*middle and right and down with pressure*. She gassed it, swinging around and leveling a shrub, then slammed on the brakes, every inch of her flush with a slick layer of sweat.

Determined, she found first gear and began creeping cautiously towards the parking lot exit, then shifted into second. She felt like she was cruising, though the car hadn't broken five miles per hour. When she turned onto the road, settling into third gear like a wisdom-weary grandmother too timid to drive the speed limit, she decided this was as fast as she needed to go.

The Division of Children Youth & Families branch of Child Protective Services, which had been her home away from home for the past ten years, was located in the Laconia District Office on Beacon Street West. And as Gertrude pulled into a parking spot, her Audi bucking and jolting until she slammed on the brakes just shy of the concrete parking stop block, she felt the swell of how much she had missed this place.

The brick two-story building, spanning an industrial three hundred yard block, sat at the foot of the Opechee Bay Reservoir, a canal that connected Lake Winnipesaukee with its smaller twin, Winnisquam. As she climbed out of her car, she could smell the sun-kissed water rushing through the canal.

The DCYF awning, blue and faded, flapped in the summer breeze, as she approached, feeling beside herself with self-consciousness. Her sweater was too thin; her pants too baggy in the rear, and the knees were puffed out loosely like bubble-wrap a child had popped. She had forgotten to shave her legs. Her calves felt prickly when she stroked one against the other, hesitating just shy of the glass door.

"Gerty!" Breathless in her excitement, Wendy hustled down the sidewalk, brown unkempt hair swaying and slacks swishing between her thighs. A blazer, black and petite and wrapped in plastic, dangled from her finger. "Got a little something here for you," she explained as she smacked the plastic up and off of it, wriggling the garment free of its hanger. "Goodwill, but I had it dry cleaned. Go on."

Quizzically, Gertrude slid her left arm into the right sleeve and Wendy immediately took over, grabbing the blazer by the collar and holding it open for her like a knowing chambermaid, as Gertrude slipped it on.

"There," she said, stepping back and giving Gertrude the once over. A satisfied smile spread across her face that her contribution had made all the difference in the world. "What about this?" She produced a scrap of black felt that Gertrude realized was a French beret when Wendy punched her fist inside it a few times, giving it shape before positioning it off-kilter onto Gertrude half-shaved head. Without so much as a stab at a French accent, she said, "Très chic."

Gertrude could only assume she looked like a vagabond that had stumbled out of a costume shop, and it made her hope that the world wouldn't notice, she did not belong.

"Come, come," said Wendy, cradling Gertrude with her soft, yet massive arm and ushering her to the door. "The gang is going to be thrilled!"

The corridor, dimly lit and stuffy, brought back a wealth of memories. How many times had Gertrude ducked out of her cubicle, stealing away to make a personal call to Doris in this dismal hallway with its smudged placards? She used to marvel at these faded awards—Public Elected Official of the Year NAWS Chapter Laconia District 2009, Social Worker of the Year NAWS Chapter Harold McNeil Representing Laconia District 2011, Susan Alby LSW Recognized for Lifetime Achievement in Social Work 2013—as Doris had blared complaints in her ear, *Can you please come home and make a little something to eat, I'm starving,* and Gertrude's put-out grumbling, *If you had bothered to take your driving test you could go to the store yourself,* and Doris' ever-rising impatience, *You know I don't retain information, I would never pass!*

God, how she missed those arguments, hunching in the hallway out of sight, seething into her cell phone, studying the framed photos of the District staff, their glazed over smiles, and remembering the days certain photos had been taken. *I didn't see a flash*, and Harry's barked order, *hold still, he doesn't use a flash*, and Gertrude standing in the back, her hair in a high ponytail, her eyes bright, her smile huge, too ecstatic to be there. Each subsequent year, Gertrude had felt less and less proud to be amongst the winners, having gradually lost sight of the good she was doing, because she hadn't been, had she? Families remained broken. Drugs kept surfacing. Children died.

She studied a photo from last year, paying Wendy no mind, not that her friend was pressuring her to get on with it. Rather, Wendy was watching over her like a patient parent in no rush to tear her child away from a fenced-in goat at a petting zoo.

In the photo, Gertrude wasn't even looking into the lens. She wore no smile, not even a plastic one for show. She seemed exhausted and dazed, but thinking back she couldn't remember why. Had something bad happened? Had she failed in some way? And then she remembered. It hadn't been work related. She had been distraught over something Doris' had told her. What was it? Gertrude searched her memory, but it wasn't there, only the fact that Doris had shown up at her house in the dead of night—*I can't live with them, I can't!*

But why couldn't she?

"Sorry," she apologized, turning to Wendy.

"I know it's challenging… you being here. We'll take it one step at a time. You're doing beautifully."

They continued down the corridor, voices billowing through the walls, phones blaring louder and louder, fingers tapping across keyboards, a sense of displaced urgency filling the air, as they neared the office suite where the glass door read DCYF in black letters across the top.

Wendy opened the door for her and Gertrude stepped in, but then paused, the frenetic energy of the place stopping her until Wendy proceeded, guiding her through the cubicles.

The conference room was in the back. She knew that much, but was momentarily confused when Wendy rounded into one of the cubicles. Then she read the nameplate that was tacked to the cubicle's cork surface: Gertrude Inman, LSW- Child Protective Service Worker IV.

Delicately working her fingertips over the cluttered stacks of ad hoc case files and strewn pens then opening drawer after drawer, rummaging as non-intrusively as she could, Wendy found a notebook. "Ah, and this should do," she said, pinching a pen from a ceramic mug that said *Life's a Beach* but had an image of a screaming toddler. "Ready?" She asked, handing the items to Gertrude, who would've never thought to prepare herself so practically for the meeting.

Her smile was a nervous frown when Wendy told her *it would be a breeze*. "Come, come," she sang cheerfully to compensate for Gertrude's ineptitude. And off they went.

A few glassy-eyed social workers glanced up from their reports as Gertrude passed by, but for the most part the employees dredged through their morning undisturbed by her return.

The Director of Children's Services, Harold McNeil, a man with a bushy head of salt-and-pepper hair and a staunch New England coldness to rival even the waspiest WASP was angrily dunking a tea bag into a mug of creamy, hot water, as though he had been seated at the conference table far too long by the time they stepped inside.

Next to him and smearing away the stray drips from Harold's mug that had soiled her notebook was Amanda Seevey, one of the Child / Family Advocates who had started last May. She was young, dim-witted, and last Gertrude could recall, had been the subject of a secret pool. The department had been placing bets on whether Amanda would quit or get fired, and on what date precisely. It wasn't so much her lackluster boredom that had inspired Malcolm Jarvis to start the pool, but rather her Louis Vuitton bag or more specifically the teacup Maltipoo inside it. *My dog helps the kids open up*, she had argued, nose nuzzling the little thing as it yapped its head off, terrified to be out of the bag. *No one objected in North Conway*. And why would they have? The yuppie town in northern New Hampshire had been built on frivolities.

"Gertrude, you're looking well," said Harold, glancing up from his tea, which must have been disagreeable. He couldn't stop bobbing the bag and grimacing.

"Good to be back, Harry. Nice to see you, Amanda."

"I didn't realize you were gone," Amanda told Gertrude through a big innocent smile.

Wendy scowled, but Amanda was oblivious or else very good at pretending to be. Gertrude was so anxious to seem professional, pleasant, unquestionably in her right mind however, that the insult had barely registered.

"Let's get you settled right here." Wendy was holding one of the weathered conference chairs out for her, having scraped it across the floor since its plastic wheels had given up years ago. The seat teetered precariously, as Gertrude sat.

With no further pretense, Harry launched into the case at hand. "Amanda's been overseeing the King family. Visits, interviews, walk-throughs, the like," he began, as Gertrude pressed her pen hard against her notepad, unsure of what to write down. "They're on Winnipesaukee," he mentioned as an aside. "First visit was three years ago, a total of five visits. Then again two years ago, then every six months, only a few visits at a time after each incident. We treaded carefully, no deep probing." Harry was skimming down a report that looked almost as old as Amanda. "You get the point. Family of four, Zhana, pronounced with a soft J then Ah-na," he explained, struggling then moving on, "and Charles married in the early nineties, a fall from grace sort of thing. Two kids, Roberta and Maude." Harry seemed bored already so he glanced at Amanda as though that would be enough for her to pick up where he was leaving off. It wasn't. "Amanda, why don't you get Gertrude up to speed."

"Oh," she smiled, lost in thought, perhaps reminiscing about something amusing that had happened to her last night. "Just read the file. It's all there. Oh, except that I haven't been there in months. What?" she sang, another big innocent smile forming across her pug-face. "I'm super busy and they're fine. They've been totally fine."

"Except that Maude killed herself," said Wendy, seething. Her cheeks had flushed and she was glaring at Amanda so hard that Gertrude thought she had stopped breathing.

"Right," she said easily, "but like I said, I hadn't been there."

Wendy widened her eyes at Harry as if to say, *she seriously doesn't get that negligence caused this tragedy?*

Harry cleared his throat and excused Amanda from the meeting. Amanda sighed, *finally!* and scooped up her tote-encased Maltipoo and left the conference room without closing the door.

To ward off the rant Wendy clearly had locked and loaded, Harry pressed his palm on the table. "We're understaffed."

"Maude was a ten year old girl," Wendy explained when Gertrude slid the case file in front of her, daunted at its volume. "The father owns many firearms." Rolling her eyes, she added, "Live free or die," mocking the state motto that hadn't been in good taste since the Civil War. "As you can imagine, we're concerned for Roberta's safety. She's seventeen and still a minor by all accounts."

"We're only focused on the environment," added Harry. "Motives for why Maude would take her own life. Could be neglect. Why was she left unsupervised with an arsenal of weapons?"

"Reckless endangerment," Gertrude supplied.

"Which we're pushing for," Wendy assured her. "But surprise, surprise, the father, Charlie, is a cop's cop."

"He's a police officer?"

"Retired," Harry clarified. "But buddies with the police. When he said he keeps his guns locked up, detectives didn't ask a follow up question. Believed him outright. Let's not wade into law enforcement's job," he stated, straightening in his chair. "We only need you to investigate the home and see if it's safe for Roberta to continue living there."

"Grief counseling," suggested Wendy with a sense of gravity so strong that for a moment Gertrude felt the suggestion had been meant for her.

Leafing through the dense report, she asked, "When did Maude take her own life?"

"A good month back," Wendy said, angling the report so she could find the exact date. "July second, it looks like."

She already knew the answer thanks to Amanda, but Gertrude asked anyway. "No one from social services stopped in since then?"

To Harry, Wendy demanded, "You need to fire that girl. She's deplorable."

"Has law enforcement removed the guns from the home?" Gertrude was shy about meeting Harry's gaze. He had one of those faces that made her cower if she looked directly at him for too long. But this time, instead of flaring up like a missile, his expression drew long and weary.

Wendy answered on his behalf. "The police have not been cooperating with us."

"Why? Because the dad is a retired coin?"

When they both stared at her quizzically, she blurted out, "Copper." A stuttering swell of frustration came next. "Retired *Cop*. Is that the reason?"

Gently and with great purpose, Wendy placed her soft hand over Gertrude's. "Get Roberta out of there. It's not safe and you need to prove it."

CHAPTER THREE

GERTRUDE EASED her old Audi onto the grassy shoulder, feet pressing intently on both clutch and brake as she jiggled the stick in Neutral and came to a stop. Through a sparse line of Maples, she spied a row of dormer windows tucked under a pitch of wooden shingles that were so weathered they had turned gray and buckled. The Kings' home was a New England Cottage far past its prime.

To get her bearings on who she would need to be—the person she had been before the accident—she reviewed her car's interior or rather the tips and instructions she had left for herself. A yellow index card with black pen marks embedded deep into the paper told her to *SMILE!* from where it rested over the center of the steering wheel. It had fallen off several times during the drive and as a result had a smudged shoe print—gray and dusty—across its right side. Another index card taped to the inside of the driver's side door said, *the truth is in-between the statements*. And six others spanned the cracked leather dash, though it had been too dusty for the tape to stick properly. Realizing that, she had stopped at Benjamin's Crafts and bought crazy glue to adhere the cards—*everyone has secrets*, and *kids want to be heard*, and *trust is built*, and *show them you're safe*. The last two, which had flapped when the windows were down, were glued to the glove box door and completely illegible, though she recalled their content: *disclosure works*, and, *connect.*

She realized the car was still idling, so she turned the key off and slipped it into the front pocket of her blazer.

The case file, thick and tattered, was resting on the passenger side seat where Doris should've been. And it might have been that association that prevented her from thumbing through it once more to re-familiarize herself with the three years of spotty visits as documented by Amanda Seevey.

Gingerly and partially anticipating the door would break off, she popped the handle and climbed out, bringing along only the notebook and pen that Wendy had collected for her earlier that day.

Getting the door to latch closed required a number of attempts, the last of which included her throwing her hip into it, but that strategy had sent her beret sliding down the buzzed side of her head on impact. She straightened her hat, starting for the gravel driveway while peering at the house through the trees, their thick trunks and billowy tops, and the lake beyond.

Once she cleared the Maples and the house came into full view, she observed that its wood-shingle siding was nearly identical to the sloped roof—weathered gray and buckling like a snake in the throes of shedding its skin. The gables were chipped. The chimney bricks looked white and powdery as though something sickly was trapped inside and trying to escape.

Doris would have a lot to say about this house. For a ragtag teen approaching her senior year of high school, it had been clear she would go into architectural design had she graduated, had she lived, had Gertrude been able to save her.

Doris would have personified the house in an instant—*an old man too grumpy to let anyone care for him,* or *a cripple in denial,* or maybe simply *Sisyphus.* And then she would point out the architectural details, their flaws, offer a prescription, much in the way Gertrude assessed her cases, houses no different than people, objects and subjects deteriorating unless you helped them.

So lost in the comparison was Gertrude that she didn't notice the planters wrapping the house, their bushes and weeds sprouting tall yet dying, until she veered up the muddy walkway and saw the hunched, squatting form—a red dress amongst vegetation—of what appeared to be a teenage girl, her knees splayed like a frog, her elbows deep in soil, her head lost between the bushes that shook and rustled, as she dug.

Gertrude spent a painstaking moment trying to figure out how to introduce herself. Should she state her name, announce her credentials, clear her throat loudly? The longer she hesitated, the worse the interruption seemed, and it didn't help that the girl was oblivious.

Deciding to take a few notes first, she did what she could to scratch the pen noisily against the pad:

August 5th, Monday. Roberta (presumably) unsupervised. Unusual choice of dress. Abnormal. Sandy blond hair. No vehicles at the home.

It slipped her attention that she had crept towards the girl, but the trance of noting her behavior helped Gertrude forget herself, and as a result, a straightforward question tumbled out.

"Roberta King?"

The girl froze then, turning her head, peered at her through a tangle of weeds like a mangy jungle cat wise to the threat of man. Gertrude was struck by her angular eyes, their indeterminate color, the narrow bridge of her nose, her cheekbones high and sharp like those of starved, third-world children that Sally Struthers would advocate for on Gertrude's TV—snow and static, as Gertrude made out a personal check, never more prone to the hardships of others than she was at two in the morning, the weight of her profound aloneness stinging her heart.

Reasoning it might not be her best move to reveal she was with Child Protective Services, and remembering her own advice, Gertrude smiled, but her lip quirked, causing her mouth to waver badly until she was sure she looked either scared or ill.

"I'm with the DCYF." Her neck felt hot, her throat dry and raspy, so to compensate she tried to hold her notebook with an authoritative air. "You're Roberta King, aren't you? This is 118 Moulton Street?"

The girl straightened up from the planters. Her forearms were stained dark with soil. Examining her hands she said, "Yeah," then smacked the dirt off and picked under her fingernails, paying no mind to the red dress hanging off her bony shoulders even after one strap slipped off.

Roberta was voluptuous and emaciated in the same breath—her arms like reeds, her legs two stilts, her breast bone ribbed, and though the dress held her loosely (low on the neckline, high on the thigh) Gertrude could see her lower abdomen sunk in with a concave curve. She had a Vaudevillian quality, as though she were a ghost from the 1920s, displaced from her troupe, lost and downtrodden that her act wouldn't translate in this modern time—*I can tap dance and sing, step right up, it only costs a quarter!*

Clearing her throat and tucking her notebook under her armpit, she explained, "I'll be your new case worker-"

"I don't need a case worker."

"I'm afraid you might."

"You *should* be afraid."

Her tone was high and melodic like a child's, and not at all as chilling as her words.

"I'm not," Gertrude said, feigning a thin smile.

Bluntly, the girl asked, "What happened to your face?"

Gertrude hadn't looked at her face and she didn't dare imagine, though her hand had drifted up to her cheek, which she was now touching.

"It's all brown and discolored."

"Your last case worker didn't have a chance to stop in for quite a few months. I'm wondering if we could get acquainted, get things up to speed."

Her mouth was a wry smirk that Gertrude couldn't read. But soon the girl turned, walking through the dying grass to the steps leading up to the porch. As she ascended, Gertrude realized Roberta was barefoot, which made her choice of dress all the stranger.

She joined Roberta on the porch, but hung back between the wooden pillars, noting their peeling gray paint and imagining them white, decades prior.

Sinewy and precise in her movements, Roberta perched on the wooden railing, setting her left foot on an aluminum barrel, which Gertrude soon recognized was a keg of beer.

"Are your parents home?"

She frowned, giving her head a quick shake, stringy unwashed hair brushing her shoulders for a beat.

"You're seventeen and have one more year of high school, correct?" She realized she sounded obvious, stating facts for confirmation. Whatever conversational grace she used to have, though she could envision it, was beyond her abilities. "Are you excited for your senior year?"

When Roberta snorted a disgusted laugh, which Gertrude hoped was her response to the question and not to Gertrude herself, she wondered if Roberta had known Doris. They were the same age and, according to the case file, attended the same school, Laconia High. Had they been friends? Rivals? Total strangers? Had they gone to the same parties or vied for the same boys?

"Why don't you tell me a little about school? Your favorite subjects? Are you looking at any colleges?"

"Can't you ask me the standard home visit questions and get this over with?"

Roberta's candor made Gertrude realize that she hadn't even properly introduced herself and she stammered, hunting through her pockets for her identification.

"I didn't mention my name. I'm Gertrude Inman. Here," she said, as she used long strides to reach her, handing over a laminated ID card.

Surprisingly, the girl took great interest reading it over and eyeing it front and back before passing it back. Gertrude clipped it to her lapel and didn't make a fuss that it hung crookedly.

"To be honest," she started, taking a shy step or two backwards, "I'm not sure how standard this visit is supposed to be. I would like to ask to come into the house, but if your parents aren't here, I'm not going to. Your last social worker did you and your family a great disservice, even though I shouldn't say that." Gertrude adjusted her beret and noticed her scalp was sweaty. "I would really like to talk to you about the tragedy, but I'm not supposed to begin with those questions." She stopped herself from going down that road, took a carefully measured breath, smoothing her hands down the front of her blazer and catching Roberta's expression as it widened—slight smirk, eyebrows rising, chin tipping downward. "So why don't we spend a little time getting to know one another."

"And then you'll go?"

"I will, but I'll be back. I need to speak with your parents, see the home, due diligence and all that."

She started scraping her teeth against the inside of her cheek as though she was considering.

"Have you received any counseling after Maude took her own life?"

Roberta's eyes turned flat and Gertrude made a mental note not to press that barrier again unless the girl indicated she was ready to go there.

"I'm a counselor, for what it's worth. I live across town on Lake Opechee. We have the lake in common." Her stream of consciousness approach had her cringing, but she told herself blathering on was better than standing silently. "I like swimming in the summertime. Do you swim?" She didn't leave much of a beat for an answer. "I'm not too good at skiing, though I've been a few times. I think the Old Man in the Mountain looks weird. Have you seen it?" Not a breath of a pause for Roberta to voice her opinion. "They should've let him collapse into the ravine. I think deer are rats that kill people."

"What?" Roberta started laughing, shallow and breathy trills of utter confusion in response to her ramblings.

As Gertrude launched into a tirade about how Wendy's donations to her outfit made her feel—*like a French performance artist*, and *a sore thumb* (though she mistakenly used the word *toe*) and *a mistake to end all mistakes*—it dawned on her that she was treating this home visit as if it were a therapy session with Dr. Hagstaff. And yet, as wildly unprofessional if not glaringly insane as she sounded—looking at herself from the outside in, mortified and begging herself to stop talking—Roberta seemed to be enjoying the show. Perhaps alarmed, her dark eyes frozen round and locked on Gertrude, her brow knit with a hint of sarcasm, smirking in a way that told Gertrude that the girl was both apprehensive and amused, Roberta took on a relaxed attitude.

Sliding off the railing, bare feet soundlessly touching down, she asked, "Why are you dressed like that?"

"I've been asking myself the same question."

As Roberta grabbed the keg's nodule and started pumping, her mirror image reflecting in the window beside her, Gertrude studied her then the window, which was rippling as if it had been hand blown—an ethereal girl and her grotesque twin.

When Roberta took the nozzle and aimed it inside a red, plastic party cup, filling it with beer, she casually said, "This is left over from the party."

It didn't occur to Gertrude to stop her. She didn't connect that a seventeen year old shouldn't drink alcohol, or that drinking at all at ten in the morning was a sign of poor judgment if not alcoholism. In fact, nothing about Roberta gulping it down in one long haul struck her as even vaguely inappropriate.

Unnerved perhaps that her social worker hadn't intervened, Roberta said, "Let me see your ID again."

Yanking it free from her lapel, her beret jostled off her head, which sent a hot rush of embarrassment across her skin. Sheepishly, she covered her bald side with her hand, extending her ID to Roberta, then quickly snatched up her hat, returning it to her head. She didn't have to look at her to know Roberta had seen the light dusting of hair that curved around the left side of her head, and had seen the track of surgical staples that would forever remain there, and understanding this made meeting her gaze a challenge.

"Don't worry about it," she said softly. "At least your scars are on the outside." She pumped the keg and refilled her cup. "When they're on the inside, nobody knows."

"You have scars on the inside?"

The wooden porch slats beneath her feet creaked when she shifted her weight, waiting for Roberta to respond.

"I wish they were scars," she said, getting a bit lost in the foamy crust of her beer. "More like cuts that never heal."

Treading carefully, keeping her tone gentle, and feeling the electric thrill of glimpsing into a young, wounded mind, she asked, "What caused the cuts?"

Roberta padded to the adjacent railing and glanced down at the plants hugging the perimeter of the house. "They're all dying. No one waters them. The soil has been raped of nutrients. They're yellow and brittle." She looked at Gertrude. "They're supposed to have flowers. I've never seen flowers here." After a brief moment sucking down her beer, she added, "It's this place, the house. It's killing them.

It was too abstract for Gertrude to grasp the thin thread connecting the girl's emotional wounds to dying plants, metaphors and symbolism too dynamic for her shattered brain.

"Maude's lucky," she concluded, her voice hollow, as she tore up a dehydrated branch. "She escaped."

"What happened to her?"

Roberta's gaze went soft, her pupils dilating, as though she was receding into herself and mentally floating away. *Dissociating*, Gertrude thought, but jotting it down, the impulse of which had a strong hold on her, would risk the girl clamming up.

"She shot herself in the head," she said easily, snapping her eyes to Gertrude, instantly present in her surroundings.

"Did you see her do this?"

Roberta clipped Gertrude's ID to her dress where the spaghetti strap fanned out into the bodice.

"Where were you?" she pressed.

"Around."

"Where were your parents?"

She frowned, eyes going soft again. "Don't know."

"How did Maude get access to a firearm?"

Throwing her head back, she let out a groaning laugh. When she leveled her gaze again, the light cut her eyes just so, revealing their color—muddy green, like a bog overwrought with peat and sphagnum.

"They're everywhere," she said once she had sobered up from her guffaw.

Nearing her though cautiously, she asked, "Are they still everywhere?"

"I don't even see them anymore." It didn't answer the question directly. "They blend in with the knickknacks and ceramics. They're camouflaged against the couch cushions and tabletops."

"So there are weapons in the house?"

Airily, she twirled, saying, "I wouldn't know. I can't see them."

"Roberta, it's very important that you live in a safe environment. I'm here to make that determination. Now, I need a straight answer from you. Are there, or are there not, guns in the house? Your father was ordered by the court to remove all firearms and I need you to tell me if he's done that."

After a beat of vacantly staring once she had turned around, Roberta swiftly rounded down the porch steps, beer sloshing from her plastic cup. "I want to ask you something," she said without glancing over her shoulder to see whether Gertrude was following.

She was, however, tracking after the girl, eyes traveling the length of her spine, something reptilian in the bones, like a dinosaur where her red dress scooped low towards the small of her back. Sickly, yet youthful like the plants.

When she passed the back of the house—its rough wooden edge demented from too many harsh winters—Roberta told her to wait there, as she disappeared under a long set of stairs that connected the backdoor to a ground-level deck. Beyond it was ten feet of sand then the lake's shore where a dock jutted out into the water.

Though the sky was clear, the lake's surface appeared choppy. Across the water, the landscape of Balsam firs interspersed with Maples looked like dabs of paint tapped carelessly over canvas. A warm breeze rolled in off the water. Deceivingly calm, she thought, not at all the killer it truly was. She wasn't sure if she would ever set foot in that lake again, but had a feeling that she wouldn't.

Roberta jogged out from under the stairs and didn't stop for Gertrude, who saw she had a photograph in her hand as soon as she slowed her pace to an out-of-breath trot around the front of the house.

By the time Gertrude trekked back, Roberta was pouring another cup of beer.

"I should've mentioned earlier," said Gertrude, huffing up the porch steps, "you're too young to drink."

The girl ignored her statement, nearing her with the photo she had retrieved. It looked damp and soil-stained, as Roberta stood directly beside her so they both could look.

A family portrait.

"I buried it," she said, perhaps making an excuse for its decomposed appearance. "They don't let me have anything to myself unless I hide it in the dirt."

Gertrude noted the photo was recent. Roberta looked the same except for her clothing, which in the photo amounted to a cropped halter-top and cut-off jeans. Standing to the left of her younger sister, Maude, her mouth was straight and her eyes looked dead. Gertrude hadn't seen Maude. The case file hadn't included a photo of the girl, who, according to this portrait, appeared sour. Her eyes were dark and wide-set under a prominent brow, but she had Roberta's nose. What struck Gertrude most distinctly about Maude, as captured in the split-second snap of the camera, was that she seemed furious—her mouth a taut snub, her arms folded, leaning away from her mother as though Zhana were diseased.

She could feel Roberta's eyes on her.

"Do we look happy?"

Her tone didn't sound confrontational, but rather curious as if she were obsessed with fragments she couldn't make sense of.

"No." After glancing at Zhana in the photo—her broad smile, bright eyes, *the camera loves me!* And then Charlie, a stiff man with a cop's rigidity, who seemed to have no awareness of the family he was posing with, she asked, "Can I hang onto this?"

"If I can hang onto this," she said, flicking the DCYF ID clipped to her dress.

"What? No." Then, off Roberta's darkening mood, "I'm sorry, but you can't keep my ID."

Roberta's expression hardened, as she walked backwards to the keg. She didn't take her glare off Gertrude as she found the spigot and lifted the already high hem of her dress, exposing the crotch of her black underwear.

Observing her do such a thing was jarring. But when Roberta placed the spigot flush between her legs and pinched the lever, causing beer to flow like piss, a dark chill washed over Gertrude.

The girl was acting deranged.

Feeling strangely in danger, Gertrude hurried down the steps, forgetting the photo in her hand and abandoning her ID. She crossed the gravel driveway briskly, all the while sensing Roberta's burning glare on the back of her head.

When she got in her car, she couldn't start it fast enough. But though she twisted the key in the ignition, the engine wouldn't turn.

CHAPTER FOUR

IT SOUNDED LIKE the mechanical chortle of some old grouch on his deathbed defying the inevitable, as she held the key into the On position for the fifth time. She flipped it off to let the car rest then twisted again only to hear the same horrid grinding, which she quickly put an end to. She didn't want to flood the engine, a notion that gave her hope only because it was a glimpse into all she used to know about cars. But when she wracked her brain for the specifics, what might be causing this problem, the particular cause at the root of this symptom, there was nothing there, only a murky sense that in her prior life she would've been able to fix it.

She cranked her window down for a little fresh air and avoided the steering wheel's advice, *SMILE!* then popped the hood.

Before climbing out of the car to investigate, she glanced through the Maples. Roberta didn't appear to be in the yard or on the porch, which made the prospect of standing in plain sight less demoralizing.

The girl's outlandish behavior, the phallic nature of her demonstration, caused remote agitation in Gertrude, like a fever, low-grade, but apt to climb. Certainly, Roberta was peculiar and shouldn't be left unsupervised. But the question remained whether or not her parents were fit guardians worthy of caring for her. Ten minutes with the girl hadn't even scratched the surface. She needed to get inside that house.

Maybe being stranded would work out in her favor. If Zhana or Charlie King returned, she could speak with them, get a feel for their aptitude in being responsible caregivers, and perhaps confirm the home had been properly stripped of firearms. Then she could develop a steady routine of bi-monthly home visits, focus on her rehabilitation, and not risk a minor's welfare because her mind was a jumbled version of its former state.

As she opened the driver's side door, the King family portrait, which was resting on the passenger seat, caught her eye. Or, more accurately, Maude's pose did. What had the little girl been so angry about that day? Why couldn't she bear to stand directly in front of her father? What compelled her to lean away from her mother and scowl? The slant of her posture in the photo conveyed a story. Something must have happened, but Gertrude didn't have the foggiest idea as to what.

When she lifted the hood and secured it with the hood prop, the tangled mess of wires and grease-slick metal gadgets she saw were intimidating she didn't dare breathe, much less attempt to locate the problem. She wasn't sure what she hoped to accomplish staring down at it like a mechanic. Any experience she might have had only qualified her for the most basic fixes—an oil change every four months, a jump start when a cold winter's morning had stunned the battery, the occasional tire replacement after discovering a nail in its rubber—and of those she remembered only obscure fragments and nothing to join them into a cohesive picture that would shed light on her current predicament.

It crossed her mind to call Dr. Hagstaff, but doing so would make virtually no sense in terms of solving her car problem. She thought of Wendy next, who would do her even less good. Then of course her sister popped into her brain. Doris hadn't known much about cars, but these days no matter what Gertrude was in the midst of, she thought of her sister—*Green jello again, I hope I can walk soon... Did Doris like green jello?* And, *Well, I peed all by myself- is this a funny accomplishment or a sad one?* Even in Roberta's company, she had thought of Doris, *Remember the time it took us all night to pick the lock on Mom's liquor cabinet? You watched me chug vodka at six in the morning when we finally busted it loose and we laughed, remember? Was that a good memory or a bad one?*

Having forgotten where she had put her cell phone, Gertrude scanned her index cards, optimistic she might have jotted down a note to herself about where she had stashed her phone. She was in the throes of crawling into the backseat when she heard an engine growling from down the road. Spying through the rear windshield, which was so dusty the road and trees beyond it were smears of muted colors, the emanating growl grew louder until a pickup truck came into view.

She raised her hand for it once she had climbed out. It slowed, tires crunching over weathered asphalt. Banged up and heavily dented, the mist-gray pickup had a metal ram on the grill, she noticed, as it rolled to a stop with the passenger side window down.

She snugged her beret down as far as it would go on her head and straightened her spine, but fell into a guarded slouch, folding her arms and feeling suddenly awkward to touch eyes with a man.

Holding his gaze, *cornflower blue* came to mind and it took her a breath to place it. Doris had been good with colors, she knew every shade on every house they had driven past. That was the color of his eyes—cornflower—a clear blue that pierced through the sun's glare and penetrated the dim hovel of his truck, as he shouted, "Hey there," over the engine's hum. "Car trouble?"

For fear she might choose the wrong word, she gave him a nod paired with a smile to confirm.

"Let me pull around."

As he maneuvered his Dodge with a three-point turn that pitted his front bumper a foot from hers, Gertrude battled her delayed reaction to encountering the stranger, nerves zinging through her gut for reasons she couldn't identify. Excitement? Terror? Relief?

There was no reason to be intimidated, though she would prefer to have her cell phone on her.

He looked like a cowboy dismounting a horse the way he confidently stepped out of his truck, which he had kept idling. His jeans and boots were basic enough, but his shirt—a Gingham button-down with a purple cast—seemed fancy. As he made his way towards her Audi, he rolled up his sleeves, his gaze fixed on the old engine.

She guessed he couldn't be much older than her, mid-thirties she imagined since his chestnut hair didn't have a hint of gray. She realized she was hanging back near the rear door of her Audi so she joined him more or less, but kept her distance.

In her head, she practiced saying, *it won't turn over* a number of times before stating the fact out loud. When she did, she didn't falter too badly, but her voice sounded small, not that he noticed. He just said, "Yup."

After examining the engine, his finger tracing certain wires to their points of origin, he asked, "Does it crank?" Off her blank stare, he added, "Does it make a sound like it's trying to turn on, or is it totally dead?"

"It has a trying noise."

Even she hadn't thought that sounded right so his puzzled glimpse, eyes wincing as he held her gaze, perhaps attempting to decipher her odd wording, was justifiable.

"I might be able to help," he said plainly, though he seemed to be taking in the whole of her as if she didn't add up—the beret, the bizarre almost English cadence (*trying?*) the brown stain left from her facial bruise. There was no worse time to be introduced to someone new. "Gertrude, right? Inman? The woman who drove into the lake?"

She hoped that wasn't how people were referring to her, but she confirmed it.

"Glad you're okay," he added as though he could tell he had struck a nerve. Returning his attention to the engine, he started rattling off a few ideas. "Could be a bad starter or if we're lucky just some mild corrosion on the ground cables or maybe the connecting cables. Can't tell one way or the other by looking at it. Why don't you start her up so I can hear what we're dealing with?"

"Ah, sure." She turned, then impulsively mentioned, "My friends call me Gerty."

As a smile formed at one corner of his mouth and he raised a single eyebrow at her, she forced the door open and ducked into the car. Once settled behind the wheel, she concentrated, taking her time. *Press the brake pedal.* She did. *Press the clutch.* With it down, the gear shifter in neutral, and the emergency braked pitched up, which she checked three times to make certain—the last thing she needed was to be known as the woman who had driven into the lake and then ran some poor bastard over—Gertrude turned the key and let the engine squeal for a good long while.

"Okay! That's enough now!"

Pulling the key out and edging out of the Audi, she asked, "What do you think?"

"It's not the battery. Let me get my brushes and clean up the corrosion. Worst case scenario, I'll give you a tow to Larry's Auto. You ever go to Larry's?"

She couldn't remember a single trip to the mechanic.

"What did you say your name was?"

He shuffled towards her with his hand out, saying, "Ah sorry, Jake Livingston. I live just down the road next to the Kings." After shaking hands—warm, strong, like a lion's paw, but gentle, she thought, touching him—Jake started for his truck's cab where he pulled a toolbox from the floor and returned.

Kneeling with his toolbox in the dirt and sorting through what appeared to be a nest of odds and ends hiding a few recognizable tools—a screwdriver, a wrench, a hammer—Jake asked, "So what brings you out this way?"

"I just got turned around."

He found a stiff bristle brush and a rag scrap, and began untwisting a particular engine cable. When it sprang free, he ran the brush over the input, really working to loosen the build up of soot and debris.

"A car this old, you ought to stick to the main roads if you can help it. You were lucky I came along when I did. Not too many homes out this way with people who can help stranded travelers."

"Thanks," she said quickly, since doing so had slipped her mind. "I'm really happy."

He paused to glance at her.

"I mean I'm really thankful." She stilled. That wasn't right.

"No problem," he said, getting back to it.

It was a moment before she blurted out, "Grateful."

He smiled, but she could tell he felt bad for her.

After attaching the cable, he freed the next and cleaned it in the same manner. It was hard to tell if it was her duty to keep some sort of conversation going. Her ability to read others, to sense their feelings, and execute basic social graces, was as mysterious as the engine he was fixing and probably just as broken.

Also, she was becoming preoccupied with an eerie feeling she had met him before or that they had talked, but she couldn't place it. Wouldn't he have mentioned if they had, and refreshed her memory? She had been getting a fair amount of déjà vu ever since the accident, which Dr. Hagstaff had explained was a mild symptom of misaligned brain synapsis. When they misfired, her surroundings—what she saw, smelled, touched, tasted—mistakenly stirred either her short or long-term memory, so that she felt as though she was reliving something that in fact, she never had. It would work itself out, he had told her. But though she trusted him, at times she had acted in strange ways to shake the feeling, singing loudly, throwing her meal tray against the wall, lying face up on the cool tiles of her hospital room and staring at the ceiling, at the dreary acrylic panels, cloudy and ruddy, which defused the fluorescent lights they covered. *I haven't done this before. There's no way I've done this before. I would remember. Wouldn't I?*

"All right. Let's hope that did the trick," said Jake, stepping away from the car as he wiped his stained fingers on the rag, which did little to remove the grease. "Want to give it a try?"

As soon as she got in her car, her feet pressing the pedals, she turned the key and grimaced at the sustained whine. But just when she was about to give up, the engine turned and her Audi maintained a healthy idle.

"Beautiful," he shouted over the slam of the hood he had eased down. Rounding to her door, which she had left open, he said, "I would get her over to my guy Larry as soon as you can. Have him check it out in case anything else is hanging on by a thread."

"Yes, okay." She was smiling, but it caused a dull ache in her left cheek.

Jake's gaze drifted over her index cards and when she glanced up at him, his cornflower-blue eyes rounded slightly, just enough to make her uncomfortable. But he played it off, shutting her door, which immediately shifted his attention. It wouldn't hold in the frame. Rather it bounced out. He tried again, but they both could tell it wasn't settled.

"Man alive. I'm afraid to try again," he laughed.

"It's okay," she said, quickly taking command of the door. She had been getting a feel for its quirks and held it open by a few inches then slammed it hard, which did the trick.

He smiled at her through her open window, but his eyes said *deathtrap*. If her last trip into the lake hadn't killed her, this vehicle certainly would.

Working the gear shifter into its tender Reverse spot, she said, "Thanks again!" But he jutted his chin at her passenger seat.

"You know them?"

"Ah," she glanced at the Kings' family portrait. "No."

He worked his mouth into a frown. "Their oldest, Roberta..." Trailing off a beat, Jake's eyebrows floated up as if to indicate the iceberg mass of which she had only seen the tip. "I don't know about that one. Pure trouble and not the innocent kind every teenage girl tries on for size."

Intrigued, she asked, "Do you know her?"

He exhaled a long breath then snorted a strange laugh. "No, and I figure best to keep it that way." Angling his gaze on her as if probing for the real reason she had come out this way, he added, "I suggest you do the same. Steer clear."

"No one's the same after a tragedy," said Gertrude, defending Roberta or more likely herself.

For a moment, he searched her eyes, his expression softening into a parting smile. "True enough." Then he tapped her hood and took a few swaggering steps backwards. "You take care now and don't forget to swing by Larry's Auto Shop."

After giving him an acknowledging nod, she reversed away from his pickup then cautiously swung a U-turn, driving off and trying not to spy him in her rearview mirror.

Moulton Street, its asphalt, salt and sun faded, was smooth as her Audi puttered away from Jake Livingston. Though the air—rich and crisp with the scent of Balsam fir—was comforting, the gusts coming through her open window were rattling her index cards like a Joker in a bicycle wheel flapping against the spokes so she cranked her window up, all the while debating her return to the DCYF.

She needed to type up her case notes and scan them into the system, but the thought of working in her cubicle with the office sounds swarming around her head—phones ringing, fax machines blaring dial tones, coworkers cursing about their reports not feeding through the printer fast enough, the frenetic buzz of the environment, pent up stress, released anger, deadlines missed—wasn't at all appealing and her aversion became overpowering. She couldn't go back there. Not right now. Later, she told herself, later today around four when it quieted down, she would return.

If her biggest regret in life was not being able to save her sister, her second biggest regret was having missed Doris' funeral. At the time, she had been immobilized, in her hospital bed, two pins in her left hip, her cheek swollen to such an extent that she couldn't crack her eyelid open—a vessel lost in an angry sea, anchored only to a row of machines monitoring how closely she drifted towards death.

Her parents had gone ahead with the arrangements, or so Dr. Hagstaff had explained. They hadn't told her in person. They hadn't written or called, except to contact her doctor—*please send her our regards*—her mother had said through Dr. Hagstaff and that was before the certified letter. Dr. Hagstaff had looked grim, barely able to touch eyes with her. He had knotted up a Kleenex in his hands, the box in his lap, so distraught for Gertrude that he had forgotten to offer her a tissue.

She had done what she could to sit upright in her bed, watching him, feeling things she couldn't identify, not precisely, a vague emptiness taking root. She hadn't felt numb, not entirely and not thoroughly shattered, but hurt, despairing perhaps, though at the time she hadn't been able to recall a name for it.

Had her parents always been that cold and hateful? She hadn't been able to recollect their typical demeanor towards her beyond a few slanted memories.

Often during her recovery she had asked Dr. Hagstaff why she was able to easily remember her work, her years with the DCYF, her months with Doris living at her house on the lake, but the bulk of her upbringing was gone from her memory almost as completely as the accident itself and the strange evening leading up to it.

He hadn't seemed to have a concrete answer, though he mentioned it was possible at this time only memories that served her to function were necessary. He had tried to make his tone sound confident and knowledgeable to instill her trust, but his expression had worked against him. He had been as equally mystified as her.

Gertrude wasn't paying attention as she drove through the center of Laconia, but even before she snapped out of her heart sinking reverie, she knew she was heading towards the Union Cemetery on Academy Street where her sister had been buried.

After parking in the small lot and then enduring a distinct and fearful twinge that if she turned her car off it might not start again, she bucked up, pulled the key out of the ignition, and grabbed her laptop satchel from the trunk. Walking towards a stone archway that marked the entrance of the cemetery, she glanced at the grassy plots, the handsome headstones, and mausoleums.

The peacefulness was striking, as she padded over the grass, noting the names on each headstone. It was warm and the air was still. She didn't hear a bird chirp or a chipmunk rustling. When she glanced at the sky, the popcorn clouds were motionless against the blue. It was as though time had stopped and all living things didn't dare appear in this sacred place.

She didn't have to wander too far before she found her sister's name.

Was that a headstone?

Gertrude stared at a granite slab, which looked more like a rock fallen from the side of a mountain than a proper headstone. Arched along its top edge was her sister's name, *Doris Inman*. The bottom edge noted her birth and death years, omitting the specific dates, and between the two was the imprint of a heart.

It looked familiar and at first she blamed her recurring déjà vu, until she recalled her dog. Nervous to live alone when she had moved into her house over a decade ago, Gertrude had adopted an old black lab from the local shelter. Old Rusty had been a sweet, lumbering dope, nearly deaf and not at all equipped to defend her home against intruders, but she had always loved him. After he had died, she had bought a memorial marker and buried him in her backyard.

Her parents had done the same for her sister.

And the great emptiness she had suffered that day when Dr. Hagstaff had forgotten to hand her a Kleenex, returned.

Her parents had been cold and hateful, hadn't they?

They had bought a pet marker for her sister's grave instead of a headstone.

Marsha and Albert Inman, *What have you done?*

CHAPTER FIVE

THE SHED WAS nestled between a haphazard row of saplings and a cluster of Birches. Quinton Avery's eyes were still adjusting to the hazy morning dusk, as he walked, careful not to trip over debris and loose rocks that littered his path. The shed's brown siding looked black and its pitched roof was lost in darkness, but the orange door was clear as day.

He didn't like having to get up so early, and he liked walking out to the shed even less. It was spooky. Fog rose up from the earth and he could smell the lake through the trees.

If he hadn't stayed up so late playing Call of Duty on his Xbox—fiercely smashing his thumbs over the controller, twisting and jerking his shoulders to force every move, hissing *yes!* on every kill and groaning at missed opportunities, all the while absorbed in the incredible glow of his flat screen—then peeling himself out of bed at 5:15 am wouldn't have felt like such a chore.

The orange door creaked faintly when he pulled it open. It took a moment to swat his hand around for the dangling string, but he found it, yanked it quickly and the naked bulb overhead flickered on, illuminating the interior but not by much.

Ad hoc carpentry tools hung on nails and wooden posts at the far wall above his dad's worktable, which was lined with rusty basins, coils of dried out rope, and other random items—hand-held gardening tools, the innards of dissected VHS players, relics of his mother's pottery, a dehydrated Christmas wreath with a faded red bow, all cast in soft, tungsten light.

For some reason the table was where his gaze landed every time he set foot in the shed, but he turned left for his bicycle, an old Huffy Rawhide, powder-coated in robin's egg blue with tarnished fenders and Belleville handlebars arching back like ram horns. The bike was good enough for his route even though it was as old as his father.

But this morning it didn't look quite right, and his foggy brain was slow to pinpoint why.

It had the posture of an obedient dog, seated and eager for a treat, and as the cobwebs cleared from his mind, he noticed the reason. There was something wrong with the rear wheel. Handling it, he realized the tire had been slashed, but that wasn't the worst of it. It was also bent out of shape, causing a number of spokes to have snapped from the rim like spiders' legs.

"Damn, Roberta," he muttered. "If you have something to say to me, just say it."

As he straightened up from his bike, not quite ready to believe he would have to walk his route, Quinton wondered just what in the hell he might have done to Roberta to warrant this level of destruction. He had been checking in on her, stopping by most mornings after his route and sneaking over with leftovers after dinner—pot roast, spaghetti and meatballs, his mom's homemade gnocchi, Roberta's demands, *Bring a liter of Coke* and his response, *She'll notice that, she's been asking where all the soda's gone* and her insistence, *Just bring it, Quinton!* Loyally, day after day and night after night, he had placed the items on the porch—offering libations to an angry god who rarely granted him what he prayed hardest for: her genuine affection.

Roberta was a goddess.

Towering over him, her feline eyes boring through him which stirred up all kinds of thrill and terror in his chest, she would stomp around, pacing the shore behind her house whenever he displeased her. It was so easy for her to ignore the effect she had on him. A bull's spirit trapped inside fluid elegance—fury mixed with refinement, cruelty wrapped in cultivated beauty—was how she would act.

But Quinton hadn't done anything wrong.

He turned the light off and closed the orange door on his way out then started through the woods for his bundle of newspapers, which the Laconia Daily Sun truck had deposited at the end of his driveway as they had done every morning since he had been hired.

His sack was resting limply at the front door so he grabbed it, tossing the canvas strap over his shoulder, then padded down the drive and collected the bundled newspapers wrapped in twine, shoving it in the sack and setting off for Roberta's house, which was half a mile down the road.

Today was going to suck.

He needed his driver's license and a car, but a year stood between him and making that dream a reality.

The landscape gradually brightened, sunlight sparkling off mist, as he made his way. Cutting through the Maples that shielded the Kings' house from the road, he spotted Roberta, ass-up in the planters, digging.

She had been doing a lot of that recently. Ever since Maude had died, Roberta had become bizarrely obsessed with the dirt. At times she was frantic and so focused, she couldn't spare a second to acknowledge him. Others she searched about lazily, digging and tearing up plants, if that's what she was doing—searching. For what, he couldn't imagine.

"Roberta."

She was flinging dirt behind her like a dog.

Louder, he said, "Roberta."

Standing, twisting, but not turning completely around, she glared at him from the corner of her eye. "What?"

He gaped at her like *duh*. "You annihilated my bicycle."

"Keep your voice down," she ordered, stalking towards him after glancing at the second floor windows.

"Well, what the hell?"

Her eyes turned innocent and he almost didn't have the nerve to break it down for her, the consequences of his newborn burden. He held his head high, in part because she was that much taller, but also to affirm that he was no wimp.

"It's going to take me literally eight times as long to get through my route, which means half my papers will be delivered late, after my customers leave for work in fact. Which means I'll get complaints, which means my boss is going to ream me out, which means I might get fired, which means I won't be able to save up for—" Fast sip of oxygen, then he barreled through the rest of his point. "A car, which means our long term plan is going to get pushed off. Don't you get that?"

He was breathing heavily. The adrenaline rushing through his veins was almost more than he could bear. The shoulder strap on his sack was cutting into his shoulder and making him stoop so he shoved it off. It fell hard to the grass.

"What did I do?"

"You talked to my mom."

"When?"

"Yesterday."

He gaped as though it might fool her then let the pantomime go when she gaped right back at him mockingly. He tried to explain. "You weren't around."

Folding her arms, which jostled her chest in a way he couldn't resist peeking at, and raising her brows as if to challenge his poor defense, she gave Quinton the distinct impression she wanted him to come clean and come clean fully.

"All right," he began. "Obviously you were around and you know. She was out here. What was I supposed to do? Run off? She saw me and said hi. She just wanted to find out how you were doing."

"So she asked you? She didn't ask me. She could any time she wants. It's not like either of us do anything except avoid each other in that house."

"Well, I didn't say anything. You didn't have to total my bicycle."

She leveled her gaze on him, her expression neutral, then her eyebrows went flat. Finally, she said, "Sorry," but her tone implied a real apology would degrade her.

Sighing, he told her it was fine.

"You can use my dad's bike."

"No way," he blurted out.

"He doesn't use it. He probably forgot he has it."

Quinton had encountered Charlie King only a handful of times, but each instance, though brief, had been more nerve wracking than the last and had haunted him for days. Charlie hadn't said much during those encounters, but when he had, his booming voice, deep and piercing, shocked Quinton's heart out of rhythm and sent him trembling.

The first had been when he caught Quinton in Roberta's room. He had kicked the door in and barked, *Hey!* In that split second, Quinton had gotten an outsider's glimpse of the scene—Roberta lounging on her back, her hand under her head, the curves and lines of her body melting sensuously into the bedspread though she was clothed, Quinton perched at the foot of the bed, magnetized, leaning towards her, on fire to be painting her toenails. With Charlie glaring at him, Quinton had kept praying *I look gay, I look gay, don't I? This is pretty gay, right?* But Charlie hadn't thought so. He had lunged at him, grabbed him by the shirt, and the next thing Quinton knew he was careening down the stairs then sprinting home.

The last time he had crossed paths with Charlie was behind the house when he was swimming with Roberta. She had stretched her bikini top under her breasts and Quinton hoisted himself onto the raft to get a better look at her as she floated on her back—she liked to tease him like that, or torture him as the case might be. Then he had heard a shot. Quinton had flinched, pissing himself and falling into the water, as Charlie straightened his aim, poised to shoot at him again. He hadn't dared collect his clothes on the shore. He had swam all the way home, holding his breath as long as he could and only coming up for air when his lungs started screaming.

"Come on. It's in the basement," she said, pulling him to get him walking then hooking her arm around his neck when he did.

He half expected a noogie to follow, but she only pitched him forward with a playful shove, as they started around to the back of the house.

"You need to change out of that thing or wash it at the very least," he said, eyeing her red dress. "You stink."

"Shut up." She ducked under the staircase behind the house and opened the basement door. "The washer's messed up. The hose is cracked and we can't run it without flooding the place."

Quinton waited for her in the entryway, as she padded through the dark then emerged, rolling a mountain bike. At first glance, the seat looked way too high, but he could adjust it.

Taking the handlebars, he relieved her of having to push the bike to the driveway where he had left his sack.

"Who was that lady that was here yesterday?"

"Amanda's replacement."

"Social services?" he asked, as he chucked a newspaper at the front porch. He had decent aim and it landed right in front of the door. "Is that going to mess everything up?"

"They'll get to her," she stated bleakly.

"Damn, Roberta," he said, his voice a thread.

"They get to everyone."

"Then don't talk to her. Is she making you talk?"

She screwed her face up, considering. "Not really. I doubt she cares much. She wanted to know about the guns."

"What did you say?"

"I didn't let her in the house. Told her no one was home. It didn't take much to get her to leave," she said darkly.

Though he knew the topic of Maude was off limits, he asked, "What does she make of Maude?"

Her expression hardened and she clenched her jaw so Quinton deflected, hauling his sack over his shoulder and finding something interesting about the mountain bike.

Then she said, "There's something wrong with her. Gertrude." She pronounced the woman's name like it was an infectious disease, which wasn't the volatile response he had anticipated. "She doesn't stand a chance against them."

"I think you should tell her."

"And what's that going to do?"

"Maybe you could stay at my house until you graduate."

"Your folks can't stand me," she countered, dismissing the idea, and he accidentally waited too long to insist she was wrong.

She held his gaze, both of them silently confirming what the whole town thought of her, that she was a tramp, demented, damaged beyond repair—a carnival of abnormal behavior overpowering this side of the lake.

"I should get going," he told her.

The sun had risen over the water behind the house, casting long shadows where they stood.

"Have a drink."

"Christ, Roberta. It's barely six."

But she was already dragging him up the porch steps and didn't release him until she got to the keg.

"I can't believe there's any beer left at the rate we've been drinking it," he commented, as she pumped it and filled a red cup.

"I paid to refill the keg," she said, handing the cup to him then pouring one for herself.

"How did you pay for it?"

"My dad has a tab at the liquor store."

She drank hers down like she had just crossed a desert then angled the nozzle in her cup for round two, as Quinton stared at the foamy surface of his beer, dreading this form of bonding.

"At least tell that social services woman about the funeral."

Correcting him, she said, "The party, you mean."

"Didn't she ask about the keg? Didn't she see it?"

"Something's off with her," Roberta said easily, but then quickly scowled at the fact he hadn't taken so much as a sip.

"All right, all right." Choking the bitter, warm liquid down, he drained his glass, grimacing all the while in such a way that beer trickled from the corners of his mouth. "Christ, that's gross."

"She acted like the funeral was her own personal debutante ball."

"That's why I don't get why you're wearing that dress of your mother's."

The alcohol hit him and he was suddenly light headed and swaying. Or maybe he wasn't swaying. Maybe that was the porch.

"I'm just throwing it in her face. Who wears a red cocktail dress to a funeral?"

"Your mother, evidently."

"Remember her teachers?" Roberta was smiling strangely, all loosened up with booze. "A bunch of fourth graders running around, not quite getting it. And their teachers wrangling them, casting sideways glances at my mom as she paraded around the living room, martini glass in hand, oblivious to how horrified they were."

Quinton didn't want to divulge the raw feeling her mother had given him at the funeral, the quavering anxiety he had felt when he had been alone with her that had been far worse than his encounters with Charlie. Maude's death had elicited in Zhana a queer need to celebrate. She had seemed strangely euphoric, a butterfly emerging from her cocoon after a painstaking metamorphosis. Or maybe that was how she grieved, but if it was, it was dark.

Setting his empty cup on the railing, he offered, "I can come back after my route," though it was a given.

"Do it. We'll go for a swim."

She draped her arms around his shoulders. He had a buzz going and because of it she felt like a dream. The same one he had gotten in the habit of conjuring each night as he drifted to sleep. However, as soon as he reached for her, reciprocating, hands nearing her hips, she urged him back and her chiseled features hardened like a warning.

He crossed the porch and when he passed the newspaper he had delivered, he gave it a little kick so it would be tucked against the door then padded down the steps. After collecting his sack, he adjusted the bicycle seat down, loosening the pinch bolt on the seatpost and sliding the seat with a twist into the frame. As soon as he secured it, he felt eyes on him and knew it wasn't Roberta. Someone was peering at him from the second floor windows. He sensed it, but was too scared to look up.

Swinging his leg over, he hopped on the bicycle then took off riding through the warm morning, its air crisp and filling his lungs.

His tires hummed over asphalt until he turned up Mr. Livingston's driveway, which was bumpy with ruts and compacted dirt. The shocks were stellar and he didn't have to stand on the pedals to save his ass like usual. When he reached the walkway, he pulled a U-turn without stopping, chucking a paper at the front door, then pedaled onward as fast as he could as though the harder he worked his muscles forcing a sweat, the quicker he would rid his system of alcohol.

It was an hour before he was rounding the Opechee Bay Reservoir, crossing over the bridge that marked the last leg of his route. Sweat drenched with the canvas sack limply flapping at his side, he turned up Opechee Street and chucked one of the few newspapers he had left into the Wongs' yard. Their eldest daughter, Jennifer, a prim girl in the grade above him, who was too smart for her own good, had gotten into a nasty habit of pretending to sunbathe on a grassy patch at the end of the driveway. Hoping to catch him, Quinton suspected. Not that she had anything nice to say. Generally, she just glared at him, while lying on her towel in the shade so that her porcelain skin never tanned. She liked to shout rudely at him, things about Roberta he had heard so many times that he was both deaf to it and highly sensitive.

He spied her in her usual spot, so he chucked the paper and hightailed it out of there, turning up the street and wincing as she called out, "Quinton and Roberta, perverted in a tree! F. U. C. K. I. N. G." Then she cackled to high heaven.

The remaining houses were quick and painless, and soon he was riding home along Moulton.

He slowed up as he came to the King's driveway, planting the rubber soles of his heels into the road and scanning for Roberta through the trees. Unable to spot her, he figured he had a few minutes for breakfast before she would notice that he should've returned so he kicked off again.

As he arched around Mr. Livingston's house, a patch of red beyond the tree line caught his eye. Roberta, hands dark with dirt, her dress tattered and sloping off one shoulder, was walking at a staggering pace along a low stone wall—old Colonial property dividers hidden through the forest. She looked dazed, zombie-like, her eyes unfocused and lolling as though she couldn't make sense of where she was, yet she seemed decisive about where she was heading, which was into Mr. Livingston's yard.

If she had been wandering onto anyone else's property, Quinton would've intervened, but Jake Livingston was not someone to mess with.

CHAPTER SIX

IT WASN'T SO much a home office as it was a hovel.

Sun-faded and dust-tarnished, the wood paneled walls were eroding, but mostly hidden behind bookshelves, framed photos, placards, and porcelain plates that depicted landscapes and wildlife, every inch of wood covered with mementos from his ancestors, grandparents, and the many generations of Livingstons that had lived in this house.

The office smelled of musty books, but that was what Jake liked about it. Books comforted him. Relaxing his eyes from his computer monitor, he glanced at one of the shelves, studying the row of stiff spines—some sitting vertically, packed tightly on the shelves, others fanning sideways. They breathed wisdom—facts and figures, statistics and demographics. Interspersed between the hard covers were criminal files he had stolen that looked like arms reaching out as if to say, *Come back, I have more to tell you.* The history of a town with too many secrets, the vast divide between what had been printed and what had actually occurred, was what these walls wouldn't let him forget.

His desk was no better. Overwrought with notepads full of research and drafts of article copy marked in red—ones which he knew his editor wouldn't print, not yet, not until he got proof—he barely had any surface space left. Every inch was covered with precarious pillars, each stacked haphazardly and threatening to spill.

His behemoth computer, or the Eye of the Storm as he had come to refer to it, glared at him, cursor blinking impatiently, as Jake sat motionless, wrapping his head around the angle he would like to take, the trajectory of his article, and how he might get away with writing his hunch even though he hadn't a shred of evidence.

Maude King hadn't killed herself.

But no one would say as much—not the cops, not the medical examiner, not the family—had uttered one word of skepticism when the ten year old girl's death had been ruled a suicide.

Hesitantly, he placed his fingers on the chunky keys and in response, the IBM, a boxy relic he refused to retire—too many good thesis' had come out of it during college, too many articles for which he had almost received awards—began humming, fans blowing noisily as if to nudge him, *get on with it.*

He couldn't turn in the article he wanted, but he might be able to get away with writing about gun control, not that the Daily Sun's subscribers would appreciate it. He would get flack no question. The county, and the state for that matter, held their second amendment rights in high regard.

A 1989 Glamour magazine resting to the left of his keyboard stole his attention. Zhana King was gleaming at him from its glossy cover. She couldn't have been a day over twenty-three when the photo had been taken. Her emerald green eyes, unreal in their color and clarity, her impossibly high cheekbones, the clever arch in her eyebrows, and a certain indescribable levity in her overall expression—grand smile, chin up, sandy blonde hair big and bold and blowing from an off camera fan, *Watch out world, I'm ready!*—had him falling into a daze.

Not even the gaudy, pastel palette of her makeup, or the horrendous yellow scarf around her neck could distract the viewer from her undeniable beauty.

She had been a burgeoning star.

In the A&P, when Jake had asked her for a photo, explaining he was in the throes of drafting another article—*After the tragic news and the article we printed, the Laconia Daily Sun would like to do a follow up, give the town hope, show the readers you and your family are carrying on,* and Zhana, her eyes brightening as she had lifted them from the gallon of milk in her hand, *How thoughtful*—Zhana had looked alive, radiant in fact.

Just as radiant as she appeared on the magazine cover.

But the decades in-between the two events, the long years she had spent tucked away out of the public eye, she hadn't been alive, not in Jake's observation.

It seemed that Maude's death had somehow freed her. She had proudly handed him the magazine—*You're a lucky man, Mr. Livingston. I don't give these away, you know. I only have five copies left.*

Not a recent family photo of the surviving members. Not an Instagram snap of her with Roberta or even a Christmas picture featuring the four of them prior to her daughter's death. In response to his request, in full knowledge that the photo would be distributed to the entire town, she had given him a piece of her former life, an image of who she had been before marriage, before kids, before New Hampshire, and before Charlie had stolen her away.

It didn't sit right with him, not by a long shot.

The rising morning sun was piercing through the window, magnifying the dust in the air, so he opened the window to get a cross breeze going. Near his desk and resting atop a stack of achieved articles was a wooden post, which he used to prop the window up, wedging it between the tarnished sill and the metal lip of the pane. As soon as he did, he noticed Roberta King creeping into his backyard.

She was barefoot. Her hands and forearms appeared dirty, and as she squatted in front of the flower bushes lining his house, he wondered why in the hell she was dressed like that, wearing a red cocktail dress, even before he questioned what she was doing.

Quick to pull on his boots when he reached the foyer, after padding down the stairs and nearly tripping into a coat rack where his winter-garb hung like a weeping willow, Jake didn't bother lacing them up. He rushed through the darkened house, passing bookshelves and boxes, weaving around the side of a cracked-leather couch, until he stepped out the backdoor where the rising heat had burned off the morning-mist, leaving the air muggy.

When he turned towards the planters and caught Roberta digging, he had an impulse to shout, *Go home*, but what had worked on old man Hadley's Doberman might not be as effective on a seventeen-year-old girl.

So he went with, "Can I help you?"

"No," she said without looking at him.

As he rounded behind her, he realized she had a copy of this morning's paper rolled in her fist, while she used her left hand to plow a hole between two shrubs.

"I'm going to have to ask you to stop doing that."

Her movements were almost frantic as though burying the newspaper was a matter of life and death, and Jake's presence hadn't deterred her in any way.

Keeping his tone friendly, but firm—dealing with Roberta was akin to scaring off a mountain lion, if threatened, she would likely attack—he suggested, "Can't you do that at your house?"

Again, a simple, "No," was her answer, and before he could ask why not, she added, "I think it's killing the plants."

Having succeeded, the newspaper now under a small mound of soil meant to mark its location, he presumed, she plopped on her butt, glancing up at him, while he struggled to comprehend her.

"I thought you would be at work," she said as though it was her version of an apology.

Leaning back on her hands, she stretched her legs out and wiggled the dirt from between her toes.

"I've been burying things at my house," she began explaining easily. "I'm pretty sure it's killing the bushes."

"Well, you know plants need water. You can't clog up their root system with objects and expect them to survive."

She considered his point, but didn't seem convinced then sprang to her feet, startling him, though only deep down—his pulse rate quickening and his throat tightening uncomfortably.

"I'll be back to check on it," she asserted like a doctor who had used unorthodox methods to stabilize a patient.

Dusting her hands off and shaking her hair out of her face, she turned to leave.

"Hang on."

When she paused, meeting his gaze from the corner of her eye, he wondered if he would regret what he was about to do, but reasoned that avoiding her at all costs, as he had been doing, had been to the detriment of the article he most wanted to publish.

No one volunteered to be alone with Roberta, no one in their right mind anyway, not since her pattern had developed where rumors mixing with truth shattered the lives of decent men. When he had heard about Tom Riley's arrest, the details leading up to it and the correlating gossip—*why did he bring her to that billiard hall?* And, *what was he thinking, going for a night swim with a thirteen-year-old girl?* And, *I heard he threatened to drown her if she didn't keep quiet*—it didn't matter that Jake had known Tom since grade school. Like the rest of the town, he had chosen to believe Tom was a predator.

But soon Tom wasn't the only one. By the third and fourth arrests—Mike Waters then Jimmy Smythe—a dark, sinking feeling had come over Jake. He didn't at all think the five men who had gravely miscalculated Roberta's advances, were guilty, quite the opposite in fact. She was a spider, spinning men up into her web, which bound them to an inescapable fate.

He had talked to Jimmy Smythe before the man got shipped off to County, and Mike Waters as well. Their experiences with her had been identical—flirting, but no sex, out all night, but no crime committed. And a day later, Charlie had ambushed each of them, his badge in his hand as good as a death warrant.

But despite all that, Jake held her liquid gaze and said, "Are you hungry?"

It might have been the light changing. Maybe a cloud had cleared the sun overhead, but Jake thought he caught a glint forming in her eyes, one that suggested he had piqued her interest in the wrong way.

As she responded with, "I am," enhancing the melody in her soft voice, Roberta tipped her head ever so slightly sideways and smiled coyly. It reminded him of the first time Jake had invited a girl to a school dance. It was unnerving.

"Come on in then."

Leading her inside, he closed the door and turned on every light—a green-glass bankers lamp oddly placed on the end table beside the couch, another that looked like a vase wearing a canvas hat, which had been his mother's, and last but not least the overheads since they were the brightest—making his gradual way to the kitchen, Roberta following behind too closely.

"What do you feel like?" he asked, facing her.

She was staring at him from where she was perched between a hanging fruit basket filled with spotted bananas and the stove, the burners of which were topped with clean pots since he had nowhere to hang them and couldn't tuck them away inside the cabinets. They were packed to the gills with archived files.

He began rattling off the options, while in the back of his mind he felt preoccupied by the bizarreness of her being in his home in the first place. "I have bagels and bread and stuff like that, or I could make a sandwich, but I don't have any lettuce or tomatoes. I think I have popcorn somewhere around here, not that it's a meal."

As he worked his way around the kitchen, more or less proving he had each item as a means to avoid looking at her, Roberta edged towards him, sliding her bare feet over the linoleum. She reached him at the toaster, but he stepped back.

"Any of this sound appetizing?"

"I'll have a bagel."

Pulling two options from the breadbox, he asked, "Raisin or poppy seed?"

"Raisin."

He felt her watching, as he cut the bagel and placed it in the toaster oven.

"Butter's fine," she added so he grabbed a stick from the refrigerator, maneuvering around her.

He rarely had company and when he did, his kitchen seemed comically small.

Busying himself, he pulled a plate from the dish rack, cleared some room on the table, and tried not to sound invasive. "How're you spending your summer?"

She grinned darkly, but he couldn't figure out why until she mentioned, "You sound like my case worker."

The toaster oven was clicking, making his pause all the more apparent.

"Gertrude Inman?"

Holding his gaze was her version of confirming, he assumed.

That explained her being out this way as well as her having the Kings' photo. He should've put it together sooner, but he had been somewhat thrown that she had no recollection they had met before. It had been brief, and the farmers market had been noisy. Unfortunately, he had asked her out since their three seconds of weather related chitchat had seemed to go smoothly. He should've known better. She had turned him down, and when she skirted off to find her sister who was raising hell at a vendor for using pesticides when they had claimed to be selling organic, Jake had kicked himself for succumbing to an impulse he knew wouldn't pan out.

The toaster clicked off and he buttered Roberta's bagel, remembering how strangely he had felt writing about the car accident that had killed Gertrude's sister, an article he had volunteered for, because he felt a strange closeness with the woman who had rejected him.

"Do you like her?" he asked when they got situated on the bar stools at either side of the table.

Looking like a flamingo perched on her stool, Roberta shrugged and watched excess butter drip from her bagel to the plate. "She only came once."

"What were some of the things you buried at your house?"

The bagel had expelled whatever prior flirtation she had attempted. She looked almost childlike, inspecting her teeth marks in the bread and savoring each bite. Once she had swallowed, she said, "Underwear."

He was sorry he had asked and the wiser side of him begged his internal investigator that generally dominated everything he did to change the subject, but after a carefully measured breath, he asked, "Why?"

"Safe keeping. Evidence, I guess."

"Evidence?" He reminded himself she was very skilled at spinning webs, but Tom and Mike and Jimmy and the others who would be locked up for the next six years were at the forefront of his fast working mind. "Your underwear?"

She chewed and swallowed the last bite. With the bagel gone, the glint in her eyes returned and a darkly clever smirk lifted one corner of her mouth, cloying at him from across the table.

"You want to talk about my underwear?"

"Actually, I would rather talk about your dad. I haven't seen him around since your sister passed away."

"Is that what people are saying?"

"That he's holed up in your house? I haven't heard that. It's only my observation."

"No, that Maude passed away?" She was nearly laughing, but it was clearly a sign of her disgust—long, airy exhales between her teeth.

"What happened, exactly?"

Planting her elbows on the table after pushing her plate aside, she coolly stated, "It bothers me that you're asking that."

"Why?"

"Your name was on the article that was written about us. You claimed to know all about us."

He leveled his gaze on her. Under a cocky exterior, she was wavering, hurt, once again childlike, so he kept his tone smooth. "It was an assignment. Only facts were printed. I'm not sure if you read it, but there weren't that many facts."

"Yeah, I read it." Warming to him again, she agreed, "It only said she died from a bullet to the head, and it implied that she killed herself."

"Isn't that what happened?" He was being too forceful. It would backfire, but he kept going. "Everyone was home that night?"

Her tone was eerily neutral when she countered with, "You think my parents killed my sister?"

Hearing her say it out loud made him realize how outlandish he must sound, if not for his hunch, then because he was endeavoring to get Roberta—the daughter of the people he suspected, a girl who could very well be scared witless in that house—to admit it.

"I don't know," he said finally. "All I know is that I haven't seen Charlie around and I used to see him all over town before this happened."

It wasn't a question so she didn't respond.

"Where is he?"

Her eyebrows drifted up and she settled into a repose that struck him as honest. "I don't know."

"So he's not at the house?" He got a bit lost down the annals of his bending mind, struggling to do the math on the possibility, but no matter how clearly it added up—that Charlie fled because he had either killed Maude or knew who had—Jake knew that until someone who could confirm his hunch came forward and said as much, he wouldn't be able to do a damn thing. "He left after Maude's death? Immediately after?"

Almost imperceptibly, she nodded. But though she had, he found her expression as challenging to read as ancient Sanskrit. Her trepidation commingling with a bold sense of daring was hidden under a thin veil of innocence. And because of it, he sensed this might be a game to her—luring him in as if she were twitching a string across the floor for him, the cat, who would pounce on any broad stroke, blind to her manipulation because he was enjoying himself too much.

"What does your mother think of that? Has she contacted him?"

"I don't know."

"Isn't she worried? Or furious at least?" Hoping to rile her up, he added, "How can he take off like that after a tragedy?"

From out of left field, which in Roberta's case was her mode of operation, she stood, peeling off her dress straps.

Red fabric fluttered down her slender body, exposing her nudity.

Utterly stunned, Jake froze, suffering from a bout of stupidity induced indecision, and then tripped his way off his stool to distance himself as if it were a more logical step than insisting she cover up.

It took longer than he would've liked to jump start his brain, but when he did, having stammered some nonsense to clear the cobwebs, he ordered her to put her clothes on and get out.

Stubbornly, she took her slow time lifting her dress and returning the straps over her shoulders. She milked each second in case he changed his mind.

When he sensed she was decent, he also sensed she wouldn't leave on her own, so he ushered her through the house and expelled her out the backdoor like a priest would a demon.

But driving her out felt like a counterfeit miracle.

The demon would return.

CHAPTER SEVEN

THOUGH IT WAS August, Gertrude wore a pair of worn-out jeans and a long-sleeved sweater when she returned to the Kings' house. Ever since the accident, she had been living with a chill in her bones as though the memory of the lake were tendrils cloying at her. Adding layers was all she could do to keep sane. The beret that Wendy had given her had become an appendage over the course of the past few days. As ridiculous as it felt to wear, she hadn't taken it off, not even to sleep.

The King family photo was tucked under the top-sheet of her notepad where she also kept a handwritten list of questions for Roberta. She hadn't covered nearly enough ground with the girl during her last visit and winging it again wouldn't do.

As she neared the house, padding over dying grass once she had cleared the gravel driveway, she noticed the curvy silhouette of a woman standing on the other side of the screen door. With her back turned, the woman thrust her rear into the screen, pushing it open, and appeared to be dragging a heavy object onto the porch. Gertrude saw that it was a giant bag of Miracle Grow, when the woman, who she presumed was Zhana King, stepped aside and straightened up to catch her breath.

In a word, the woman was stately. As she ran her arm across her brow to wipe away sweat, her blonde hair, which was carefully styled in a bouffant coif and shellacked with hair spray, didn't so much toss as shift like a helmet. And her Capri pants and tailored blouse seemed equally stiff. But her face—the cheekbones, wide mouth, and dramatic arch of her eyebrows—had an almost feline fluidity, as she assessed the gardening materials that were laid out on the porch—a trowel, pruning shears, a coiled rubber hose, foam kneeling pads, and gardening gloves. If she sensed that Gertrude was watching her, she didn't acknowledge it.

"Excuse me, hi," said Gertrude from the foot of the steps, getting her attention.

"Can I help you?"

Gertrude rode through the awkward sting of being sized up, as the woman looked her up and down, her narrowing emerald-green eyes full of judgment that contradicted her plastic smile.

Gertrude could tell Zhana found her hard to look at, but plowed ahead regardless, clearing her throat to say, "I hope so. I'm with Social Services. Gertrude Inman. You're Roberta's mother?"

"Oh," she interrupted, waving her hand and smiling as if dismissing the matter. "We're doing just fine. My husband should've made sure your department closed the file. I'll remind him."

Gertrude couldn't have felt smaller looking up at the tall woman, who from the porch, was towering.

Confused, Gertrude asked, "Close the file?"

"I don't understand that stuff either." She let out a breathy laugh as though they were in this together, but it seemed contrived. "We would like our privacy during this difficult time. I'm sure you can understand."

"I do. Certainly. And you can trust me to keep this private, but I do need to talk to you and your husband and Roberta."

"Well," said Zhana, taking the information in and keeping her attitude light, though her breezy attitude caused Gertrude's stomach to clench. "I hope you don't mind if I do a little gardening while we speak. These bushes have been nagging me all summer."

She wasn't exactly asking for permission to carry on as she held Gertrude's gaze. It felt more like she was daring Gertrude to stop her, knowing full well she wouldn't.

After a beat she trained her attention on the Miracle Grow bag, forcing it open by tearing its top edge, while Gertrude stood there wrestling with her crippling doubts, Zhana's personality rendering Gertrude inept.

"See this?" She asked, leaning over the railing and brushing her gloved hand over the yellowing fronds of one of the bushes. "It's purple Lythrum. It should have axils of small purple flowers sprouting out of it this time of year. Such a shame."

As concerned for the plant as she seemed, when Zhana started chucking fistfuls of Miracle Grow at it like an exterminator bombing pests, it dawned on Gertrude that she wasn't the only one out of her element.

Continuing the assault by working her way across the porch and throwing an ungodly amount of lawn fertilizer down, Zhana said, "These are Japanese rose bushes, but do you think I've seen a rose? Not in years! And the Hungarian bromes have all but shriveled up."

"Let's talk about Maude."

Pausing, Zhana pressed her mouth into a hard line. "Such a disturbed little girl."

"What makes you say that?"

"Ms. Inman," she said, smirking at Gertrude as though she was at a loss for communicating with an idiot, "Maude *killed* herself. If that's not disturbed, I don't know what is."

"Sorry, I thought you were implying there were signs."

"There weren't any. Not even one." Zhana sighed, sinking into her hip, on which she planted her fist and gazed out at the yard with unfocused eyes.

During the interlude, Gertrude stole a quick glance at the keg of beer tucked into the far corner of the porch.

"Teenagers," Zhana said with a pretty smile, having caught Gertrude spying the beer. "Impossible to control. Truth be told, I've loosened my parenting since Maude's death. Roberta doesn't need me policing her. She's grieving, I'm sure, and I don't think it's fair to put additional pressure on her."

Not wanting to insult Zhana outright, which wouldn't serve to gain her trust or help Gertrude ferret out the actual details she was after, Gertrude held her tongue and didn't mention that Roberta needed structure, rules, and firm parenting. Instead, she waded into the issue at hand of whether or not Charlie had removed the guns from the house as he had been ordered.

"Could you tell me, by your account, what exactly happened the night Maude died?"

"Please," she said impatiently, "come in. Let's have a seat."

After a moment of appearing pained to leave the plants in dire straits, she pulled the screen door open for Gertrude, who smiled with relief that she would finally get to the bottom of this.

Following the woman, Gertrude stepped inside the New England cottage and noted the interior was as aged and manicured as Zhana—scuffed wooden floors, chipped and peeling navy-blue walls, and a blue checkered couch with matching chair, both in need of being reupholstered. Gertrude imagined, in its heyday, the home might have been the envy of the neighbors, but it was clearly nearing disrepair.

"Have a seat," said Zhana, indicating the coastal dining table beyond the couch. "Care for a drink?"

Gertrude didn't get the feeling she was offering anything but a cocktail, so she told her a water would be fine, as she settled onto one of the wooden chairs.

"I recommend a hard drink," said Zhana. "I'll certainly need one."

Without waiting for her response, Zhana rounded the half-wall separating the living room from the kitchen, and with her back to Gertrude started making what appeared to be martinis.

In Gertrude's observation, the woman's movements were pronounced, but also faintly glamorous as though she exuded old Hollywood grace.

When she finished, she carried over the martini glasses, filled to their brims, and set them gingerly on the table, and then she sat on the chair adjacent to Gertrude, who by this point found Zhana's need to drink glaringly inappropriate.

"The fact of the matter," she began after pursing her lips to her glass and drawing in a slow but long sip, "is that I don't know what happened to Maude. No one does. It was very late at night and I had gone to bed." Pausing as if to collect her scattered recollections, she trained her gaze on her drink.

"Take your time." Gertrude pulled the pen she had clipped to the top of her notepad and found her list of questions, flipping the sheets back, careful not to spill the family photo.

"The sound of the gunshot woke me," she went on. "And at first I was too scared to get out of bed. I don't know if I was in my bedroom for a minute or an hour, I really don't. It felt like an eternity."

"What did your husband do?" When Zhana furrowed her brow, seeming unsure, Gertrude clarified, "Wasn't he in bed with you if it was so late?"

"No," she said in a far away tone, "he wasn't."

Gertrude made a note.

"Why are you writing that down?"

In response to Zhana's distrustful scowl, she mentioned, "It's nothing to worry about."

"You're not a detective," she said in a stern tone. "We've already spoken to the police."

"No, I know. I'm just being thorough for my report. It's all internal."

Zhana studied her for a brief moment, perhaps scrutinizing the validity of her statement as if she would be able to tell whether or not Gertrude was lying.

"I guess Charlie was down in his office and I imagine Roberta was in her room. I was terrified it might have been an intruder and so I listened for Charlie, thinking he would take charge of the situation, but when I didn't hear anything, I ventured out and immediately saw her."

Explaining as much as she had seemed to age her and this time when Zhana paused to drink, lifting her martini with a trembling hand, she drained the glass.

"You don't understand," she went on in a quavering voice, low and weak. She swallowed hard. "The shot. Her head. She had blown her face off."

Giving weight to how difficult this was for Zhana, Gertrude sat with her in a long moment of supportive silence then asked, "She took her life in the hallway?"

Shaking her head, she corrected her. "No, Maude's bedroom is directly across the hall from ours. Her door was open. That's how I saw her."

Gertrude considered the few pieces she had collected. The timeline, according to Zhana, was disturbing. Though Charlie and Roberta were at home, as much as an hour could've passed and the first person to reach Maude was the only one who had been asleep? It didn't sound right. But Zhana had prefaced her statement by mentioning it might have only been a minute, she had been too frightened to process how much time had elapsed.

"What happened next?"

"I screamed," she said. "Charlie came racing up the stairs and Roberta came a few minutes after that."

"So he heard you scream but didn't hear a gun going off?"

"I really don't know," she sighed. "I had assumed that he had heard the shot and came running."

"The house isn't that big," she countered, looking around.

Eyeing the martini she had made for Gertrude, Zhana perked up, reaching out and asking, "Forgive me, are you going to drink that?"

"Please." Gertrude scooped the glass up and there was a careful pass-off between them, then Zhana brought the drink to her lips. When it seemed Zhana had relaxed, having overcome the massive hurdle of recounting the sequence of events that night, Gertrude set her pen down and laced her fingers together with an air of authority. "Mrs. King," she began, formulating choice words in her head before speaking them, "in your opinion, how was it possible for Maude to get her hands on one of your husband's guns?"

Straightening her back, her tone became direct. "Do not misunderstand this household," she warned. "Charlie is very careful with his firearms. We're not reckless."

Not only did it not address her question, it also contradicted Roberta's statement that there were so many guns strewn throughout the house that the girl had become desensitized.

"That may be," she said as though it were a verbal olive branch. "However, Maude is no longer alive-"

"Do you have any idea how determined these suicidal types are?" She challenged, eyes firing angrily. "How could we have stopped her from killing herself when she seemed fine? She was determined," she said, reiterating how tenacious those fated for suicide could be. "She hid her anguish and torment from us. She stole that weapon. She made no mistake. She had a dark mind and she succeeded at taking her own life."

Gertrude couldn't press the issue without causing her to shut down, but backing off entirely wasn't an option.

Before she could angle in further, however, Zhana groaned as if recalling something then spoke up in a milder tone. "The funeral was an utter disaster, all those unruly children crawling over every inch of this house, too ignorant to understand. But," she shifted her tone again, this time sounding strangely optimistic, "we really are fine and there's no need for you to be here."

"I know Charlie was ordered to remove all the firearms from the home," she stated in response. "I'm under the impression he hasn't."

"No, he hasn't."

That she had admitted it was almost jarring. Suddenly, Gertrude was aware of her pounding heart. This was a victory. Charlie had violated an order and once she filed the paperwork, she could get Roberta placed in a safe environment.

"You don't know what it's like here with Roberta." It sounded like her mouth had gone dry, and Zhana seemed to wilt, explaining, "If Maude had a reason for killing herself..." but she trailed off, unable to finish the thought.

"So, there may have been a reason?" She asked, surmising as much.

"I didn't want to have to get into it, because I don't want to blame Roberta, but Roberta's been in some trouble. None of it was her fault," she quickly clarified. "But over the years she's gotten involved with a few characters, a handful really. Men. We tried to shield Maude from it, but, you know, children can be very observant."

"What kind of trouble? Inappropriate behavior?" she asked with her pen poised to document the details.

"Oh please." Zhana placed her hand over Gertrude's, stopping her. "Please don't tie it up with Maude's death. Please."

Her widening eyes and sickened grimace gave Gertrude the impression she would shatter if what she were about to say was recorded so she set the pen down, listening.

"There were some charges, not against Roberta mind you; but, well, the young men she had become involved with were arrested."

Horrified in her assumption Roberta had been gang raped, she nearly gasped.

Catching Gertrude's near slip, Zhana immediately said, "Separate incidents. Over the past few years, that is. Charlie was convinced she was being victimized, but I never thought that. Anyway, that's how we got roped into all this social services business." She fanned her eyebrows up as though the connection was beyond her. "The point being, Maude was probably traumatized by these ordeals. Maybe she feared another ordeal was on the horizon."

"Can I speak with Roberta?"

"She isn't here. Probably off with that neighbor boy from up the street. Running wild and deflowering the neighborhood virgins," she explained, waving her hand in an exasperated yet graceful gesture, embarrassed but smiling.

"What about Charlie?"

"He's not here either. I can have him give you a call if you like?"

Flipping through the pages of her notebook to return to the top sheet, she realized she hadn't any business cards so she began writing her office and cell phone numbers down. Her hand felt vaguely limp and her fingers wouldn't fully grip the pen. She fought to keep the numbers legible, all the while a burning self-consciousness that she was taking too long roiled through her. When she finally tore off the information, she tried not to cringe. It looked as if it was written by a small child.

Zhana looked it over once Gertrude set it down in front of the empty martini glasses then met her gaze, saying, "That's an interesting hairdo."

Feigning a smile, Gertrude said, "It wasn't my doing," and got up from the table.

After Zhana rose as well, shedding her grief as though she only felt it at the table, she touched her blonde coif, disclosing, "Mine's been falling out." She forced a sheepish smile. "So it would seem we have that in common. Oh, not that yours is falling out," she quickly added as if the possibility of offending Gertrude pained her. "But I'll be bald soon, I'm sure." Then she clapped her hands in conclusion. "I'll walk you out."

Hoping to get her ID back from Roberta, but knowing it would have to wait until the girl returned, she followed Zhana through the house, and onto the porch where they stepped carefully over the array of gardening materials and went down the steps.

"When should I expect you back?"

As Zhana sank into her hip and smiled expectantly, Gertrude became distracted when she thought she smelled something odd like sour refuse, which seemed to be coming from the plants. Shaking off the notion, she met Zhana's gaze.

"Tomorrow."

The woman's smile hardened, though it retained a pleasant sheen. "I look forward to it."

Giving the bushes one last discreet glance—the rank smell could be in her head, brainwaves misfiring,—she pivoted, tearing her gaze away and starting down the driveway.

Walking across the gravel towards her car, which she had parked on the grassy shoulder of Moulton beyond the tree line, Gertrude found herself latching onto what it must have been like for Roberta to hear a gun go off in her own home. For as troubling as it was to try to make sense of the long delay between Roberta, Zhana, and even Charlie hearing the shot and finding Maude, if Gertrude was in the exact same situation, she couldn't be sure she would be quick up those stairs either.

But why was that? Why did she feel so certain that she would've hidden out, too terrified to investigate, if a shot had rung out in her house?

Just as she reached the driver's side door of her Audi, a rush of memories washed over her, transporting her to a time when she and Doris were living in their parents' house.

Doris had been perched at the end of her bed, flipping through the glossy pages of Better Homes & Gardens and dreaming of a different life, Gertrude had guessed, from where she had been reclining against the headboard.

She could remember watching her sister, but she had felt rattled, as though someone downstairs was percolating, readying to boil over in a rage. Her breaths had been shallow, her ears alert as if being poised, hyper-aware of the activity in the house could save them both from some terrible, impending fate.

As soon as the gun went off in her memory—Doris: startling to her feet in a jolt, gaze widening with hers, Gertrude: jumping off the bed to make sure the door was locked then holding her sister in their hiding spot behind the far side of the bed—Gertrude yanked the car door open and collapsed inside.

In order to ground herself like Dr. Hagstaff had advised, she squeezed the steering wheel, focusing on what her eyes were seeing beyond the windshield—late afternoon sunlight striking through the trees and illuminating the Balsam firs' bushy needles, the white Birch tree trunks, the faded asphalt road that wrapped around the bend and disappeared.

But though she hadn't entirely slipped back into the disturbing memory, she couldn't get her mother's face out of her head—Marsha's serpentine grin, her poised, dark eyes, the way she had looked down her nose at Doris and her with disdain, loosely slurring her words, *You'll live*, before shutting the door.

Marsha had used the same nonchalance as Zhana.

Rejecting the eerie comparison so that she wouldn't spring a panic-attack, Gertrude angled the key into the ignition, which called to mind how badly she was shuddering. But after five calming breaths, she managed to turn the engine and put the car in gear.

As she drove home, having determined she was in no condition to return to the office, she kept breathing deeply and every time her thoughts wandered into a territory that felt dangerous, she concentrated on using the tools Dr. Hagstaff had taught her.

It wasn't ten minutes before her Audi was crawling into its spot in front of her cabin, a modest two-story log home she had mortgaged directly after college.

She remembered that she had built it herself with the help of a few contractors and of course, Doris, who had a lot to say despite never lifting a finger, but she couldn't remember the details of the excursion, only that she had loved stacking the stone foundation, watching the logs erect into walls, chinking the seams when necessary, and marveling at the pattern of interlacing notches, the support beams of the deck where they met the pitched roof, the simple glass windows that somehow let in so much natural light.

All of her memories of Doris revolved around this house and the family they had become; just the two of them after Gertrude had helped get Doris out of their parents' house.

Realizing this brought on an eerie surge, as she padded quickly across the deck then opened the front door, which she had been forgetting to lock.

The house was dim and she did nothing to change that as she made a beeline for her bedroom. As she spilled onto the bed, dark recollections entwining tightly with nightmarish visions seeped into her mind, and she couldn't separate fiction from fact before slipping into a fitful sleep.

CHAPTER EIGHT

THE NEXT DAY, Gertrude woke in a panic, bolting upright, reeling from tangled dreams, and struggled to place where she was. *Her childhood bedroom?* No. *Brain injury rehab?* No. *Her cabin?* Once she had a grip on it, *she was in her cabin!* she flung the covers off and darted for the shower.

As the dawning sun bled across the tangerine sky, gradually turning it blue, she drove to the DCYF.

When she reached her cubicle, after passing her coworkers' cubicles, she popped the front of her blazer open single-handedly, unwilling to set down the morning paper.

Though it wasn't covered in ash, her desk reminded her of Pompeii and Herculaneum—perfectly preserved, life frozen after an unforeseeable act of God, items where they had always been, yet untouched for far too long.

The stacks of case files, reports, her notes written in sloppy cursive—some stained with coffee rings, others curling from humidity—would've been overwhelming had she not recognized each and every one of them.

Her spotty memory was a constant source of intrigue and frustration, but at least in the office she didn't feel lost.

As she began organizing her workspace, returning files to stout cabinets that were tucked under her wrapping desk, she mentally reviewed her afternoon with Zhana King. During their hour together, Gertrude hadn't jumbled her words. Her mind hadn't gone whiteout blank. She had held her own, covered more ground than she could've hoped, and had gained a real foothold, accomplishing precisely what Harry had instructed.

She should be feeling good, but instead an indistinct rawness had taken hold. Booting up her computer, she made an honest effort to pinpoint why that was. As the screen flickered to life, it occurred to her that because Roberta no longer had a sibling, because she was undeniably alone, because she didn't have someone like Gertrude to turn to like Doris had, she might never feel saved or safe no matter where she was placed.

Impacting her worry in this regard was an overpowering sense of guilt. She felt badly for Zhana. The guns, which Gertrude had seen no sign of when she had walked through the living room, spent time at the dining table, and peered into the kitchen, weren't Zhana's, but her husband's. Nevertheless, Zhana would be punished just as severely as Charlie, if either of them felt that having their only living daughter taken away was a punishment.

For one brief and flashing moment, Gertrude sensed an eerie potential. She had lost Doris,

Roberta was on the precipice of being displaced from her own family, but Gertrude pushed the kismet into the outer reaches of her thoughts. It would be, after all, wildly inappropriate even to consider.

Instead she pulled up a 10-1C template on her computer and began reviewing it. Filling out an Application for Temporary Removal of a Child would be the first step in placing Roberta in a temporary home.

As she typed, the cubicles around her began filling, lights flickering on here and there, conversations and telephone calls billowing up louder and louder, and soon the office was buzzing in full swing with its morning rhythm.

After completing the form and sending it to her printer—an old Dot Matrix that munched up the accordion of tractor-fed paper behind it and stuttered the application out onto the tray—she grabbed the morning paper, thinking she would give it a read in the meantime.

Gertrude nearly did a double take when she saw Zhana staring up at her from the front page. Shocked, she scanned the article without really taking a word of it in, as though the fact of its existence was too much to process. She slowed. The headline read, *Rift Emerges Among Gun Owners Over Safety of Our Children*, and was juxtaposed with a decades-old magazine photo of Zhana King. It made for a disturbing message. And if that weren't alarming enough, she caught the name of the journalist—Jake Livingston.

Wendy surprised her, appearing at the edge of her cubicle and booming a loud, *Morning!*

"Harry wants to see you in the conference room." Gertrude must have looked concerned, because Wendy quickly added, "For an update, don't look so scared. I'm going to sit in with you." Taking a beat and giving Gertrude the once over, she smiled. "You look sharp, Kid. That beret is working out."

"Thanks."

She rolled over to her printer and tore the application along its perforated edge, as Wendy slurped coffee noisily from her mug that was captioned with, *I survived another meeting that should've been an email*—her teeth clinking against the rim all the while.

"Got your notes?" She said when Gertrude joined her, a question Wendy would've never asked before the accident. "Crossed the T's and dotted the I's?"

"Yeah, it's right here," she said, indicating her notepad.

"Cup of Joe? Shouldn't be a long one, but with Harry you never know."

"Ah, I'm fine," she said, unsure but declining. She had been perpetually jumpy ever since leaving Dr. Hagstaff's care and the Brain Injury Rehabilitation Program's insulated environment. The last thing she needed was a caffeine induced heart arrhythmia.

As she followed Wendy—lumbering footfall, bohemian skirt swaying, greeting each social worker she passed with an exuberant *hiya!* or *get 'em tiger!* or sometimes *fresh coffee in the break room!* overcompensating if there had been friction with that individual in the past—Gertrude puzzled over the fact that the man who had fixed her car was a journalist for the Laconia Daily Sun.

In the conference room, Gertrude sat nervously and fell mute while Wendy chattered on about the finer details of her trivial hobbies like an estranged aunt desperate to connect with her child-niece who showed zero interest—*I nearly super-glued my finger to a ceramic cat last night!* (awkward laughter followed) *My husband tinkers with that old motorcycle nonstop, but won't let me help and I know a thing or two!*

Harry was the last to arrive and when he did, he wasted no time.

"Where are we at with the Kings?" He eased into a chair at the head of the table.

Fumbling through her notepad, she explained, "Roberta seems to be drinking freely under her mother's supervision and Zhana admitted the guns were still in the house. Here." She slid the application towards him for review.

Holding her breath while Harry skimmed the 10-1C checking she had filled the fields out correctly, Gertrude wrestled down the impulse to confront him, but ultimately succumbed.

"Sir, I learned that Roberta had been victimized by a number of men, who were eventually arrested for statutory rape."

Wendy looked grave and deferred to Harry to take this one. And Gertrude immediately felt as though she had done something wrong. But his expression—pained yet firm as though he was willing to work with her—was uncharacteristically reassuring.

When he didn't point out her oversight, she quickly apologized. "I must not have remembered the details after I read the file."

"Gerty, look." He choked out a heavy sigh, leaning forward.

But before he could elaborate, Wendy interrupted. "She's getting into the swing of things. Don't blame her."

"I wasn't going to. Gerty, you're a strong investigator," he began, but the compliment made her want to cringe. She had been good at her job, whether or not she had retained the skill was up for debate. He glanced over the application. "This form looks good."

"I can look over your notes next time," Wendy offered as a means to boost her confidence.

"Don't placate her," he barked, annoyed and defending Gertrude just as fiercely. "I have my suspicions about the Kings. I don't like that Charlie has the influence he does over his cop buddies and the velocity at which those men were arrested. I don't believe there was sufficient time to collect evidence, and I also don't believe the evidence documented wasn't somehow..." He seemed to wince, "*altered* and I know I shouldn't say that. Gerty, I know you can go in with a fresh pair of eyes. Truth be told I don't know what's going on, but the police have been stalling and sometimes sabotaging this department. You're doing good work."

Gertrude was struggling with his use of double negatives.

"The goal remains," he announced. "We're going to keep taking steps to place Roberta in a safe home." He rubbed his eyes, drawing in a deep breath, then glanced over the application. "This is solid work. I'll see if I can't file it. In the meantime, before we get her out, I'm still making efforts to get the guns removed. I've pulled a few strings with the DA to put pressure on the police to actually go in and seize those weapons. As soon as I receive word, Gerty, I'll let you know. I would like you to be there with Roberta to make sure Charlie doesn't do something rash."

"Okay," she said, though she hadn't the foggiest idea how she might prevent the man from doing something rash especially since, in this context, she had to assume that Harry meant *violence*. Recalling Zhana's suspicion, she asked, "Do you think the statutory rape incidences are connected to Maude's suicide?"

Validating the question, Wendy trained her concern on Harry as well.

"I don't know what I think except that this is a royal mess and that damned article is only going to make things worse."

He was rubbing his eyes again.

When her brow knit, Wendy quietly asked her, "Have you read it? The Livingston article?"

"The headline looked promising," said Harry, preparing to fill her in, "but the slant was that this office effed up."

Gaping, Gertrude asked, "It said we *effed up*? Social services?"

"No mention of Charlie other than his stellar reputation."

Irate, Wendy nodded, backing him up.

"Jake Livingston made Zhana King out to be some kind of oblivious clown," he added, rising from the table, application in hand. "To be fair, he did make a few valid points about gun control, but it was soft, national statistics, nothing that directly blamed the laws around here." When he reached the door and pulled it open, he turned, purposely making eye contact with Gertrude. "I should've reminded you about the statutory rape charges. We're glad to have you back. This is a family." Once his apology landed, he concluded, "If we're going to get Roberta out, our reports and applications have to be laser focused on the hazards in that house. We have to prove that there is evidence of reckless endangerment."

"Right," said Gertrude.

Wendy didn't let her leave when they were alone, placing her hand over Gertrude's.

"Be careful with those people."

"I will."

Wendy tapped her hand, giving her a smile, and then hoisted herself up from the table.

"Coming?"

Rising from her chair and collecting her notepad to show that she was right behind them, Dr. Hagstaff crossed her mind. Maybe she could take an early lunch or make an excuse for ducking out now.

When she reached her cubicle, she gave him a call, hunching secretively with her back to the room. With each ring, her anxiety elevated until she could hear her pulse pounding in her ears, and as soon as a female voice came through—his administrative assistant?—she interrupted with a sharp tone.

"I need to see Dr. Hagstaff."

"May I ask-"

"It's Gertrude." Confused silence on the other end had her blurting out, "Inman. Gertrude Inman."

Not that she was being met with resistance, his assistant Abby was kind and efficient and didn't object to her heading over, though she put her on hold, but Gertrude feared her rising panic would culminate into a career-ending breakdown. She couldn't get her speeding thoughts to slow down long enough to figure out why in the hell this was happening.

Before Abby could return on the line, Gertrude grabbed her purse and laptop satchel and was darting through the office and out the door.

She nearly broke the car door off its hinges, yanking it open, then collapsed behind the steering wheel—*SMILE!*

She ripped the index card off and shredded it, her vision blurring and tone whimpering like a wounded animal, as the pendulum of her emotions swung up into full-blown, hyperventilating gasps.

Focus on your breathing.

But her breathing—convulsive hitches, desperate straining, a thread of oxygen flossing up and down her tightening throat yet never reaching her lungs—was all too apparent.

She was sure she would pass out before she got a grip, but then as suddenly as the attack had seized her, it dissipated. Squeezing the steering wheel, she glanced around the parking lot and up the sidewalk, embarrassed she might have been seen, but there was no one around. She started the car, found Reverse, and backed cautiously out of her parking spot.

As Gertrude drove along Beacon Street West, passing brick buildings that never seemed inhabited and green-awning shops that looked just as sleepy, the rapture of adrenaline cooling in her veins gave her the mild shakes, but she stayed alert to the traffic around her vehicle, used her blinker at every turn, and was soon merging onto the Daniel Webster Highway, which would take her to the rehabilitation center.

She kept the speedometer hovering around forty miles per hour and didn't glance at the cars whipping around her in the left lane, but she looked in her rearview mirror and noticed a truck was coasting just shy of her bumper even though there had been plenty of opportunities for it to pass. Her hibernating panic began simmering all over again.

"Go around me," she said, waving her hand, not that the driver could see.

She jerked her Audi back into its lane when she realized she had drifted, holding her eyes on the rearview too long.

The truck lurched at her bumper, sending a fresh jolt of adrenaline searing through her veins. What were they doing? She tried not to glance at the mirror again, but a hot flash of sweat broke out across her skin at the thought of not looking.

Flipping her right blinker on to indicate she was about to veer onto the shoulder, if not exit the first chance she got, and checking the rearview mirror, she saw the truck buck forward.

It hit her.

The impact was stark and her head snapped back against the hard curve of her seat. At first she assumed another vehicle had rear-ended the truck and it was about to be a pile-up, but glancing back for a split second, her instincts told her that wasn't the case. She slammed her foot on the gas, gunning it, and locked her eyes on the empty road ahead.

The needle on the speedometer angled around, passing fifty miles per hour, then sixty miles per hour, then seventy miles per hour, and finally it passed eighty miles per hour, and she came upon a sixteen wheeler. She eased her foot off the gas, stealing a peek at her mirrors where the truck was nowhere to be seen.

No sooner than she returned her eyes to the road and sighed out a shuddering breath of relief, she heard sirens wailing behind her.

Looking in the rearview mirror again, a state cruiser was gaining on her.

"Please don't be for me," she groaned.

But the cop car was flashing its headlights at her and she knew if she didn't pull over, the power speaker would come on next.

Squeezing the brake and easing onto the shoulder, Gertrude wracked her brain for where the vehicle registration might be. As soon as she came to a stop, she hunted through the inner door pockets, then the stow-away compartment between the driver and passenger seats, and finally the glove box. Luckily, she found it sprouting out of the Audi manual.

After placing it and her license in her lap and cranking her window down, she watched the patrolman, a state trooper in a forest-green button down with a golden crest on the sleeve, tan tie and slacks matching his Mountie hat, approach her vehicle. He rested his hand on his glistening gun where it hung on his hip, as he neared her window, boots crunching glass and gravel.

His posture was erect—rigid gait and boxed shoulders—like a drill sergeant just itching for confrontation. But when he stared down at her through the open window, the texture of his skin—deeply creased around the eyes, ruddy cheeks, taut jowls along his jaw—didn't match up to the fight and fire in his coal-black eyes.

He didn't ask for her license and registration, but angled in on her, snorting as though the sight of her hadn't lived up to his expectation.

"There was a truck," she explained. Her voice cracked so she cleared it and tried to speak loudly so that she would be heard over the sounds of cars whipping by. "A truck rear-ended me from behind. I was trying to get away from it. I wouldn't speed otherwise." She felt scattered, searching her memory for the truck's make and model, but even the color eluded her. "I'm sure there's damage if you check."

His tone was like feedback through an amplifier, horrid and sustained, startling her. "Every inch of your car is damaged."

She resigned herself to the ticket she had coming and slumped back in her seat.

Removing his hat and leaning his forearm along the sill, he scowled, his steely eyes boring through her as if she both amused and sickened him. She shrunk deeper into her seat, recoiling in response.

"You know everyone thought so highly of you, fighting your way up from the bottom of Lake Winnipesaukee like that." He sucked his teeth for a beat, glancing out at the highway, then steadied his gaze on her. "Losing a sister like you did, well, I would've thought you would be understanding."

In danger of trembling, she broke eye contact, lowering her gaze, which happened to settle on his badge—a golden eagle soaring over a ship and a branch of laurels underneath. Then she caught his surname clipped beneath the badge: King.

She hoped her tone would come out steady and not stutter, as she asserted, "I would like to file a police report against the truck that rear-ended me, Officer, please."

"No, I don't think you would."

He was too old to be Charlie. Factoring his weathered face and white hair, she pegged him for sixty-five, maybe sixty years old. If he was related to Charlie at all, and she had no question that he was, he had to be his father.

"People round here are probably a bit riled up, you poking around a family in mourning and all."

This was his excuse for why a truck purposefully rear-ended her?

"I'm thinking you'll do the right thing. Maybe take a little more time for yourself. Lord knows you're probably scaring off the children you work with, your face busted up like that." He clenched his jaw then worked his cracked lips into a brittle smile. "Why don't we chalk this up to a warning?" She knew when she was being threatened, though it rarely happened. "For speeding, that is. I know you'll do the right thing otherwise."

The way he was staring at her, she had to assume he expected confirmation. When she didn't give it, he snorted a laugh and started back towards his cruiser, whistling a death tune as he went.

What were the Kings after, she wondered? What was so vital about keeping both Roberta and the firearms in the house? And why didn't any of them seem grief-stricken that Maude had taken her own life?

As Gertrude signaled onto the highway, accelerating hard and shifting fast, ironclad determination to uncover their secrets formed around her like a shield.

Yet her instincts told her that when it came to the Kings and their peculiar grip on this town, she was facing an uphill battle, plain and simple.

Trust no one, she thought, and she might have a prayer of staying alive.

CHAPTER NINE

"I WISH YOU had called instead of showing up unannounced." Zhana was flitting about the porch, tidying up her gardening tools and making the place look slightly better as if for Gertrude's benefit. "I would've made sure Charlie was home."

Barely acknowledging Gertrude, Roberta appeared bored from where she was perched on the railing, her bare feet on the keg, toes exploring the edge of the barrel as she watched her mother.

"Roberta," said Zhana.

The girl's eyes were glazed over, but she said, "Hmm?"

"Why don't you pull those lawn chairs out of the basement?"

She slid off the railing, her red dress snagging, but she jerked at it and the material snapped off the splintered wood. Zhana eyed her as her daughter padded down the steps and circled towards the back of the house, disappearing.

A silken handkerchief with purple and mauve swirls—a 60s pattern—wrapped Zhana's head, but she pulled it off and picked its knot open then shook it like a flag. Her hair wasn't styled as precisely today. It flowed when she ran her fingers through. A few strands fluttered down and she wiggled others over the side of the porch.

Observing her, but feeling odd—there was something awkward about watching Zhana finger-comb dead hair off her scalp—Gertrude asked, "So where is Charlie?"

"I apologize. I really can't tell you. He's off somewhere."

"You don't know where he is?"

"Sorry." She shrugged with a little wave of her hand, looking across the dusky yard.

There had been no delays or pitfalls with the 10-1C application. Apparently Harry had received confirmation from the Laconia Police that they were planning to move forward with the court order and were scheduled to arrive shortly. Gertrude thought it would've taken longer than a day to process and, considering her bizarre encounter with Peter King on the highway, she had actually assumed the order had been shredded and shoved in a recycling bin at the precinct.

It was probably for the best that Charlie wasn't here. This might actually go smoothly.

Roberta returned, dragging a folded lawn chair across the grass then up the steps, but Zhana snatched it, grumbling about her daughter's carelessness.

When she unfolded the chair, placing the rickety thing near the railing, Gertrude realized its legs weren't three inches off the ground.

"There you are," said Zhana, indicating she could have a seat. "Would anyone like a drink?"

"Thank you, no." Gertrude was hesitant to sit so she made an excuse of glancing at Roberta, who seemed to be debating what she would like, but she also declined, returning to the railing.

After Zhana went inside, the screen door slapped shut, bouncing a few times in the frame.

"You're here a lot," Roberta commented. "I thought you guys were supposed to come once a month."

"Considering everything that's happened, we feel that checking in on you frequently is necessary," she explained, as she sat down in the low chair.

As soon as she did, she regretted it. She felt like a dog looking up at its master.

"What's really going on?"

"I just want to make sure you're safe," she said quietly. Through the screen door she could hear Zhana faintly clunking around in the kitchen.

"Is this about the article?" She didn't wait for a response. She was shaking her head and glaring through the screen door. "I doubt she gets it."

"Have you had any counseling since..." trailing off, she wasn't sure how to phrase it delicately then said, "since the attacks, by those men?"

"It's not what you think," she said, implying there was no need for therapy.

Gertrude struggled to divide her attention between Roberta and listening for Zhana in the house. In terms of making a drink, Zhana was taking a while, and Gertrude grew nervous she might make a phone call, warn Charlie, or worse, tip off her father-in-law, who Gertrude hoped to never see again.

"What should I think?" she asked the girl.

Roberta took her time and seemed to reject a few replies that formed in her mouth. Then, finally, she stated, "The way things are here, you're not going to be able to change them."

"Why do you think that?"

Turning sullen, her gaze fell and she frowned, started swinging her leg.

Zhana returned and a graceful balancing act ensued, flipping on the porch light with her elbow and using her foot to kick open the screen door since her hands were full with two martinis—both for her, Gertrude assumed, though part of her was curious to see whether or not Zhana would hand one to her daughter.

Though the light was soft, it caused the darkening dusk around the house to look like a black abyss. Shadows covered the driveway, the road behind it a mere tracing. Gertrude could see the lake, the moon's glow across the water, but only if she turned her head.

"So," said Zhana, bending at the waist and setting one of the drinks at Gertrude's feet, "what would you like to talk about this time?"

Roberta cut in with a biting idea. "Why don't we talk about that article?"

"You want to talk about it?" Zhana snapped. "You think I'm happy?"

"You're the one who gave them that magazine photo. What did you expect?"

Looking up at them as they hissed like two rattlesnakes lashing out at each other, Gertrude got the impression they had forgotten she was there and their overlapping jeers—*I had every right to use that photo!* and Roberta trumping her mother's intensity, *You're the joke of the town* and Zhana shouting, *That's the pot calling the kettle black,* then *You would like to find me with a bullet in my head,* and simultaneously *Just wait until Charlie gets home*—culminated into a crescendo when Zhana exploded, screaming: "Take off my dress!"

In a tone so resigned Gertrude almost didn't hear her, Roberta said, "Fine," pulling the straps over her shoulders and letting the dress fall to her feet, which left her standing with nothing on but a simple black bra and plain underwear.

Accusingly, Zhana said, "You're the reason my hair is falling out." She gulped her martini to compose herself then snapped, "People can see you-"

"There's no one out here."

"I'll not have you conducting yourself without dignity. Go inside. Put some clothes on."

"I don't have any clothes."

"Yes, you do."

"They've been sitting in the hamper. I'm not going to wear dirty clothes."

"Ah," Zhana groaned, as if agreeing, then mumbled distractedly, "I have to get that washer fixed."

Gertrude, who had been watching the exchange with unblinking eyes, noticed a set of scars over Roberta's right thigh—fine lines, as close-set as wood grains—wrapping from her inner thigh to her outer hip bone.

"Can I wear something of yours?" Roberta asked her mother.

Having given up, Zhana sighed in defeat. "Pick out something sensible and nothing too expensive." Then she glanced down at Gertrude, giving her a vexed smile as if to say, *See what I have to put up with?*

But Roberta didn't pad into the house. She simply pulled her mother's red dress up and slid the straps over her shoulders, having finally been clever enough to get Zhana's permission to wear the dress.

"I can't take your games!" Zhana muttered, pacing away. "I just can't with this!"

Startling her, Gertrude's cell vibrated in the front pocket of her jeans. When she stretched her leg out to fit her hand in her pocket, she accidentally kicked over the martini glass. "Damn." She reached for it, but it was rolling away, spewing vodka across the porch and arching towards the steps.

Roberta grabbed it and used her foot to spread the puddle so it would drip between the wooden slats, as Gertrude checked her cell phone.

Swiping the screen, she saw a text message from Harold McNeil, which read:

More BS. Cops aren't coming.

"Excuse me," she said, getting to her feet and moving absentmindedly down the porch steps, as she composed a reply. After she sent it—*aargh okay*—she turned and found Zhana staring at her. "I might have to take off."

"Very well," said Zhana, her eyebrows rising. She shot a warning glare at Roberta then pulled open the screen door. "Goodnight."

Gertrude watched the door thwack shut then gave Roberta a parting smirk and started off down the driveway for her car, but Roberta padded after her, catching up.

"Don't you want your ID back?"

She stopped, saying, "Yes, I would."

As if negotiating, Roberta asked, "Why are you really here?" Gertrude's hesitation seemed to provoke her. "Look, you're obviously trying to accomplish something. The other woman almost never came and when she did it was barely five minutes. And the woman before her came once a week and it was usually scheduled and she only talked to my mom then made sure I was breathing. So what are you doing?"

"We have your best interest in mind," she recited. It was right out of the manual.

"But you were waiting for someone, weren't you?" Then urgently, she asked, "You're trying to get me out of here?"

Roberta looked miserable and the optimistic glint in her eyes was gut wrenching, but she wasn't sure giving the girl hope would be responsible. "It's a long process," she began. "And it's complicated. Your dad was ordered to remove his firearms from the house and he didn't, so I was expecting the police. In terms of removing you, it might work in our favor that we can't seem to get the guns out. It proves the environment isn't safe. My boss is filing an application with the court, but it'll take time to get the order. Is that something you want?"

"Does it matter what I want?" she asked as though she was genuinely interested.

"At this point it might not," she admitted.

"Where would I go?"

"A foster home." When Roberta's expression turned fearful, she added, "It would be a family around here. You would go to the same high school. It would be a big change, but you would retain a lot of your usual life and you would see your parents under supervision."

Her brow furrowed as if bearing all that in mind was worrisome, but she managed a doubtful smile, which soon dropped, her face going long.

"He'll stop you," she said.

"Your dad?"

Scraping her teeth over her lip, she nodded. "The police are never going to help you."

"Yeah, I'm realizing that."

She twisted her big toe into the gravel and when she glanced up again, backlit by the dim porch light yards behind her, she looked ghostly, her black eyes staring up.

"People keep telling me it'll all be over soon, you know, because I'll be eighteen. They think I'll be able to leave, but I won't. He's not going to let me leave. Sometimes I think about running away. He would find me, though." She fell silent, searching Gertrude's eyes. "He wants me to do *it* to Jake."

It took a moment to place precisely what she was referring to then the five arrested men sprang to mind.

"He had you do that to those men?" Gertrude felt like the earth was tipping off its axis, realizing the entire criminal justice system was corrupt. "Why?"

"I don't know the particulars. I just know what happens if I don't do what he says." She swallowed grimly as if choking a memory down. "They got in his way somehow, doing something, I don't know."

"So they never actually assaulted you?"

"Assaulted? No. But I slept with them. Well, some of them. All you really need is semen to get them locked up, so technically, you don't have to have sex with them."

Horrified, Gertrude almost couldn't believe what she was hearing, and Roberta's easy nature, her casual tone, was alarming. She nearly insisted they go to the police station right now to give a statement—if Charlie was coercing his daughter into sexual acts to entrap men, Gertrude could take Roberta out of the house right this instant—but the police weren't an option and wrapping her head around that hard fact made her wince in frustration.

Working it through out loud, she asked, "Your dad told you to seduce Jake Livingston?"

Ashamed, she went back to twisting her toe in the dirt. "Yeah."

"Because of the article?"

"No, I mean, he probably didn't like what Jake wrote, but the article came out this morning," she said as though Gertrude was a bit dense when it came to the timeline. "I don't think my dad wants anyone living within five miles of our house."

"Charlie is sending men to prison because they live too close to his house?" She gaped, astonished. "What the hell is going on inside your house?"

"All kinds of crap," she stated, intentionally stirring up intrigue, or at least that was how Gertrude read her.

"Tell me."

"Why? You won't be able to do anything about it."

"I'll find a way," she asserted, but Roberta smiled and began swaying coyly, which gave Gertrude the strange feeling this was a game to her. "Are you messing with me?"

"There's something wrong with your brain, isn't there? Something happened to you."

Straightening her spine, she countered with, "What makes you think that?"

"You're better today," she observed, evasively. "You didn't ramble at all." She was stepping in close and studying Gertrude's face. "Did someone hurt you?"

"No, it was a car accident."

"Were you driving?" Her eyes widened, catching the moon's reflection.

With night falling, the air was cooling off. A thin veil of fog crept towards them from the lake.

"I was."

Reaching her hand up, she nearly touched the bruised side of Gertrude's face. "You slammed against the window there. Doctors had to shave your head?"

"It's growing back," she pointed out, taking a step back. "I don't remember anything, so there's no sense in asking me."

Roberta held her gaze, as she folded her arms against the eerie chill that was sweeping through.

"I had a sister," she went on. "She died. Wasn't wearing her seatbelt, I'm told. She was your age, maybe you knew her, Doris Inman?"

"I don't have that many friends at school."

Gertrude got the feeling she was being polite, that perhaps Roberta didn't care for Doris, but she couldn't be certain that was the meaning behind Roberta's narrowing eyes.

"My brain is fine. Using the wrong word here and there is just superficial damage," she said, which wasn't true, but Roberta didn't need to know that. "And I'm a rambler anyway, so, no change there."

"I'm sorry you lost your sister."

"I'm sorry you lost yours."

Holding each other's gazes, Gertrude felt an immense urge to embrace her. She wanted to grab hold of her, pull her in, feel the realness of her body, maybe even feel Roberta's heart beating against her own chest, feel her warmth, smell her hair, and scream and cry. But knowing it would be impossible to reach through a living girl to touch a dead one, she simply closed her eyes for a long moment.

When she opened them, she asked, "Can I get my ID now?"

"You can get it any time you like." Registering Gertrude's confusion, Roberta quirked her mouth into a funny smile. "It's in the dirt."

Then she turned on her heel and started for the lake, looking like a skeleton gliding through mist. Gertrude watched her until she vanished, fog billowing up around her so thickly it swallowed the red of her dress.

As Gertrude set off for her car, she sensed more than saw someone walking on the road. Training her gaze and squinting her eyes, she realized it was a kid, a boy rather, fourteen or perhaps fifteen, though if he was fifteen he was short for his age.

His thin, long limbs and sloping shoulders, which should've made him seem taller, actually made him look frail, like he would snap if you squeezed him too hard. He appeared to be carrying a Tupperware container in his petite hands. Dressed in a basic pair of jeans, a tee shirt, and Converse sneakers, there was nothing distinct or remarkable about him. He looked like every kid she had ever seen, but his features, she realized as they passed one another, were delicate and mousey, unusual—dainty dark eyebrows, a tight narrow mouth, and a slightly oversized nose.

When she felt it wouldn't be obvious, she turned, watching him stalk up the Kings' driveway. He slowed, behaving somewhat cautiously as he came to the porch steps. He didn't ascend them, didn't cross the porch or knock on the door.

For some reason, he piqued her curiosity. Maybe it was because the overall feel of him was so incongruent with Roberta's that she couldn't imagine them being friends. In fact, Roberta was so odd she couldn't imagine her being friends with anyone. She knew if Doris were alive, she would tell Gertrude the real deal about Roberta.

Grieving this extra layer of loss, she climbed in her car and started it up. As soon as she was buckled in and about to shift into First gear, the image of a scarred thigh popped into her mind. She knew it was supposed to be Roberta's, the marks she had seen when the girl had let her dress fall off, but for some reason her brain was associating the image with her sister.

The memory was faint, but real.

She had seen the same scars on Doris.

Without question, she had. Her sister's scars had been in the same exact place—the upper thigh. Self-mutilation. Why had Doris been doing that to herself? She knew it was a symptom, but of what?

Clinically speaking, she knew the reasons behind self-harm. Overwhelming emotional turmoil—sadness, distress, anxiety, and confusion—could become so extreme that a teenager, at a loss for a healthy way to cope, might seek to alleviate the internal pain by hurting themselves.

At least you have scars on the outside. Roberta had said that to her the first day that Gertrude had shown up at the house. She had said that she didn't have scars on the inside, but open wounds that never healed.

Did Doris?

Roberta had clearly been compelled to reflect those internal wounds on her body, cutting her skin, bleeding, darkly soothing her emotional pain.

But why had Doris done that?

Gertrude could feel the answer deep within her memory, dodging around her brain, evading her. She sensed with absolute certainty that her sister's cutting had revolved around the real reason she had moved in with Gertrude. And Gertrude even sensed that the particular reason somehow dovetailed into the car accident, but the truth behind it all remained hidden in corners of her mind she couldn't access.

Her frustration built as she racked and racked her brain. But she felt like sifting sand through her fingers in search of a pearl on a five-mile beach, and soon she was furious. Because of it, and for reasons she couldn't explain, Jake Livingston came to mind. Though it was borderline insane and devoid of all logic, directing her anger at him and at his article felt satisfying. He had glorified Charlie King, ridiculed Zhana, and most egregiously of all, he had blamed the DCYF for Maude's death. And recognizing all of this—who and what he really was—she realized that despising Jake Livingston felt more than satisfying. It felt right.

She had every intention of giving him a piece of her mind.

CHAPTER TEN

THE FLOODLIGHTS that were angled over the front door of his cabin shed just enough light for Gertrude to recognize Jake's pickup truck parked in the driveway.

The journalist was home.

She parked on the grass, killing the engine before she even came to a complete stop, and started for the front door, as fog undulating over the yard crept towards her.

Jake lived in a saltbox house that looked at least a century old. Swallowed in gnarly Birch trees that were emerging from the soil, the roots of which threatened to shift the foundation, the architecture looked as dilapidated as the Kings' house.

As soon as she reached the door ready to pound on it and demand answers, it popped inward and Jake, surprised by her arrival and a bit confused, asked her if she had broken down.

"What the hell was that article about?" she blurted out.

"Provocative," he said, but it sounded more like a guess. "I can explain."

"Provoking who?" In the throes of confronting him, her thoughts scrambled and articulating herself was shot to hell.

"Can I invite you in?"

She hadn't anticipated that, hadn't planned this beyond unloading her frustration. His welcoming tone, his easy stance, the concerned glint in his eyes, and his cooperative attitude had her thrown.

"Come in, please," he said, making room as though doing so would summon her inside.

"Did you get a chance to get your car over to Larry's?" he asked when she hadn't moved.

"Not yet."

He lifted his eyebrow at that and plowed his fingers through his chestnut-brown hair, drawing attention to its cowlicks.

"Really, we can talk inside." He scanned the dark road behind her as though he didn't trust it.

Giving him a quick glance as she debated, she noted worn-out jeans and a thin, moth-eaten tee hugging his relaxed posture, both of which gave her the impression she had caught him unwinding. And when she followed him into his cluttered living room and spied a bottle of beer on the coffee table, it confirmed as much.

"Feel like a beer?"

Without thinking she said, "I can't drink," but didn't know why.

As Jake feigned tidying up, clearing files and old newspapers from the couch and making excuses for the disarray that sounded more like fibs—*Usually it isn't this bad,* and *I'm this close to hiring a maid* peppered in with misplaced compliments *I wish I couldn't drink* and *You must be a morning person*—Gertrude wondered why she thought she couldn't drink.

Images of her kitchen over the years flashed through her mind—white wine in the refrigerator door, liquor in the cabinet above the stove, beer bottles in the recycling bin. It wasn't that she couldn't drink. It was that she shouldn't, but why?

The answer came clear as a bell as if there was a second person in her head—because of the accident.

Had she been drinking that night?

Gertrude nearly touched upon that memory, when the sight of Jake plucking up his beer, causing dew droplets to roll down its side, yanked her back to the present time.

"I'm not happy with how the article came out," he started. "For what it's worth, I didn't write half of it." In response to her skepticism, he added, "My editor must have rewrote most of it, because what they printed wasn't what I turned in."

She wanted to doubt him, but he carried himself with an air of honesty she couldn't overlook.

"Really," he insisted when she screwed her face up, her expression lagging behind the speed of her thoughts. "I can show you what I turned in." Nearly interrupting himself, he blurted out, "But it's upstairs. You would have to come up to my computer. It's not a laptop."

She hadn't even sat down.

"I'm not going upstairs with you."

"Right, no, I know. I wouldn't either." He glanced around, seeming to take in her perspective. "And I didn't mean it like that."

Suddenly awkward about tipping her off that the thought of her upstairs in some other capacity had perhaps crossed his mind, he took a moment to drink some beer—big, nervous gulps. Then he sat, pushing a precarious tower of files behind him on the couch. If she had been inclined to sit, he hadn't left her much room.

"All that stuff printed about the DCYF wasn't me," he went on.

He seemed sincere, but she couldn't understand why it was so important to him that she should believe it. Why did he care what she thought?

"Has Roberta approached you at all?" When he studied her instead of responding, she stated, "I think she's being coerced," but his rising eyebrows told her that she had been too vague. He couldn't make the leap from her first point to her second. "It's obviously no secret I'm her social worker."

"Yeah, I got that," he said, a crooked smile forming at the corner of his mouth.

"She confided in me." Before she could go on, she drew in a deep breath, mourning the loss of her ethics for what she was about to reveal. But then she stopped herself. Jake didn't have to know about the real reason five men had been incarcerated for tangling with Roberta, and he shouldn't.

She needed to be extremely cautious about what she told him. He could print anything, or worse, his editor could pervert it to Roberta's detriment.

"I think she might try something with you." It wasn't enough for him to catch on, so she added, "Seduce you. Make claims. Get you into serious trouble."

"Like the others…"

"So you know?"

Holding her gaze was his confirmation.

She asked, "Has she tried anything with you?"

"I'll watch my back. You should too."

Offended on Roberta's behalf, she asked, "You think she's responsible?"

"You think someone else is?"

"Off the record," she warned, so there would be no misunderstanding. When he agreed with a nod, she disclosed, "She indicated that Charlie had put pressure on her."

He stilled, studying her, and though he grew serious the light behind his eyes brightened.

"I want you to see something," he said, jumping off the couch. "I'll be right back."

He padded up the stairs and as she sat, angling herself onto the corner of the couch and assessing the three feet beside her to estimate whether or not he would have room, she heard him hunting around overhead—objects clanking to the floor, Jake muttering swears.

When he returned, he was so focused on a sheet of paper in his hands, which looked as if it had been shredded then taped together, that he sat on the couch, oblivious to their close proximity. His leg brushed against hers and if she hadn't crossed her arms and pressed herself against the arm of the couch, their shoulders would've touched.

"I found this," he said, tilting the sheet so she could look at it with him. Bold letters at the top of the form read: Homicide Report. She noticed it was only partially filled out. "My guess is that the responding officer filled it out, but was discharged, and the form was shredded."

"Where did you find this?"

"Dumpster diving." Two seconds after he admitted it, his face flushed red, then he added,

"There's a lot you can find out rummaging through trash."

"I'm not judging."

Returning her eyes to the report, she skimmed over the content.

"See here?" He pointed to the Details of Offense section.

"Weapon not present," she said, reading out loud. Then she repeated the detail, mumbling under her breath as though the tighter she mentally grasped the information the more disturbing it became. "If she shot herself, the gun would be in her hand if not a few inches away depending on how she hit the floor. How could there be no weapon if she killed herself?"

"Exactly."

"Unless," she countered, playing devil's advocate, "Charlie or Zhana didn't want this coming down on them and they removed the weapon."

"But that wasn't how things were framed in the police report that *was* filed."

When she glanced at him, their eyes locked and she sensed he wouldn't look away unless she did.

"The police report on file," he went on, "was a different form first of all, one for suspected suicide. And it notes that a GLOCK 27 was found near her right hand."

"What?"

"Here's what I think," he said, setting the stage. "When the Kings called the cops, the responding officer arrived, looked at the scene, found no weapon, and immediately thought it was a homicide. I doubt he would draw up the report then and there. That's not how it's done procedurally. But maybe he was a smart guy, and got a bad feeling when his superiors showed up. Maybe when he got back to the precinct, he went ahead with filling out the homicide report. Maybe he was going to submit it to someone he thought would believe his account, someone above the cops who were behind the cover up. Or maybe he was so green he did start filling out the report on the scene and got shut down. Either way, someone at the house that night, one of the cops, didn't find a weapon, and made this report. And get this; the GLOCK 27 noted on the report, which correspondingly was logged into evidence at the precinct, was only logged in the system. My contact at the station told me the actual gun isn't sitting in the evidence locker."

"And that's why Charlie has refused to turn in his weapons?"

"At this point, I doubt if anyone over there would dare to match the firearms against the registrations, apples-to-apples, but if they did, they might have come across the murder weapon, or more likely would not find a match, which would be evidence someone discarded the weapon after using it to kill Maude King."

Gertrude needed a moment to absorb the magnitude of it all. She wanted to believe the Homicide Report was some kind of horrendous administrative error, that it wasn't an indication of a conspiracy, but there was no way for her to make the leap.

"If Maude didn't kill herself," she said finally, "then who did? And why?"

"That's what I would like to know."

She felt him staring, as chills washed over her.

"Hey, are you okay?" he asked when she started trembling.

She had hoped it wasn't obvious. "Yeah. Fine." Crossing her arms tighter, she added, "Just cold."

But she wasn't. She was riveted.

"I wanted to talk to whoever wrote up the Homicide Report," he went on, "but the bottom wasn't signed. So I asked my contact at the precinct, an HR guy. He told me that just three days after Maude's death, on July 5th, one of the officers dropped off the payroll. A guy named Kevin Robinson. I tried to get in touch with him, but was told he had left town. There was no forwarding address, no indication as to where he went. It's like the guy disappeared."

If Maude had been killed, if people who knew were disappearing, it meant that Roberta was in danger far graver than she had ever anticipated. Roberta had revealed her father's twisted nature and how she'd had to do things though she hadn't understood the greater picture of why. Was obeying her strategy for staying alive? Had Maude not risen to the same potential?

"Do they know you have this?" she asked, taking the tattered report from him to skim it.

"I've been careful. But if Roberta's aiming to get me locked up..."

"Then they probably know," she supplied, then began thinking out loud, refining the motive to a razor's edge that might cut to the core of this thing. "The other men lived around the Kings. Do you think they saw something at the house and were *eliminated* because of it?"

"I don't know. They wouldn't tell me."

She sank into deep thought, engulfed in fears that this case was way over her head, her supervisor's head, insurmountable.

"Hey," he said, as concerned as he had been before, reading her expression and gently touching her shoulder—his hand warm and strong. "Let me give you my numbers."

He worked his cell phone out of the front of his jeans and started tapping the screen with both thumbs. "What's your number?"

Vacantly, she recited it for him, and when he tapped the screen a few more times and shoved his cell in his pocket, she felt her own phone vibrate once in her jeans.

"Are you going to be all right getting home?"

She said, "Yeah," but her voice was a thread.

"Let me walk you out."

Getting up from the couch, he took the report from her and set it beside his beer on the coffee table. When they reached the front door, he held it open for her and she paused on the mulch walkway, while he closed up.

"You can call me any time," he mentioned as they walked out of the floodlights' glow and into darkness—shadows upon shadows throughout the woods surrounding them.

Abruptly, she turned to him when they neared the driver's side door, asking, "You think Charlie killed his own kid?"

"At this point, all I know is that Maude didn't kill herself. And her murder, I believe, is a very small piece to a very big and dark puzzle."

Consumed with that notion, she opened her car door as if floating through a nightmare, but then felt his hand clutching her arm. He softened his grip now that he had her attention and stepped in, angling his face so near hers that her breath hitched in her throat.

Softly, he said, "Thanks for the heads up." Then he released her, adding, "But I would never mess around with Roberta."

She tried to smile, but it wavered badly, as she climbed in behind the wheel. He helped her close the car door properly then backed away, watching her as if he wouldn't head inside until her car started up properly.

As she drove off, tires grinding over gravel and the shock of headlights illuminating both the beaten road and the green dusting of vegetation that flanked it, Gertrude kept her gaze on the black horizon as if it held answers, real but hidden and lying in wait.

Jake was burning in the forefront of her mind, distracting her from dreadful thoughts of Doris, the dark connection between her unexplainable reaction—*I can't drink*—and the night that had taken her sister. Soon her scattered thoughts focused into a laser beam.

She sensed more than remembered they had gone to their parents' house that night. Something had happened, but she couldn't place what.

Doris flashed through her mind—cardigan hems pulled over her palms, her chipped nail polish, her fingernails tapping the counter of the bar as if to say *hurry up*, her eyes, blackened with liner, staring Gertrude down as if she could evoke guilt if she glared hard enough.

They had stopped in a bar. Gertrude had needed a drink, her bones buzzing from the confrontation—*Just one drink,* and *One more and that's it,* and *Don't give me that look, we'll leave after this one, last one, I promise.* The pit stop had sent Doris into a silent rage.

The memory cleared, leaving the road ahead and a crippling knot of remorse in her throat that she couldn't choke down. Would they have crashed into the lake that night if she hadn't stopped for a drink?

The accident, the particulars, the cause and effect, were still beyond her recollection, but the overwhelming sense it had been her fault was all too clear.

She turned off Opechee into her driveway, as a pair of deer flitted across her front yard, their white tails erect and catching the light. *Rats that kill people*, she thought, cringing at the stupid comment she had made to Roberta, as she got out of her car and carefully shut the door.

She hadn't explained to the girl what she had meant by that, how deer had a tendency to dart in front of cars at night, causing the driver to swerve, hit a tree, or God knows what.

It suddenly occurred to her, though fuzzily, had she swerved that night? Had something jumped in front of her car?

The question flew out of her head when she saw the front door of her cabin.

It was open.

When she eased inside, she saw candlelight flickering across the floor and lapping up the living room wall. Shapes and shadows played off the bookshelves, the column of framed photos beside it, and a wooden rocking chair in the corner.

Cautiously, she crept deeper into the room, as she scanned the bookshelf, seeing but not understanding. The sight was too complicated to process.

Spray paint?

A giant red circle had been drawn over the books, the wooden shelves, and the wall. Within the red circle was a five-pointed star, also red, and at its center was a pair of eyes.

When she glanced at the row of candles on the floor, she startled. There was a dark heap of mangy fur on the floor, too, illuminated by candle light. Then the smell hit her—cold, damp soil mixed with a faintly rotten scent.

A carcass.

Gasping and sputtering as she realized what it was, her heart leapt up her throat. Her stomach clenched hard, and nausea swept through her.

Someone had exhumed her dead dog from where she had buried him in the backyard.

The entire scene looked satanic, and when Gertrude examined the red symbol that had been painted on the wall, she realized that it was drawn in blood.

CHAPTER ELEVEN

QUINTON COULD hear them. They were deep in the woods, far away, but he could still hear their creepy voices seeping through the walls of the shed where he was.

The sounds of their chanting set his teeth on edge.

If Quinton hadn't known better, he would have thought that the chanting voices were nothing more than the wind. But Quinton *did* know better, and a cold sweat broke out across his chest because of it.

Seated on a cracked milk crate, his heel pounded like a metronome on high tempo, as he watched the shed's door, studying its shadows as though it would calm him.

He debated turning on the light. Its naked bulb, bright and stark, had made him queasy when he had first stepped inside, yanking its string. Somehow he felt better with the light off. Or at least it had—hiding out unseen, covered in darkness, denying the role he was about to play. But his fears had found him in the shadows, and now he was itching for a new way to expel them.

Alert, his ears pricking up at the sudden silence in the distance, he nearly eased realizing the chanting had stopped. But the lapse was fleeting, and when they began booming out another sustained tone, beating their rawhide drum at intervals and prolonging the ugly ritual, Quinton's anxiety swelled into full-blown panic.

Roberta should have been here by now.

He pushed off from the crate and the plastic cracked in terrible timing with the faint pattering of bare feet over twigs outside the shed.

Her soft whisper came urgently through the closed door. "Quinton?"

Guts burning in relief they hadn't reneged and snatched her, he rushed to let her in. "Keep the light off," he ordered when she reached for the string. "I don't want my parents to know I'm not in my room."

"Okay," she said quietly, as she eased the creaking door shut.

She looked ghostly, shadows forming in the hollows of her cheeks and across her eyes, her mouth a dark line. The only evidence she was of this world was the rank dress she refused to take off.

Roberta investigated the camera in her hands then padded over to the dusty window where a patch of moonlight shined through. With the camera pressed to her face, she pinched one eye shut, twisting the lens, adjusting the aperture, and getting the settings just right then passed it to him, helping the strap over his head.

It felt like a noose.

Last time, Roberta hadn't been able to steal her mom's camera and in a scramble of desperate measures, they had bought a disposable one. Only when they had returned to CVS to pick up the prints and had seen the sheer horror on the clerk's face, did they grasp the critical error they had made. An oversight they wouldn't repeat. Charlie's reach had been far and wide, and the manager had intervened, dismissing the clerk and handing them the prints. The clerk never reported what he had seen in those images as they had scanned out of the printer. And Quinton never saw him again either.

"Come on," she whispered, leading him outside. "I know he's home."

Every cell in his body was screaming. He didn't want to do this again, but he put one foot in front of the other, pinecones crunching under his sneakers and twigs snapping, the misty night dampening his hair, his sweat-slick face, as they wove through the sparse trees that would eventually connect to Jake Livingston's backyard.

Roberta seemed tense. Her gait was stiff, not swaying like she usually moved.

Stealing peeks when he wasn't squinting through the darkness straight ahead, he glimpsed her downward gaze, her somber eyes, eyelids slack. She seemed dreadful.

Here and there a sapling branch whipped his face, surprising him, and he flinched from the sting, as they trekked deeper. Like Quinton's family and the Kings', Jake's house was on Lake Winnipesaukee, but the faster route, which would've been along the shore, could risk exposure if anyone was night fishing on the lake. All told, he would've preferred running that risk, as opposed to veering through the woods and walking along a thin strip of wilderness that the clan could easily spy. It felt like tempting fate. He was terrified they would go back on their word and harm Roberta if their paths crossed.

Roberta winced when a fallen tree branch snapped under her foot but not because it cut her. The crack had been loud and they were nearing the gathering where the chanting had risen to wails. Crossing undetected behind scattered trees and in patchy shadows would require the stealth of a cat burglar, a quality neither of them possessed.

As they worked their way through at a snail's pace, taking painstaking care where they stepped—avoiding twigs, muscling over loose rocks, and shifting their weight with the utmost precision—Quinton caught sight of torches blazing in the brushy field beyond the trees.

The sight of cloaks and hoods, the dark circle of joined hands, flames licking silhouettes, sent his heart punching up his throat.

He didn't know, not fully, not really, the things they had done to Roberta. He had only seen the disastrous effects—her rage, refusal to eat, the hot clips of whimpering, teeth bared like a wild animal when her mind couldn't reject the truth of what her body had been through. Each time was worse than the last. It took Roberta longer and longer to recover, and when she did an eerie calm would come over her. Vacant eyes. Slack jawed gulps of booze, a slow restoration until she had blossomed with characteristics he recognized.

But it didn't matter that she could recover. It was chipping away at her, eroding her spirit with each passing year. She was crumbling from the inside out.

Quinton had agreed to help her take the photos, jeopardizing his life for no other reason than to save her from *them*, from the weeks of grueling recovery, from the probability that if she went through it again, endured another soul-murdering night, she would come back as nothing more than a shell.

Following behind Roberta as they hooked left, cutting straight through the woods, no longer within the clan's sightlines, Quinton picked his pace up to a jog. The camera rattled even though he held it tightly in both hands. He prayed it was working, that they wouldn't discover some kind of mechanical malfunction and have to do this all over again.

Through the trees, the windows on Jake's house glowed softly and shimmered across the lake's rippling surface. Roberta keeled over and planted her hands on her knees, catching her breath when they reached the edge of his yard.

"That's the living room window," she explained, softly padding across his yard towards the shore to stay in the shadows. "The couch is right there so I'll get him in that area. Make sure the flash is off or else you'll get a glare from the windows."

Quinton eyed the camera, but had no idea what all the gadgets represented. Handling it, she pushed the flash down into the camera body for him.

"You're going to have to sneak up close to the window, but you have time," she went on. "And Quinton, be sparing. There aren't that many frames."

The camera was rattling in his grasp and he realized he was trembling. Jake wasn't a simpleton. He wasn't a drunkard or impulsive or nearsighted. He was clever and calculating. Jake played life like a game of chess, every move planned with exquisite precision, his sights set on the endgame like a heat seeking missile—as dangerous as Roberta, if not more so.

Years ago, Jake had become involved with a woman who had a mental disorder and was rumored to have killed a homeless man living out in Opechee Park. An urban legend had formed quickly amongst the neighborhood kids, Quinton included, that if you were at the park after midnight, Weird Wanda would crawl out of the lake and eat your face off, as the homeless man was rumored to have been found—drenched and faceless. Despite the keen interest they had taken in Weird Wanda, spying on her and throwing rocks at her shopping cart that was full of trash and blankets, it hadn't been the kids who had ruined her life. It had been Jake. Posing as her protector and confidant, he had aimed to substantiate rumors since the police had done nothing to investigate the murdered homeless man. He had ended up falling just shy of his goal and almost earned some fancy journalism award Quinton had never heard of. More homeless men had been found dead at Opechee before they locked up Weird Wanda, and new rumors formed surrounding Jake, but the kids didn't taunt him anymore. They had been truly terrified.

"It'll be fine," she said, shifting her attention from his hands and touching eyes with him.

His stomach bottomed out like a mallet to an anvil, but he steadied his grip, nodding to prove he was ready. And in return, she gave him a brittle smile. *Fine* was not what this would be.

When he had learned of Gertrude, of her title and reason for checking in on Roberta, he had found it impossible to manage his expectations—high hopes at a high cost. He had ached for her to expose Charlie's degradation, Zhana's ignorance, and the reasons for Roberta's abnormal behavior. But here they were again, scared beyond comprehension in the dark, scrambling to buy time, and knowing it would only be borrowed and expire far too quickly.

Quinton wanted to tell her he was sorry, that he loved her, that he wished he could shoulder her burden—the fits of dread that cloyed up her throat, strangling her—but as he studied the lines and angles of her skeletal face, the desperation in her sinking eyes, he knew it would be too little. Words and wishes were too damn small.

"If anything goes wrong," she said. "We meet back at the shed."

"Right."

He thought she might hug him, but she only offered him a smile that didn't reach her eyes, and asked, "I look okay?"

"Mm-hm," was all he could muster, any vowels and he would've screamed and thrown himself into the lake.

Though she looked sprightly, bounding into the wash of light across the backyard, she still exuded the same raw urgency that had him crippled. And perhaps because of it, because she both dreaded this and needed it to be over already, Roberta paused when she reached the planters, hanging back near the bushes and allowing them to distract her.

She started sniffing around, feeling the leaves and investigating each branch, and then as if forgetting herself, she began digging.

For the life of him, he couldn't understand why.

CHAPTER TWELVE

GERTRUDE WAS PERCHED at the forefront of Jake's mind and nothing he had done all evening had been able to get the woman out of his head, not chipping away at his next article, not tidying up the living room, and not standing in a scalding-hot shower, lathering and scrubbing and feeling the burn.

As he adjusted the shower dials, making the water hotter, he cringed at himself, recalling how predatory he must have sounded when he had invited Gertrude upstairs. He shook his head at the impression he must have given her, having offered her a beer then asked if she wanted to *come upstairs*.

Ugh, terrible.

Fixing her car, reviewing the police report while they had sat closely beside one another, and listening to her melodic-sounding voice had made Jake feel strangely alive, like Gertrude had awoken the animal in him and he couldn't tame it, and didn't want to.

The hot water turned suddenly cold so he turned the shower off then grabbed a towel from the nearby rack while he stepped out. He wrapped the towel around his waist, figuring that air-drying would help him clear his head.

As he had been doing all night since she had left, he challenged himself not to think about Gertrude.

By the time he reached the refrigerator downstairs, he had already failed and decided he would try the next best tactic—drinking another beer. He had drunk three already and wasn't sure if they were helping or making things worse; probably worse, but at least they would blur his fixation for a little while.

He cracked the beer bottle open and drank, as he walked into his living room that looked like a strange clone of itself now that he had cleaned up. The room was too neat, he realized. It made him vaguely uncomfortable.

All that remained on the coffee table were the police reports that he had done a shoddy job of piecing back together and a notepad that was filled with messy handwriting—ideas for his next article.

But when he sat, stealing his notepad into his lap and leaning his beer against his towel-wrapped waist, he couldn't focus on either.

He kept fantasizing about Gertrude coming back, not that she ever would. He envisioned her pretty face, which was shaped like a heart.

Jake had seen a world of regret lurking behind Gertrude's dark eyes, as well as a ton of determination. Competing characteristics. Her pale lips had looked so smooth...

This wasn't even remotely productive.

If he couldn't focus, he might as well put some clothes on. The shower dew on his chest had dried.

Clutching his beer and holding his towel so he wouldn't lose it, he padded around the coffee table to go upstairs, but the sounds of fingernails tapping against glass stopped him.

Roberta was standing on the other side of his living room windows.

What the hell?

She tapped her nails again then spread her fingers, pressing the palm of one hand against the glass pane.

Jake pointed to his backdoor then met her there after depositing his beer on the coffee table.

As soon as he met her gaze he realized his error. Her eyes traveled the length of his bare chest, lingering on his towel, the particular placement of where his hand held it closed, and when she glanced up at him again, a kittenish smirk spread across her face.

"What are you doing here?"

He realized that she was holding a branch in her hand, which he vaguely recognized.

"Did you yank that off one of my bushes?" he asked her, annoyed.

Holding the branch up in front of his face, she said, "It's dead."

"Roberta," he groaned. "It's late. You need to go home."

A flirtatious glint filled her eyes and suddenly Gertrude's prior warning came to mind.

"Are you expecting someone?"

"I'm expecting to go to bed," he said dryly.

"In your towel?"

His attempt to stare her down was backfiring terribly.

Movement near the lake caught his eye. He scanned the dark shore. He must have been seeing things. Maybe he had drunk too many beers. There was nothing out there but cattails rattling in the wind.

"What do you want?"

"Can I come in?" Again, she shoved the branch under his nose. "I want to ask you something."

"As you can see, I'm not dressed-"

"I don't mind."

"Ask me what you want to ask me," he ordered.

"Well, I'm hungry…"

"This isn't a diner."

"Ah-ha," she said, nodding as though she had just figured out why he was in a bad mood. "Your booty call stood you up."

"I don't have time for games," he said, unimpressed.

"Why do you think your plants are dying?" she asked, changing the subject back to the branch in her hands. "The same thing has been happening at my house. I know the answer. Whatever I bury in the dirt kills the vegetation."

Jake needed to put some clothes on, and he'd had enough of Roberta's nonsense, so he told her:

"Stop burying things near the plants. Problem solved. Goodnight."

When he tried to close the door, her palm smacked against it.

"I have the information about Maude that you want," she told him…

… and like an idiot, he fell for it. "What?"

In a snap, her entire demeanor had changed.

And so had his.

"Let me in."

When she pushed into his house, Jake didn't stop her, even though alarm bells were going off in his head.

"Tell me what you know," he demanded, following after her.

Instead of charging into the kitchen, which she would have done if she truly had been hungry, she rounded into the living room.

"Loosening up, are we?" she asked, eyeing his beer on the table.

"I need to put something on," he said, excusing himself.

"How about some music?" she called after him, but he was already padding up the stairs, unnerved.

In his bedroom, he threw on a pair of jeans and an old Nirvana tee shirt that had shrunk in the wash, but not enough to look clownish, and when he returned, Roberta was draped on the couch, drinking his beer and reading the police report like she owned the place.

"You're not old enough to drink. Put it down."

Like a brat, she chugged the entirety of his beer in response, draining the bottle, then placed it delicately on the coffee table as he had asked.

"Is this going into your next article?"

"Give me that." Snatching the police report then folding it to fit in his back pocket, Jake mentally reviewed his options both in terms of getting her talking and getting her out of his cabin with as few games as possible. "What did you want to tell me?"

"Sit down," she said, then qualified the suggestion by adding, "You're making me nervous."

There was a sofa chair adjacent to the couch, which seemed like a safe distance so he sat there.

"Is that what your next article is going to be about? This," she indicated the police report, "and whatever I tell you?"

Figuring the truth would get him farthest with her—no danger of being quoted if his theories never made it to print—he reacted naturally, exhaling a long sigh. "I don't have enough yet and I don't know when I will. I'm still looking into things."

She frowned, thinking his position through.

"I would still like to get a detailed account from you."

"For another puff piece?"

"It might not get printed, and that wasn't a puff piece." His tone was strained. Statements like hers always touched a nerve with him no matter how seasoned he had become as a journalist. But he cleared his throat, aimed for an even, unemotional response with a biting undercurrent. "Doesn't it bother you that your perspective was absent from my article? It didn't have to be. It still doesn't. I can write anything about you that you want, as long as I substantiate the article with tangible information."

"Like Robinson's report," she clarified.

"It was Robinson? You're certain?"

The way she was holding his gaze was confirmation.

"Yes, like Robinson's report if you can corroborate that there wasn't a gun in Maude's bedroom when the police arrived."

She smiled crookedly and leveled her eyes on him. "And give you an ace in the hole? What do I get?"

"What do you want?"

"I'm not sure anything you have to offer compares to what I have to offer," she said, though her tone was contradictory, its melody highly suggestive.

"Well then there's nothing to negotiate, is there?" He shrugged as if reverse-psychology might work, then for good measure snuck in, "You're too smart to be duped, right?"

Contemplatively and in a far away voice, she said, "It's weird how someone can die and three days later there's a funeral, like that's all the time you have to get over it."

The way her vulnerability suddenly shined through softened him, and he wasn't sure what to say at first.

Gently, he offered, "No one expects you to get over it by the time the funeral wraps up, Roberta. That's not why funerals happen a few days after someone's death. You can take all the time you need."

"No," she said in a small voice. "I can't. They're already over it."

"Your parents?"

"Everyone."

"Roberta, did they hurt your sister? Did Charlie kill her?"

"What happened to Weird Wanda?" she countered.

Her sudden woolgathering, the meandering to feather-touch random subjects, made him realize negotiating had been far more promising. Even tit-for-tat had seemed a more worthwhile exchange.

"Weird Wanda is schizophrenic. She's getting help."

"You got her to trust you, then you locked her up."

"Is that what you think?"

"Isn't that what happened?"

"No," he said easily with no intention of clarifying the real chain of events.

"Has she eaten anyone's face off in the asylum?"

It was a stretch for Jake not to react strongly to that. "I hear she's doing well."

"Why did you dump her just because she went to the loony-bin?"

"I didn't dump her, because-"

"Why were you dating a street person?"

"Why are you asking me about this?"

Shrinking demurely, not that he would buy it, she said, "I like talking to you. You're nice."

He sighed, pinching the bridge of his nose and hoping she wouldn't be here when he opened his eyes. But she was.

She was staring at him with childlike interest.

"I think we've gotten off topic."

Abruptly, she dropped her innocent act along with her dress, shocking him so instantaneously, that he could barely process it—Roberta: standing, lines and curves, skin, all skin; Jake: somehow on his feet, urging her back, not wanting to hurt her but wanting to shove her off—as she wrestled him towards the couch.

"Get off. Roberta! What the hell are you doing?"

She had wrapped herself around him like a barnacle and it seemed that she was trying to fall with him to the couch. As soon as he had peeled one arm off, her other slapped around him, in an ugly tangle of limbs he couldn't control.

"Are you crazy? For Christ's sake, stop!" he yelled and finally used the force he was hoping he wouldn't have to use, throwing her hard to the couch where she bounced at an awkward angle and tumbled to the floor.

Heaving to catch his breath, Jake became momentarily stunned at the sight of her nudity then grabbed her red dress and offered it, his eyes glancing sideways to avoid her.

"Are you hurt?"

If she answered, the loud, tinny ring of his kitchen phone drowned it out and he started through the room, confused at who would be calling at this hour.

"Yeah?" he said into the receiver, as he turned to see Roberta slinking her dress on and then shaking the beer bottle as if she might not have finished it.

"Hi, Jake?" A cool and even tone, though soft and melodic, hit his ear, causing it to prick up, thrilled. "It's Gerty."

"Oh," he said, eagerly.

"I know it's late, I..." It sounded like she pulled the phone away from her mouth for a moment. "I wasn't sure who to call. I've been debating for hours."

Listening so hard he was leaning into the wall, turning his back to Roberta, and willing the strange girl to stay silent, Jake asked Gertrude what was going on.

"I..." Again she trailed off and it made his heart punch in his chest. "I think you should come here. I'm at my house."

"Yeah, I'll be right over."

As soon as she recited her address, he promised to see her in a few minutes and quickly got off the phone.

He returned the phone to its cradle on the wall and smiled.

Then he remembered Roberta.

"I don't know what the hell you think you're doing here, Roberta, but I have to head out which means that it's time for you to go," he stated firmly, as he returned to the living room.

But the girl was already gone.

CHAPTER THIRTEEN

"WHAT HAPPENED?" Jake asked, as he approached the front door of Gertrude's cabin. He looked as though he had come running from his parked pickup truck and had slowed up only because she had appeared in the doorway. "Are you hurt?"

It took some effort, but she met his gaze and shook her head.

"I'm okay."

She had popped a total of four Xanax in the hour it had taken her to scrub the blood off the wall, off the bookshelf, and off the floor. It wasn't until now that she realized she had taken too many pills. Looking into his eyes, which were shadowed with the porch light behind him, magnified the drug's effects, and suddenly Dr. Hagstaff's warning rang true—*Only take one pill every four hours or else you'll feel woozy, disoriented, and dangerously at ease.*

"I'm fine. I didn't know who else to call," she said, even though she was pretty sure she had already mentioned that when she had called him earlier.

Jake's heavy breathing calmed, as he glanced past her, which called to mind the fact that she hadn't invited him inside yet.

Before allowing him in, she told him, "What you find in there has to stay off the record."

He nodded, which was all the confirmation she needed, so she stepped aside and he entered.

His attention locked on the wall, the bookshelf, and the smeared blood stains that no cleaning product she owned would lift out. The living room smelled of bleach and lemon-scented cleaning products. Gertrude was hyper-conscious of the strong smell now that she wasn't alone, so she opened the windows behind the couch to air the place out.

After staring at the wall, Jake seemed to take in the room as a whole, and as he did, Gertrude was able to perceive the vandalism with fresh eyes. She had thought that she had cleaned much better than she really had, but in fact she had only managed to spread the stain, making it worse. She hadn't bothered getting rid of the candles. She had only blown them out, and the carcass of her old dog was exactly where she had found him. For the most part, that was why she had called Jake. She couldn't bring herself to handle poor Rusty on her own.

She was hit with a sharp swell of déjà vu when Jake faced her.

The bottle of Xanax in her back pocket nagged her. But she knew taking another would be a mistake. If anything, she ought to flush the pills out of her system, which should clear the haze that had built in her head and turned her limbs to rubber.

"Is that a dog?" he asked without looking at it again.

"They exhumed him."

"Who?"

"Whoever did this?" Heavy footed, she walked to the bookshelf, gesturing at the shelves. "It was blood," she said, staring at but not quite seeing the stains now that she was closer. "It couldn't have been my dog's."

When she glanced at Jake, he was studying the wall as if he could get an impression of the symbol that had been there. His hands were planted on his hips, causing his tee shirt to pull taut across his chest. Then he eyed the candles, pacing towards them until his boots were inches from the dog.

"A satanic symbol?" he guessed when he went back to analyzing the bookshelf.

"I thought so, but have you heard of anything like that going on out here? I haven't."

Jake seemed thrown.

"I would really like to get my dog buried," she said, implying this was the primary reason she had asked him to come, but the suggestion didn't reach him. He was too deep in thought.

"What did it look like, a circle?"

Nearing him, she explained, "Yeah, a circle and a star inside of it and at the center of the star were two ovals." She brushed her hand over a particularly dark smear where the blood had been stubborn. "They looked like eyes to me."

"Did they break in?" he asked, meeting her gaze and drawing attention to how close they were standing.

She took a few shy steps backwards and cringed to tell him her oversight.

"I didn't lock up." Before he could gape at her stupidity, she rattled off theories and excuses, anything to get the look off his face. "It's safe around here and I usually lock it. I must have been rushing out and forgot. I don't know if it's connected, but a truck rear-ended me on the highway."

"What? When?"

"Yesterday afternoon."

"Why didn't you mention it to me?"

Heated, Jake angled his eyes on her with such intensity that she couldn't get her words out. And yet, she knew he wasn't furious at her, but at the missed opportunity, as though somewhere along the line he had volunteered to protect her even though she couldn't place when or why.

"I'm still getting my bearings," she said finally.

"Meaning, you forgot like you forgot to lock your house up," he pointed out.

It sounded like an accusation. "I hope you're not suggesting this is my fault."

"No." Softening, he added, "I'm just worried about you."

"I'm not handicapped so you can stop looking at me like that."

"That's not what I think, but I noticed you haven't remembered things."

Jake didn't know the half of it, not by a long shot, but she didn't defend herself further since anything she said along those lines would only add fuel to his fire. He seemed to drop it, as well, turning his attention to the dog.

"Do you have a wheelbarrow?"

"Out back, but it won't fit through the doorway."

"Okay," he said, assessing the dog. "We'll need a blanket. One you don't mind never seeing again."

Leaving him, Gertrude stole away to her bedroom where she flipped on a lamp that was resting on the nightstand beside her bed. A soft glow came over the room, warming the rounded log walls, white bedspread and wooden headboard, and a wood stove across from the foot of the bed.

Rounding through and careful not to clip her knee on the footboard, a mistake she had made several times living here over the years, she couldn't think of a blanket she wouldn't mind parting with. But when she reached the closet and took inventory, she decided on a woolen one that Doris had brought with her from their parents' house.

They had gotten into a stupid fight over it. Gertrude hadn't wanted it in her house and Doris had yelled at her that there wasn't a stove in the living room. She would freeze on the couch if she didn't layer on the blankets. It had been the dead of winter and though Gertrude hadn't a leg to stand on making her argument against the blanket—she couldn't offer Doris alternatives, because she didn't have any—she had ripped the blanket from her sister's grasp and declared Doris would sleep in Gertrude's room with her.

Why Gertrude hadn't taken the extra step of burning the thing or at the very least getting it out of the cabin was lost on her. And looking back, she couldn't understand her volatile reaction, except that she knew nothing of her parents had come into her cabin and she needed to keep it that way. The alternative would've been very bad, and though she didn't know why, she sensed that at one point in time she had.

When she returned, she found Jake hunched on the couch, his elbows planted on his knees. He glanced up at her, getting to his feet.

"I'll get the wheelbarrow," she said, handing him the blanket. "Do you need work gloves? I think I have some in the closet."

"Yeah, we shouldn't touch him."

The closet was in the hallway between the living room and her bedroom so Gertrude doubled back with Jake in tow.

Opening the door, she sensed him near her and when she reached for the nest of gloves that were balled up in a hanging shoe rack, he reached for them, and his position had trapped her.

Jake slapped a pair against his thigh, getting the dust off then handed them to her and by the same token christened a second pair for himself.

Turning towards her, he asked, "Where's the wheelbarrow?"

"This way," she said, but couldn't actually move with him blocking her in.

He lingered and a fresh billow of tension swelled between them, or so she thought until she decided it made more sense to figure she was crazy for reading anything into this. He stepped aside, freeing her, and Gertrude padded quickly through the house and out the front door, sensing all the while that Jake was at her back.

Fog was rolling in from the lake when they rounded the cabin. They walked out of the dim porch light and into darkness. The shore wasn't eight yards from the back of the house, and Gertrude could smell the cool, marshy scent of the lake, and the wet sand along the water.

Tucked against the cabin siding where an alcove stored winter wood that was now too soggy for her to make use of come November, was the wheelbarrow, its wooden handle laced with cobwebs, its basin filled with wood and rainwater.

Gertrude smacked the cobwebs off with a gloved hand, saying, "I never use this thing."

But Jake took charge, grabbing hold of the handles and tipping the wheelbarrow on its side. The water splashed out, wood clattering into the weeds.

They made their way silently around the front of the house, Jake pushing the wheelbarrow, his arms straining to steer it, and Gertrude stealing shy glances at him, wondering how awkward she should find this midnight dog burial when the only thing that unnerved her was realizing that Jake's help made her feel calm. She reasoned that her instincts must be off and concluded she would bring it up with Dr. Hagstaff as soon as she saw him.

Jake set the wheelbarrow down on the deck, having hoisted it with a jolt over the lip that separated the wooden slats from the gravel driveway. And then he started through the cabin, Gertrude close behind.

"Lay out the blanket, would you?"

She did, spreading it on the floor and smoothing it out.

Stooping, Jake carefully scooped the dead dog into his arms with an air of remorse as though it was a child who had died too soon. She wondered if he could see the real dog, Rusty, alive through the eroded corpse, the mound of fur and bones and encrusted mud, to which her pet had been reduced.

He set him on the blanket just as carefully then eased back.

"What was his name?"

"Rusty," she said, watching him. "He was a good dog."

"How did they find him if he was buried?"

She studied the lines of his face for a moment when he looked at her, and felt suddenly raw like she didn't have skin or flesh or bones and the deepest part of her, her essence perhaps, or her soul if such a thing existed, was exposed to him. Strange intimacy she couldn't resist.

"I had a pet marker in the yard, you know, a headstone?"

He seemed to mull that over then folded the blanket around the dog.

"He's not heavy. I can carry him."

Again, Jake scooped him up in his arms and muscled to his feet then followed Gertrude out to the wheelbarrow where he laid the bundled dog down gingerly in the basin.

"Thank you so much," she blurted out, having realized she had completely forgotten.

A thin smile formed at the corners of his mouth, which he suppressed as he held her gaze. "No problem." After a beat, Gertrude thumbed the edge of the blanket, finding relief in breaking eye contact, and he added, "I'm glad you called me."

"The grave is back here."

She walked along the side of the cabin then cut left into the yard, stalking through tall grass and listening to the ruddy thumps of the wheelbarrow's wheel plowing through the bumpy brush behind her. Somewhere an owl hooted, long and low, and the wind rustled cattails along the shore. The afternoon heat had burned away hours ago and the night air felt cool and damp.

When she reached the grave—a four foot hole, jagged edges, loose soil matting the tall grass in haphazard mounds—she scanned the dark grass for the pet marker, as Jake lowered the wheelbarrow beside the hole and breathed deeply, whether to catch his breath or steady his nerves, she couldn't decide.

She spotted the marker a few yards off. Face down, the rounded granite looked like any other rock out there hiding in vegetation, but she fetched it and by the time she returned to the grave, Jake had lowered Rusty's remains down into the grave where he belonged.

Together, they grabbed dirt by the fistful and began filling the hole. It crossed her mind to mention she should've gotten a shovel, but then she remembered, she didn't have one.

Offhandedly, he asked, "How *is* your memory?"

"Good enough to go to work, evidently."

"You don't remember me?"

She paused with dirt balled in her fists, and stared at him. Had she met him? Maybe she wasn't plagued by déjà vu, but was actually scratching the surface of things that had happened.

"We know each other?" she asked.

He released the dirt from his hands and it spilled onto the blanket. "We didn't *know* each other, but we met," he began. "I met your sister, too. Or saw her, I should say. At the farmer's market with you, a few months back, but you don't remember, do you?"

"No," she said, intrigued.

Jake shot her a self-deprecating smile and shrugged. "I guess I didn't make much of an impression."

"What happened?"

Pushing a mound of dirt into the hole, he said, "I asked you out."

Hearing that, a wave rolled through her, ratcheting up her fascination.

"Did we go out?"

They had filled the grave and Jake started patting down the soil, perhaps using the task as a means not to answer. But then he said, "No, you turned me down."

"Oh." It surprised her and she couldn't imagine why she wouldn't have wanted to get to know him. "Sorry."

He shrugged and she was well aware he hadn't looked at her, but when they got to their feet, he shook it off with a brittle smile.

"I'm sure you had your reasons," he concluded, taking hold of the wheelbarrow.

Gertrude placed the pet marker in the center of the plot, working it into the dirt to be certain it would stay put.

"It's not just you," she said. "There's a lot I don't remember. It doesn't make sense and my doctor can't explain it. Most of my childhood has been wiped out. I don't remember the accident. I barely remember my teenage years, yet I have no difficulty remembering the minutiae of every day at the DCYF. I remember Doris in terms of the months she was living with me here at my cabin, but not in terms of all the years we spent growing up." She frowned, getting lost in the dark pattern of grass at their feet.

"I don't want to scare you," he said, his tone turning serious. "But if someone tried to run you off the road, and now this? It's connected."

"I know," she said, her stomach bottoming out.

"I think it has to do with the Kings."

She did as well, but was too scared to say it out loud. To confirm his suspicion would make it real and some part of her was hanging on to the false hope it was random, a mistake, kids at the wrong address.

"Will you be alright here alone?"

"Yeah," she said quickly, as if doing so would make it true.

"You've got locks on all the windows, the door?"

"If I use them, yes."

"Do you have a gun?"

"No, I hate guns," she said even before she realized the root of her aversion.

A gun had gone off that night, hadn't it? Jake was saying something about being cautious, but she couldn't hear him, as a sealed corridor in her memory suddenly sprang open, sucking her down it—a foggy windshield, Doris messing with the glass, the silence between them, the gunshot, then Gertrude swerving the car, but why?

It hadn't been that she had driven too fast or that the bend in the road had snuck up on her or that she shouldn't have had those drinks. She'd had to swerve. She hadn't had a choice. She had tried not to hit something.

"Gerty?"

"Yeah?"

"Do you want to head in? It's cold."

"Yeah."

Jake left the wheelbarrow beside the deck when they reached it and she led him inside where he closed the door and locked it then collected her gloves, stripping one then the other off her hands and returning them to the closet, as Gertrude stood puzzling over the fragments of that night that were trying so desperately to touch her.

"I have a few contacts in Grafton County," he said, nearing the blood stained bookshelf. "I almost wish you hadn't cleaned this."

"Contacts?"

"We can't trust the police around here. I would like to find out whose blood this is, wouldn't you?"

"Hmm," was all she could say, images of the night of Doris' death clouding her thoughts.

Systematically, Jake examined book after book until it appeared he found one he liked.

"Do you have a plastic bag?"

She made her way into the kitchen and found a cluster of old shopping bags under the sink.

"A few, if you've got it," he called out and when she returned with two, he used the first to wrap one of the candles and the second for the book.

"Do you know what time Maude was shot on July 2nd?" she asked him.

"Zhana told police around two in the morning, but I've lost faith in terms of trusting those reports."

Two in the morning was when she and Doris had driven home from the bar that night. Her accident had been on July 2nd.

All of a sudden, she saw a flash from that night popping into her mind as stark as a strobe. There had been a figure in the fog that night. Someone had walked out into the road and Gertrude had swerved the car.

She could remember flying over the bridge, driving fast with Doris in the passenger seat. Hearing the gunshot had followed, and then someone had stepped out onto the road. The fog had been so thick that night.

Her memories were a blur, but it was becoming undeniably clear to Gertrude that the Kings had killed her sister.

CHAPTER FOURTEEN

LIKE A GOPHER, Wendy had been popping up to peer at Gertrude over the cubicle wall they shared all morning.

Coffee?

Need help?

Did you say something?

Each time, Gertrude had responded with, *I'm fine,* or *Gotta work,* or *Wendy, please!* as though dealing with Wendy was like playing a game of Whack-A-Mole she would never win.

Gertrude was due back at the Kings' house that afternoon. Harold McNeil had called in every last favor he had with the District Attorney to push through the 10-1C Application for Temporary Removal of a Child, and finally the Belknap court had granted the DCYF the right to remove Roberta King from her home. Which meant that Gertrude had less than five hours to coordinate the necessary arrangements for Roberta. In light of the pressure Gertrude was under, Wendy was being more distracting than helpful.

It also didn't help that Gertrude kept getting sidetracked with the mind-bending correlation between Maude's death and her sister's. Complicating matters was the *satanic* aspect, which gave a whole new meaning to the scars that she had seen on Roberta's thighs. Self-mutilation scars.

But every time Gertrude attempted to contemplate all the pieces and how they linked together, she became bogged in wooly confusion.

In many ways, she was struggling to differentiate Roberta from her own sister. Doris had harmed herself in the exact same way, she had remembered.

And it was for this reason that Gertrude had gotten very far filling out the forms on her computer.

She stared at the blank "Foster Family Recommended" field of the online template, and ignored Wendy's sudden appearance:

Snack? I could use a sugar bump!

Gertrude responded, *NO THANK YOU.*

She fantasized typing her own name into the blank field.

Could Roberta stay with Gertrude?

Wendy shuffled past her desk, making her way towards the breakroom, and Gertrude pulled up the webpage for the New Hampshire Department of Corrections on her laptop, which she had positioned to the right of her desktop computer.

Plugging in her DCYF access code, satanism came to mind.

It puzzled her.

But she had to ask herself, was there a satanic cult in New Hampshire?

It seemed so unlikely. Considering Charlie King's absence, Maude's death, the homicide cover up, the suicide report, the uncanny connection between Maude's death and her own accident car accident, which had killed Doris; and considering all the other cogs and sprockets that made up this twisted machine, she couldn't imagine how satanic rituals and sadistic cults might fit in.

And yet, the vandalism at her cabin *had* been satanic, and Charlie King had locked up five men for messing around with his daughter. It was possible that men like Tom Riley, Jimmy Smythe, and Mike Waters would have insights as to precisely how it all tied in. Whether or not they would talk to her was an entirely different matter. Regardless, she pulled up the correctional facility's contact page and began scheduling appointments at the prison.

As soon as Gertrude set her desk phone in its cradle, Wendy perched against the wall that separated their cubicles.

"The Wongs could take Roberta King," she said offhandedly and blew on her steaming mug of coffee. "They live over on Opechee, near you, as a matter of fact. And they have a daughter, Jennifer, I believe, who's Roberta's age, give or take." Wendy racked her brain, mumbling to herself, then mentioned, "I believe the girls go to the same high school."

"I'm still reviewing the options."

"If you want Roberta spending her senior year at the same high school, I'm afraid there aren't many options." Wendy shook her frizzy hair out of her eyes and smiled encouragingly. "The Wongs are good people."

Gertrude swiveled her chair so she wouldn't have to strain her neck continuing the conversation.

"I've built a fair amount of trust with Roberta," she began, keenly reading Wendy's reaction in case she would need to pull the plug. Wendy had always been her confidant and biggest supporter, and had consistently guarded Gertrude against career mistakes. If Gertrude wanted her advice and help, she would have to be delicate in her presentation. "Roberta has disclosed things to me, and she has expressed that she would like to live in a different home."

"Well, that's half the battle right there."

"She has also voiced her concerns. I think she's afraid of where she might end up."

"A perfectly natural reaction," said Wendy before sipping her coffee. "Just remind her that you'll be there every step of the way."

Her chest felt tight and her scalp, where her hair was growing in under the beret, was hot and itchy, so she pulled her hat off and grazed her fingernails along the side of her head.

Gertrude proposed, "What if she stayed with me?"

Wendy looked stunned. She froze awkwardly with her mug hovering beneath her mouth.

"Social workers have done it in the past," Gertrude argued.

Regaining her faculties, Wendy gently said, "Not in this division."

"But it's not unprecedented," she pointed out.

"Gerty," she said with a sigh, as she set her mug on the edge of Gertrude's desk. "Why would you want to do that to yourself? It'll put you through a hell of a lot, and you're still recovering from the accident, aren't you?"

"It was just an idea." As if to brush it off, though Wendy's disapproval stung, she turned to her desktop computer. "I'll see about the Wongs."

"I think that would be best." Wendy took hold of her mug and gave Gertrude one last look, then rounded to her side of the wall and disappeared into her cubicle.

When Gertrude returned her fingers to the keyboard, her gaze locked on the blank "Foster Family Recommended" field.

She typed her own name in and hit Submit before doubt could creep in and stop her.

Later that day, she walked through the shade outside, making her way to her Audi, which was parked between Wendy's dusty minivan and a row of hedges.

She had spent the majority of yesterday taping new index card reminders all over the interior of her car, so when Gertrude climbed in behind the wheel, she was momentarily bombarded by commands that didn't apply—*Lock the front door!* and *Windows shut?*—and a few that did make sense—*Where's your cell phone?* and *Stay off the highways!*

Setting her laptop satchel in the backseat, she scanned the parking lot, checking for spying eyes. When she faced forward, she found Reverse on the third try and backed out slowly, the glare from the azure sky reflecting off her windshield as soon as she hooked around the hedges.

Then she shifted gears and drove off, heading towards Route 3 at fifty-five miles per hour, which would take her south to the prison in Manchester.

A one-story brick structure with a rotund glass entrance and watchtowers, the correctional facility housed convicts from all over the state. According to the prison warden, Tom Riley had been charged with a Class B felony for felonious sexual assault, which had earned him seven years behind bars, though as of today's date, he only had three more years to go, or he could get released on parole if his behavior remained good. Mike Waters and Jimmy Smythe hadn't been so lucky. Both men had been sentenced to twenty years for Class A felonies, which was the result of the slightly different charges they had faced.

While Riley had been convicted of felonious sexual assault, Waters and Smythe had been convicted of *aggravated* felonious sexual assault.

As far as Gertrude could tell, Charlie King had worked hard to get all of the men Roberta had been with locked up. But he had coerced Roberta to entrap the men in the first place.

Why?

Most disturbing was the fact that the other two men who had been incarcerated for messing around with Roberta—Raymond Soule and Maxwell O'Malley—had been killed in the prison during a riot that had broken out four months prior.

As Gertrude walked through the parking lot, squinting up at an American flag that hung limp in the summer heat, she was struck by the serenity of the landscape. There were white, popcorn clouds inching lazily across an azure sky, and rolling hills surrounded the prison compound. The beauty felt like a lie.

Inside, a security guard inspected every item in her purse but when she walked through a metal detector, the alarm started screaming.

"I have metal pins in my skull," she explained, removing her beret and showing him the bald, scarred side of her head as proof.

Grumbling, the guard fished a wand out of a bucket beneath his folding table, which was near the metal detector, and flipped it on. He used the wand to check every inch of Gertrude, making sure she had no weapons on her, and sent her on her way.

Approaching the Reception Center, she returned her beret to her head and found her driver's license in her purse.

"Gertrude Inman," she told the guard behind the counter. "I have a noon appointment with an inmate, Tom Riley."

He slapped a clipboard on the counter and told her to fill out the forms, as he collected her ID and verified the appointment.

"DCYF?" he asked, finally meeting her gaze.

"That's right."

"I need the ID number."

"I lost my badge," she explained, pressing her pen against the form in a white-knuckle grip. "Will that be a problem?"

He eyed her for a tense moment then told her it was fine.

After filling out the forms and sliding the clipboard over the counter, she asked him where the visitors center was located. When he told her, she walked through a set of double doors and found another security checkpoint. Again, she presented her driver's license to another guard, who punched a code into the keypad on the wall, opening the door for her.

Entering the visitors center, she noticed an inmate dressed in orange was reuniting with a loved one, their hands knotted together on the table. In another corner of the room, a variation of the same story unfolded between an inmate and his son.

Gertrude chose a table near the windows so she could look out at the hills while she waited, but when she turned her attention, the door at the back of the visitors center blared and a guard ushered an inmate through.

Wearing an orange jumpsuit, the man looked like every gas station attendant who had ever filled up her tank—a broad forehead and tight facial features, winter-weathered skin, and aged eyes. The man locked eyes with her and she knew he had to be Tom Riley.

When he reached her table, he looked down at Gertrude, and her heart started punching in her chest.

"Tom?"

He settled onto the seat across from her and planted his elbows on the table.

"What's this about?"

"You were living on Moulton Street next to the Kings' house?"

Standoffish, his brow furrowed as he waited for an explanation, and when she didn't provide one, he said, "So?"

"I'm not sure you should be in here."

Cocking his head, Tom's expression eased with interest.

"I want to ask you about the events leading up to your arrest," she said.

"You're going to get me out of here?"

"I might be able to improve your situation," she offered.

"How's that?"

"Well, there's a pattern that I've noticed regarding Roberta and-"

He snorted a laugh. "Yeah, a lot of people have noticed. Nothing has been done about it."

"Could you tell me about what happened?" She quickly interrupted herself, though. "Not about your night with Roberta. I don't need to hear about that. But did you notice anything at the Kings' house, or see anything, before you got together with Roberta?"

"Who sent you? Are you with the court or with the cops?"

"No," she said, hoping she wouldn't lose what little confidence she had sparked in him. "I work for the Division for Children Youth and Families."

"A social worker." He mulled that over and Gertrude saw the light in his eyes dim out. "Yeah, I read about what happened to that little girl. Shot herself in the head, right?"

"She died, yes."

"So, what? You're going to protect Roberta? She doesn't need protection." He snorted another laugh and suggested, "She needs an exorcist."

"Tom," she started, mentally composing her point in her head and choosing her words carefully before saying them out loud. "I suspect you were set up, and I'm trying to understand why that would be. Maybe you saw something, or maybe Roberta told you something and Charlie felt threatened by what you might do with the information."

She let that hang in the air between them, giving him a chance to respond. But he didn't. He only scraped his teeth over his bottom lip as if debating.

"Anything you could tell me..." she prodded.

"Do you have any idea how long it took me to put two and two together?"

After a beat, she realized that he expected an answer so she shook her head.

"Roberta didn't have to throw herself at me and set me up. Hell, I didn't even know what I had seen, and I didn't think any of it had to do with the Kings, anyway. I didn't give it a second thought until I got locked up in here and had nothing else to think about."

"What are you talking about? What did you see?"

Leaning back in his chair, he shook his head and decided, "There's nothing you can do for me."

"I can help the truth to come out," she offered.

He shrugged and admitted, "Bottom line, I'm guilty. I had sex with her. Whether I was set up or not, it happened, which is why I was convicted."

She was losing him. Knowing that she had virtually nothing to offer him that would change his life, Gertrude began sweating, frustrated.

"Someone came inside my house and vandalized my living room," she blurted out, forgetting her composure. She let her words, as distressed as they sounded, tumble out of her. "They dug up my dead dog, my pet that I had buried years ago, and left him on my living room floor. There were candles and a horrible symbol painted with blood on my walls. It looked satanic."

"You better watch your back," he said in a tone that implied he knew what would come next if she didn't heed the warning.

"I have a map here," she said, pulling a folded map from her purse and spreading it on the table. "It shows the property lines along Moulton Street." Tracing her finger along the divisions, she walked him through the landmarks. "This is Lake Winnipesaukee and along the shore here is the Kings' property. North is where Mike Waters lived, and directly south is the house Jimmy Smythe was living in. Then you're over here," she went on, circling her finger. "And this is the field that connects the four residential properties."

"And Ray was over here," he added to prove the geography lesson was just that. "Max was on the east end. And that schmuck reporter, where is he?" Tom found Jake's plot on the map. "I bet you anything Jake Livingston will be in the jail cell next to mine any day now."

"Who owns the field?" she asked.

"I have no idea. Might be public land that no one's aware of."

Shifting on his seat, Tom leaned towards her and folded the map.

"It was chanting," he told her.

She studied him, waiting for more.

"That's all I heard. Chanting."

"Coming from the field?"

"Yeah. I heard chanting coming from the field, and the next thing I knew, Roberta had seduced me."

Gertrude's gut told her there was a lot more to the story.

"I didn't give a damn about the chanting." He threw his hands up, referring to his surroundings. "All this because the sound of chanting carries through an open field."

"That couldn't have been all you did to bring this on," she argued.

"No, all I did was go for a walk."

"Into the field?"

"Down the damn road. I had too much to drink one night. It was hot in my house. I went for a walk. When I heard a truck coming, I moved onto the shoulder to let it pass."

"Okay," she said, trying to grasp what Charlie might have found detrimental about Tom's drunken night walk.

"I didn't see the truck's license plate." He started rattling off facts, as he counted on his fingers. "I didn't see the driver. I didn't follow the truck. I didn't give a damn. I noticed that the truck bed was full, but I didn't say anything about it to anyone because I didn't think anything about it." He laughed then ran his hands down his face like he was coming undone, but when he returned his hands to his lap, he looked dead serious. "But then later, I saw the same truck at Opechee Park. This was another night; a pure coincidence. Again, I didn't see the driver." He looked suddenly ill. "But I saw him drag something out of the bed of his truck. Whatever it was, the driver left it right there in the park. It was something wrapped in a blanket. Then he drove off."

Tom drew in a queasy breath like he was reliving it.

"I was feeding bottles into the recycling depository to get enough money to buy a drink. And when the guy drove off, I got curious." He swallowed hard and his foot started tapping beneath the table. Using his teeth, he tore a piece of skin off his finger, then went on. "I shouldn't have opened that blanket. It looked like a zombie apocalypse had claimed its first victim."

Confused, she screwed her face up, trying to understand.

"I don't know if it was a man or a woman or a kid, but it looked like their face was eaten off, and the person was most definitely dead. I ran to my car and peeled out of that park so damn fast, you wouldn't believe it. I guess that was what gave me away, the sound of screeching tires. They saw me. They put it together that I was the guy who had been out for a walk that night." He pushed back in his chair and forced a long exhale. "You should talk to Mike. He saw some messed up stuff go down in that field." Shaking his head as though the image of the faceless corpse was haunting him, he added, "That poor woman."

"I thought you said you didn't know the gender of the dead person."

"No, Wanda. That homeless chick, who used to live in the park; you didn't hear about her? Weird Wanda?"

If Gertrude had, she didn't remember.

"Come on," he gaped. "Everyone knows about Weird Wanda. Hell, after they locked me up, I kept my ear to the ground, and I still do to this day. A few more bodies like the one I saw turned up and Wanda was arrested. As if she had it in her to eat someone's face off, like that's what homeless people do. She's got some kind of mental illness so they institutionalized her." Again, Tom leaned in and turned severe. "Someone in those backwoods is doing some seriously messed up stuff, and the wrong people are getting locked up for it."

"Do you think Charlie King is behind this?"

Tom frowned to confirm. "Charlie King and his cult."

CHAPTER FIFTEEN

DAYS PASSED. GERTRUDE went to work and kept her head down. Harold McNeil said nothing about her name being listed on the foster care application for Roberta, which led her to assume he had yet to review it. Every time he filled his office door, she startled, anticipating he would call her in and relaxed only a fraction when he barked out another social worker's name. Every time he sat with her in the conference room, she turned rigid with nerves, keeping her responses brief to hasten their meeting. She sensed it was only a matter of time before he would ream her out for being a bleeding heart or worse, self-serving. It wasn't lost on her how transparent it looked—volunteering to take Roberta in. She had seen it in Wendy's eyes, the look that said, *it won't bring Doris back*. Several times she had the impulse to march into his office, close the door, and preemptively confess, just to get it over with, but she stifled the urge.

She was edgy enough as it was. Being alone in her cabin, especially at night, had provoked her anxiety. For two nights she had barely slept, alert to every sound—the wind at the windows, the faint moans of the wooden floor swelling from humidity, the hum of the distant highway—as though it could be the cult ambushing her.

At Tom Riley's advice, she had met with Mike Waters. Like Tom, he hadn't initially made the connection between what he had witnessed in the field and Roberta's sudden advances. But unlike Tom, what Mike had seen in the field was undoubtedly cult activity. And it had scared him silly.

As Mike had explained it, gnawing on hangnails and picking at his eyebrows like a nervous wreck, he had wandered into the field late at night and spied roughly twelve men—their figures draped in cloaks, faces concealed with hoods—gathered in a circle and chanting, an eerie torchlight glow brightening their silhouettes. He had crept towards them through the tall grass, but never got closer than twenty yards. Mike had divulged to her that he had been more terrified of what he *hadn't* seen than what he had. He had sensed someone had laid in the center of their circle, he could intuit their agony, though he hadn't heard them. Watching them beat their drums and stomp, he had felt with absolute clarity he was witnessing a murder only he didn't know who or why. The next day, he had returned to the field and found blood in the grass, and though the summer sun had been shining brightly, he said the field was as dark as the devil himself.

By Thursday, Harry informed her the DCYF had received the court order to remove Roberta from 118 Moulton Street and that Gertrude was to transport Roberta back to the Division where, presumably, her foster guardians would be waiting to take her home.

"And who would the foster guardians be?" she asked, edging into his office with cautious steps.

Seated behind a mountain of files at his desk, Harry plowed his thick fingers through the only part of him that wasn't polished, his salt-and-pepper hair, which looked months overdue for a trim. He groaned in response, lifting and sorting through the haphazard stacks.

"Pull it up online," he suggested, implying that if the application approval was around here, he certainly hadn't read it. Having given up his search, Harry leaned back in his chair and worked the tension out of his jaw. "I want you to keep a close eye on Roberta. Swing by twice a day if possible. She's old enough and clever enough to take off if she doesn't like the living arrangements. And she needs to be enrolled in grief counseling."

"Right, no problem."

As she turned for the door, eager to escape before her secret was discovered, Harry stopped her by barking her name.

"It's been a full week. How are you holding up?"

"Good, I think. Glad to have only one case. I'm not sure I could handle more." She smiled, but it wavered badly.

"Do you have an idea of when you *will* be able to handle more?"

The answer came fast and hard, but only in her mind—*never.*

"I really can't say," she stammered. "At least a month."

Pressing his mouth into a frown and glancing over the files on his desk, he seemed to take his workload into account based on her timeline, which didn't seem to please him so she quickly offered, "I'll keep you posted, though."

He dismissed her with a nod and turned his attention to his computer.

After collecting her laptop satchel and purse, and printing out the necessary forms in her cubicle, Gertrude walked out into the muggy afternoon and deposited her belongings on the passenger seat of her Audi. When she got behind the wheel, she flipped open the manila file containing the court approval that granted Roberta King into her guardianship. As she stared at the document, reading her name over and over again, an incredible lightness took hold.

In the most abstract way, she felt like she was getting her sister back and in the same breath knew that it meant she was beginning to truly unravel.

When she got to the Kings' house, Gertrude pulled off onto the grassy shoulder as always, and it occurred to her that if there really was a cult behind this—the destruction in her cabin, the five men arrested, Maude's and murder—then bringing Roberta to her house might put the peculiar girl in more danger than she already was.

As she drove through Laconia, Jake's advice about getting a gun came to mind and because of it, her stomach clenched.

Whipping the door open and jumping out of her car as if fleeing the notion, she started up the gravel driveway when she reached the Kings', the sweltering summer sun beating through a canopy of branches overhead and roasting the beret on her head.

She rolled up the gray, cotton sleeves of her shirt, helping her slick skin to breathe, as she neared the Kings' porch where Zhana was using a trowel to pick mud out of the tread on her sneaker. Immaculate as always wearing well-tailored khakis and a crisp white tank that hugged her with vacuum packed exactness, she straightened, rolling her shoulders back and letting the trowel slip from her fingers. It was then that she realized she wasn't alone any more.

"I do wish you would call ahead," she said, planting her fist on her hip and lifting one corner of her mouth into a wry smile, which she quickly released.

Apologizing, Gertrude took stock of the yard within view and hoped Roberta was inside the house. When she returned her gaze to Zhana, she noticed something off about the woman and gradually narrowed it down to her hair.

Far from its usual bouffant style, her blond hair looked thin and straggly and soon Gertrude understood why. It appeared to have been falling out in clumps.

"Can I offer you anything?" Zhana asked with a heaving sigh as though she was going through the hostess motions without a shred of enthusiasm. "A drink perhaps?"

"No," she said, following up quickly with, "thank you," which these days was far from the tip of her tongue. "Is Roberta home?"

"Not that I'm aware of." Zhana padded down the steps and decisively rounded the side of the house where a gardening hose was coiled behind the yellowing bushes. Grunting, she yanked it loose, muscling it back around until it was taut. "Do they look better to you?"

"The plants?"

"Honestly, I can't tell." She took a moment to eye the plant then began inspecting each crisp leaf until a branch accidentally broke off. "Nothing helps."

When Zhana ran her fingers through her hair and a chunk came loose in her hand, Gertrude couldn't help but notice the glaring similarity between the withering woman and her dying plants.

As Zhana drew her silken handkerchief from her back pocket and proceeded to wrap her hair, Gertrude asked, "Where does Roberta go when she isn't here?"

"She runs around with her little boyfriend," she said easily. "There's a field out back they like to disappear in and Quinton lives up the road so they go there sometimes."

Recalling the scrawny teenager she had seen heading towards the house the other day when she had been walking to her car, she said, "I didn't realize Roberta had a boyfriend."

"Oh, well," she laughed, breathy and amused. "He's not really her boyfriend, but you know, he's not a girl so I tease. Quinton's better than most of the characters she gets tangled up with, I'll say that. But she's too strong willed for him. She rubs off on him more than he rubs off on her." She shrugged then fiddled with the spray nozzle on the hose as though it were as complicated as navigating Windows 10 after an automatic update. She took to shaking it like it would help jostle the thing into spraying. Surprisingly, it worked, but the pressure was uncontrollable and the hose whipped out of her hands, soaking her. "Oh for Christ's sake!"

"Zhana, we need to talk."

The woman kicked at the hose then stomped away from it up the porch steps where she paced in a circle, shaking her head. "I don't see what we have to talk about," she complained. "Haven't you talked to us enough? I told you I don't know where Roberta is. If only you would call ahead, you wouldn't miss everyone so frequently."

Holding Zhana's gaze was enough pressure to drive the woman into the house. She held the screen door open for Gertrude then glided through the living room and into the kitchen where she wasted no time plucking a bottle of Grey Goose out of the freezer.

"Why do I have a feeling I'll need one of these?" She chortled over her shoulder, though the sound she made was strained.

Clutching the manila folder, Gertrude eyed the dining room table, but couldn't bring herself to sit. Getting comfortable for a confrontation would only make this more difficult.

Zhana slapped a tin cap on her tumbler and vigorously shook the martini, ice clanking noisily inside, then poured the chilled alcohol into a long stem glass and swayed her way into the living room.

"Let's get this over with. I've had a hell of a day and the sooner I have time to myself, the better."

She eased onto the couch then drew her drink to her pursed mouth and ingested the entire glass in one, long gulp. It was alarming.

Settling into the adjacent lounge chair, awkward swells flaring in her chest, Gertrude realized she was holding her folder so tightly that she had bent it.

"Zhana, I need to ask you..." She trailed off, her mind going blank then producing phrases and fragments that seemed all wrong. She winced sharply with embarrassment then stumbled through her point. "Some... information has been brought to my attention..." It wasn't quite what she meant to say.

Zhana was perched like a dove on the edge of the couch, not at all concerned. "Regarding?"

"Have you noticed, over the past few years, there have been..." Gertrude scrambled for a term other than *satanic*, "gatherings in the field behind your house? Gatherings at night?"

"I'm not sure what you're referring to," she said, though her eyes went dead. "But if there have been noise complaints, I'll address the issue with Roberta directly."

"No, I'm not referring to noise complaints." She was being too delicate. She needed to come out with it even if it provoked a side of Zhana she hadn't thought was there. "I mean... a cult."

With a big smile, tipping her head back, she let out a cackle so loud it set Gertrude's teeth on edge. When her laughter subsided, she locked her bright green eyes on Gertrude, her expression knotting up like a ball of yarn, the fine lines in her face becoming deeply creased. "My dear, what in God's name are you talking about?"

Zhana tried to keep her laughter going, but the sound dried up, and the way she abruptly hopped up to refill her glass told Gertrude the woman knew something and was deflecting.

Speaking up so that Zhana's performance of making another cocktail more important than this conversation wouldn't deter her, Gertrude said, "There have been accounts from a number of residents. Some have heard chanting out in the field, and others claimed to have seen criminal acts."

"*Claimed* being the operative word, wouldn't you agree?" Zhana turned her back, as she pulverized her martini, shaking it violently and releasing her outrage. Pouring her drink, she asked, "I fail to see what this has to do with either of my daughters."

"Have you considered the possibility that Maude didn't kill herself?"

Zhana didn't have to be facing her for Gertrude to see that she had cracked her wide open. When Zhana managed to turn around, which she did slowly—a ballerina pivoting within a jewelry box—her air of perfection was stripped. She looked wounded. Honest and miserable, and most distinctly, she looked afraid.

She spoke with a thin voice. "You think my daughter was killed?"

"I wonder if Maude saw something," she supplied. "Something that someone thought she shouldn't have seen."

"And who would that be? Who do you think would shoot her in the head in the middle of the night with me sleeping across the hall and her father downstairs and her sister in another room of this house?"

Zhana seethed, her chest heaving, her fiery eyes burning through Gertrude, who couldn't have felt smaller sinking into the soft lounge chair.

Then Zhana's eyes widened and she gaped. "You rude little twit."

Gertrude was stunned speechless.

"How dare you come into my home," she raged, advancing on Gertrude as she paced into the living

191

room, "and accuse my family of killing my precious daughter."

"Mrs. King, please calm down." She was on her feet, backing away with very little room to go—stumbling around the couch, tripping backwards into the coffee table, meeting the bookshelf behind her. Gertrude minced and mangled her words. "Blame is against my ethics… I mean… I'm not blaming you or accusing you, I mean. I've heard accounts of bizarre singing that's coming from the field."

"No," said Zhana in a deathly quiet tone, silencing her. "You *are* accusing me. And you must be insane."

"Have you seen any cult activity?" she demanded.

"I want you to leave here and never come back."

As if dismissing her, Zhana returned to the couch where she sat stoically, her eyebrows lifting and face long. She pulled a dusty magazine off the coffee table, set it in her lap, and began flipping through. Her eyes glazed over at the fawn-eyed models peering vacantly up at her, their plastic smiles and hollow advice—*pesky pubic hair no more!* and *rev up date night!* and *reverse-cowgirl for G-spot orgasms!*

Without looking at her, she said, "I would appreciate it if you let yourself out."

Gertrude drew in deep breaths of air, squaring her shoulders and clenching her jaw, and didn't stop inhaling until it hurt. All the while, it didn't feel to her like she was staring the woman down. Instead, she felt like an ignored child whose problems could never be big enough to match an adult's.

Regardless, she stated, "I am here to take custody of Roberta. I will not leave without her." When Zhana lifted her gaze, growing so appalled that she seemed to turn white, Gertrude produced the document, marched forward, and deposited it on the coffee table. Zhana didn't even look at it, but stared at her as though aliens had just beamed down into her living room.

Then, without warning, she burst into tears, wailing and covering her face, as she collapsed into a miserable hunch, her shoulders quaking, the silken handkerchief she wore slipping down the back of her head.

Slinking closer, cautious not to rouse her, Gertrude retrieved the document and tucked it into its folder then asked, "Is there anything you would like to tell me?"

"Yes," she said, keeping her face shielded between trembling hands. "Go to hell."

It wasn't until Gertrude got outside on the porch that she felt raw, used up, spent, and at the core of her exhaustion was the sharpest prick of sorrow. So much of her life, the memories and recollections, were as lost as her car at the bottom of the lake. But the emotions, the memory her feelings contained, were anchored to distinct points in time.

She had felt like this before—clawing at the walls for answers, finding her mother balled on the couch, Gertrude urgent to make a pact before her father got home, failing, sabotaged, betrayed by Marsha's ugly silence, dreading Albert's iron fists.

Where the hell was Roberta?

Decisively, she padded down the steps and started around the house, her black Keds brushing over dying grass with each stride. The lake shimmered, its shore not ten yards away, as she rounded the back of the house. The yard looked months overdue to be mowed, but even with the growth, Gertrude could see the dividing line where the yard ended and the field began a good five acres out.

As soon as she collected Roberta into her custody, she wouldn't be able to investigate the field. Now was her only chance.

If the map she had pulled from the county records was accurate, the field was twenty square acres and enclosed by sparse woodlands where the properties were divided among the seven houses—five previously owned by the incarcerated, Jake Livingston, and the Kings themselves. Only the Kings' and Jake had lakefront property. The others were tucked in the woods along Moulton, which hooked around Lake Winnipesaukee but with meandering bends.

Jake came to mind, as she high-stepped through the foxtail and sweet-grass fronds that were as tall as her chest. He had been reluctant to leave her the night he helped bury her dog, and she had lingered on the deck as well. She had felt like she was falling towards him at that moment, the Xanax long since worn off. It had been her energy, or his, strange magnetism they both had resisted. She couldn't believe she had turned down a date with him before the accident when he had asked her out. When Jake had told her the other night, it had seemed incomprehensible. Why wouldn't she have jumped at the chance to date him?

Her daydream cleared the moment she realized the tall grass up ahead appeared matted down.

She spilled into the clearing. There a thin puddle of water. Her eyes locked onto a deer carcass that was lying on its side in a bloody heap in the puddle. Flies buzzed around the dead animal, making a terrible noise.

She froze, disturbed, and a zing of adrenaline rushed through her veins, which caused her temples to start throbbing. Her chest tightened and her legs turned rubbery.

But she crept closer and closer, nearing the dead animal, and discovered that a symbol had been carved into its hide. The same symbol she had found painted in her cabin.

Even more disturbing was the deer's face. It wasn't there.

Blood and bone and teeth in a startling mess that she could barely make sense of was all that was left of it.

Then, all of a sudden, she sensed that something was wrong. She could feel it—an instinct that comes on hard in the gut.

She was in the presence of pure evil.

As her nerves ratcheted up, she whipped around and found Peter King glaring at her.

"Didn't I tell you to keep to yourself?"

CHAPTER SIXTEEN

GERTRUDE WAS ISOLATED with Peter King in the field.

There was nothing but wilderness and vacant houses in the distance.

Her stomach twisted into hot knots and her skin pricked up with gooseflesh.

His eyes looked black and gleaming under his pronounced brow. The angle of the sun caused a hard shadow to cut across his face. Peter seemed to enjoy the effect he was having on her.

She felt severely intimidated, which meant she probably looked it.

"What happened to this deer?" Her hand reached into her back pocket where she kept her cell phone, but she was petrified at the thought of trying to get someone on the line. Peter would stop her. Would he attack her? And who would Gertrude even call for that matter? The police? What good would they do if they were buddies with Charlie and Peter King? Should she call Harry or Wendy or someone from the office? No, they were too far away. Jake perhaps…

"I have no idea what happened to the deer," he said easily without even looking at the thing. "I'm never out this way."

"This isn't your family's property, is it?" she asked even though she knew that no one owned the field. However, if Peter denied ownership, she would have all the more right to be here.

"Whether it is or isn't, it certainly isn't your property." He rested his right hand on the butt of his holstered gun to threaten her. "You're not going to make me drag you off the premises, are you?"

"There have been accounts of cult activity in this field," she asserted. Yelling was the only way to get the words out. "Look at that deer! That's a satanic symbol carved into its hide! Someone broke into my cabin and painted the same symbol on the living room walls! Homeless people have been turning up dead with their faces eaten off just like that deer's missing face! I'm determined to get to the bottom of this!"

He was annoyed with her, as if she were a child spouting fiction.

"I have no idea what you're talking about. My family had nothing to do with that deer or your house. But I do know this, your business with Roberta has concluded."

"No, it hasn't."

Though she was trembling, she dismissed him by pacing away and pulling her cell phone out of her pants. When she found the camera app on her phone, she stooped down next to the deer carcass and snapped a few close-up photos of the satanic symbol and the deer's bloody face.

"If you think you're taking Roberta from this house, you're dead wrong," he warned.

The warning told Gertrude that Zhana must have called Peter moments ago.

Gertrude held her ground.

"I have a court order and you can't stop me," she stated.

She turned her back to Peter and started for the house.

He lunged and grabbed her arm.

"Get your hands off of me!" she said, trying to jerk free.

"For your own good, you leave well enough alone, you hear?" he ordered.

"Where's Charlie?" she demanded. "Did you kill him?"

"He's taking some time to himself, which isn't against the law. I would know, since it's my job to uphold it, or have you forgotten that I'm a cop?"

Yanking her arm free, squaring her shoulders at him, and fighting the sunlight in her eyes, she glared up at Peter. "I know about the original police report." A voice in her head was screaming at her not to tip her hand, but accusations started flying out of her so fast, there was no controlling herself. "Your granddaughter didn't kill herself and I'm going to find out who did."

In response, he hardened. Rage rolled off him like steam from an engine. It was enough of an indication that Peter knew exactly what had happened to Maude, and he looked about ready to kill Gertrude to keep her quiet.

"You're out of your mind," he said, his tone so deep and raw it cut through her.

"I have proof," she warned, but her voice quaked. Swallowing the hard lump in her throat, she tried to steady her trembling hands, as she barked, "I have the document."

"You don't have *anything* except for a brain that doesn't work. You should've stayed in that hospital."

She had to get away from him *now*. Taking off, she walked quickly across the matted grass and when she reached the tall foxtails, she separated the fronds like a curtain and stepped through, making her way across the gnarly field towards the Kings' house.

"Watch yourself!" he called out after her. "If you keep talking crazy like that, you might end up in the loony-bin."

Like Weird Wanda had?

"Or worse!" he threatened. "You might end up dead!"

Whipping around, she could barely see him through the feathery fronds as they shimmied in the breeze. She shouted, "If anything happens to me, Jake will publicize it, and it won't matter the hold you have on this town! Everyone in the Tri-State area will suspect you and your family! You'll be destroyed!"

"Jake Livingston, huh?" Rocking back on his heels, he grinned. "I doubt Jake will be a problem for much longer."

Gertrude continued on her way. She couldn't move fast enough. Prickly fronds slapped her face and the tall grass sliced her forearms like paper cuts, peppering her skin with tiny lacerations.

In a delayed reaction, her heart was beating out of her chest, the pressure in her veins causing her hands to shake violently. She felt dizzy. Several times she envisioned herself fainting.

This particular brand of terror felt strikingly familiar, though she didn't let herself make the mental leap and connect her fear to her own family.

Instead, she focused on how she might find Roberta.

In a stroke of good luck, when she reached the front yard, she spotted Roberta running in the tattered red dress she always wore, her stick legs punching over grass, her boney-arms pumping, her mud-green eyes wild.

Gertrude couldn't figure out who the girl was running away from or where she was sprinting to.

"Roberta!" she yelled, running after her, as the girl cut around the far side of the house.

In response, Roberta turned on her heel and nearly lost her balance. She staggered sideways, her bare feet shuffling over dying grass.

"What's wrong?" Gertrude slowed to a jog until she reached her.

She heaved, out of breath. "They're after me. He's not home."

"Who's not home?"

Roberta gasped for air, wincing through a stitch in her side. "Quinton. I hide out in his shed sometimes. He's not there."

Gathering that Roberta's teenage friend sometimes offered her a safe haven, she hooked her arm around the girl and began ushering her towards the driveway where she had parked her car.

"Come with me."

"What?" asked Roberta, panicking. "Where?"

"I'm taking you away from this place."

The girl slowed her step when they reached the driveway. "Should I get my things?"

"There's no time." She explained the situation. "I have a court order that gives me legal permission to remove you from your parents' custody. There's nothing they can do."

"I don't want to live with a bunch of strangers," she yelled, shoving Gertrude off her.

"You won't. I promise." But it wasn't enough to keep the girl moving, so she said, "You'll be staying with me."

Screwing her face up, Roberta stared at her as though the information was a riddle wrapped in an enigma that she couldn't figure out.

"It's only temporary," she said urgently, prodding the girl forward. "Now come on."

Gertrude sensed that the men who had been after Roberta were somewhere nearby. She could feel their predatory eyes spying from the shadowy woods, but when she glanced over her shoulder at the house, she only saw Peter and Zhana arguing on the porch.

"Quickly now."

Finally, Roberta hurried along, using long strides and keeping up with Gertrude.

When they reached her Audi on the grassy shoulder, Gertrude opened the passenger side door, keen to its quirks, and helped Roberta inside. Gertrude moved the girl's dress out of the door jam and firmly shut her door, and when she climbed in behind the steering wheel and started the engine, she saw a truck idling up the road just shy of the bend.

As she pulled a U-turn, tires kicking up grass and dirt, Gertrude peeked at her rearview and saw the truck barrelling down the road after them.

"Who are they?" she demanded, as she stepped on the gas pedal. Her car began vibrating with the juts and buckles of the scarred asphalt road.

"My dad's friends." Roberta leaned forward and watched the truck in her side view mirror.

"Why were you running from them?" she asked, quickly upshifting as they gained speed.

"So that they wouldn't catch me."

Roberta leaned back in her seat and took stock of the index cards that covered every inch of the Audi's interior. The texture of all the index cards reminded her of reptilian scales. She stroked her hand down the dashboard, feeling the texture.

"They're following us," Roberta remarked, her tone strangely resigned as though she had been through this before and had accepted that all roads would eventually lead back to Charlie and Zhana's house.

"It'll be alright," said Gertrude, feeling a twinge of guilt for lying so blatantly. Someone from the satanic cult had been in her cabin. Things were far from alright.

Randomly, she asked, "Are you married?"

"What? No."

"Am I going to have to share a room?"

Gertrude glanced at her quickly to get a read on the girl's main concern and determined she was worrying about the characters she might have to deal with in her new home. But sharing a room was a good question regardless of the fact that it would be just the two of them at Gertrude's cabin. Doris had stayed in Gertrude's bedroom. Sisters could get away with that kind of closeness, which wouldn't at all be appropriate with Roberta.

"I'll figure something out," she said, then stammered, promising, "You won't have to share a room."

"Why are you doing this?"

She could feel Roberta's gaze burning into the side of her head and penetrating her thoughts, as if the girl was trying to understand the real reason why Gertrude was helping her.

"I don't trust anyone except for myself," she said eventually, the only statement she could make that resembled the truth while at the same time concealing it.

Perhaps satisfied with Gertrude's answer, Roberta leaned her head back and watched the road twisting and dipping through the windshield.

It wasn't until they turned onto Messer that Gertrude realized the truck was not only still behind them, but gaining on them. She hit the gas and soon she felt the floor beneath her foot, having pushed the pedal as far as it would go. The engine squealed, as the Audi accelerated. Roberta grew tense on the passenger seat and gripped the armrest.

"You're going really fast," she said nervously, as they bounced over the asphalt lip before the bridge.

Gertrude shifted her gaze back and forth from the rearview mirror to the bridge ahead, but forgot about the hairpin turn just after the bridge.

"Slow down!" Roberta yelled, pressing her tight body against her seat, as the entire vehicle shook, tires vibrating against the wooden slats of the bridge.

But Gertrude was deaf to her, a jarring surrealism taking hold, déjà vu commingling with nightmarish panic—*Doris? Is that Doris beside me?*

Screaming, Gertrude ordered again and again and again, "Put on your seatbelt!"

Yelling over her, as she scrambled to comprehend what had come over the social worker, Roberta insisted, "I did! I did! Slow down!"

Gertrude slammed on the brakes the second they cleared the bridge and the front tires hit asphalt.

She cut the wheel and the vehicle slid sideways onto Opechee Street, centrifugal force sending Roberta careening into her, though the girl had braced the door handle in a white-knuckled grip.

When the Audi slammed down, Gertrude realized the car had taken the turn on two wheels, but the second she straightened out and saw the gleaming lake on the right-hand side, she was consumed with an incredible feeling of lightness.

Lake water wasn't filling the vehicle. They were still on the road. She had cheated death. And all the risks she had taken were forgotten.

She checked the rearview mirror and saw the road was empty behind them. She whipped her gaze over her shoulder at the bridge. It was desolate.

Had there been a truck? Or had she imagined it?

Returning her gaze to the road ahead, she caught sight of Roberta whose eyes were wide in astonishment.

That's when it slipped. "Doris, put your seatbelt on."

A look of sheer terror came over Roberta, flushing the color right out of her cheeks.

Slowly and cautiously, she told Gertrude, "I'm not Doris."

"No, I know," she said, feeling suddenly mortified. "I muddle words sometimes. I know that your name is Roberta," she stated to prove that she knew who was in the passenger seat. "You're all buckled in?"

"Ah, yeah." Roberta slouched, becoming very small, and started neurotically biting her fingertips "I need to call my friend," she said, as Gertrude pulled up her driveway, coming to a stop in front of the cabin. "So he knows where I am."

"Sure."

Harry crossed her mind, as she stepped out of the car. She had agreed to deliver Roberta to the DCYF to make introductions with the "foster family," whom Harry had no idea was Gertrude. But she decided to deal with him and any subsequent fallout only after she got Roberta settled.

"I'll make you a key," she mentioned, as she unlocked the front door and welcomed Roberta inside.

The cabin smelled stuffy, she noticed, as she led the girl into the living room. The low light and disarray from her effort to clean up with Jake made the place far drearier than it ordinarily seemed.

If Roberta thought the same thing, she didn't let on, as she slowly walked around, eyeing her new surroundings—the wooden coffee table, the texture of the couch upholstery, a lamp with an off-kilter shade. She appeared to be deliberating, as if assessing whether or not she could see herself living here.

"Are you hungry?"

"I'm always hungry."

Gertrude listed the options and asked, "Would you like to take a shower while I whip up sandwiches?"

Her eyebrows furrowed as though Gertrude had used a foreign word.

"I have shorts and clean tees," she offered, "and flip-flops and a pair of Keds in size eight."

"I'm seven and a half."

"I might have that size."

Roberta was a non-responsive statue so Gertrude padded up the hall into her bedroom.

She had left Doris' clothes in her closet. It had never entered her mind to donate them to the Salvation Army or even pack them in a box to store in the attic. She knew every garment as intimately as if it were her own, and hunted for the gray tee shirt that Doris used to lounge around in, along with her dead sister's favorite pair of jean shorts, hoping that Roberta would like them. At the bottom of the closet were her sister's many shoes interspersed with hers. She plucked up a pair of purple jellies that Doris had broken in. They felt soft in her hands.

When she returned to the hallway with the clothes and jelly sandals in her arms, she found Roberta in the bathroom with the door wide open. She was using her dirt-stained fingers to comb her greasy hair, and she appeared to be examining her scalp. Then she inspected her fingers, as she wriggled a few loose strands into the trash bin beside the toilet.

"I keep waiting for it to come out in clumps," she explained, as Gertrude set the clothes on the toilet lid.

"The faucet is a little tricky," she said, starting for the shower stall. Turning the water on and rotating the dial, Gertrude got the temperature just right. "There's shampoo and conditioner," she stated, pointing out the obvious. "Soap. Disposable razors are beneath the sink if you need one. And maxi-pads, tampons, all that stuff is down there, too, just help yourself."

A faint mist of steam wafted around the shower curtain. Not at all shy, Roberta let her red dress flutter to the tiles and Gertrude diverted her gaze, sharply turning but also catching sight of a fresh cut on the girl's thigh among the patterns of fine scars that she had already carved into her pale skin.

She paused when she reached the door and before closing it to give Roberta privacy, she said over her shoulder, "I would like to get you in to see a doctor before school starts."

"Why?"

"For a Tetanus shot," she stated, as she wrapped her hand around the edge of the door to draw it shut. "The orange soap bar is antibacterial."

"Got it," she said, implying she would take it from here.

Gertrude eased the door closed, and once she was in the kitchen, she collected bread and luncheon meat to get started on the particular sandwich Roberta had requested—a ham salad sandwich.

As she did, toasting bread in the little glass-front oven, spreading mayonnaise onto thin slices of ham, and listening to the crunch of her knife slice through the layers, Gertrude got lost in the similarities between Roberta and her own sister.

The comparison was strong. Roberta was causing all kinds of memories to resurface. Yet if Gertrude tried too hard to recall a specific detail, she realized an entire memory would suddenly disappear from her mind.

Her parents had been harming Doris. She sensed it, but couldn't see the memories, couldn't pinpoint any precise event. Gertrude had gotten out, leaving her sister behind and hating herself for it. But years later, Doris had shown up on her doorstep. She had helped Doris. And when the dust had settled, the sisters went back to their parents' house to confront them. Confront them about what specifically, she couldn't say, and it was driving her crazy.

She was so close, her mind brushing the rough surface of what had happened. Taking the turn onto Opechee too fast with Roberta in the passenger seat had jostled up hints from her subconscious, but they were intangible, abstract, nothing more distinct than eerie feelings. Peter closing in on her in the field had been too familiar. The terror of it had felt strangely common, as well as the shakes that had followed.

As she set the plates on the coffee table and heard the bathroom door pop open, Gertrude was suddenly consumed by the image of Doris ill in bed—sweat beading on her forehead, the comforter pulled to her chin, a stiff winter draft seeping through the window pane, her mother complaining that Doris wouldn't eat, soup growing cold on the nightstand, Doris refusing. *I would rather die than eat that,* her eyes had said.

Roberta also wouldn't eat, would she? Starving was how she looked, the result of living with the Kings. Eager had been her response when Gertrude had offered. She would eat here.

Doris in her cabin filled her thoughts—scavenging her kitchen the second Gertrude had taken her in, desperately stuffing chips in her mouth, a hindrance to the meal she had started, too hungry to wait for the pasta to boil, she would need more hands to eat and cook and revive herself.

Gertrude jolted from her reverie when Roberta stepped into the living room.

"Smells good," she said with a wide smile, looking bizarrely like Zhana. "Toast is my favorite smell."

In three long strides she was on the couch. Wrapping her hands around the sandwich, she stuffed it into her mouth as though she had been deprived for days.

Gertrude took small bites of her own sandwich, watching her. Roberta's hair had dried along her forehead and ears—blonde wisps drifting away from damp locks. The tee shirt fit her well, but the jeans pulled taut at her thighs, riding up and cutting into the flesh.

"Let's talk about what's going on," she suggested when Roberta devoured the last scrap and set the ceramic plate on the coffee table. "I've been awarded temporary custody and your parents don't have the right to take you, though they could appeal."

She startled as if remembering something important and blurted out, "I have to call Quinton!"

If she asked her to wait, she wouldn't have Roberta's full attention so she said, "The house phone is in my bedroom. Could you make it quick?"

Roberta disappeared down the hallway and Gertrude heard a quick series of murmured phrases, which she assumed would stretch out into a long, lingering conversation. She imagined Roberta playing with the coiled cord, her head tilting, her feet kicked up in the air as she splayed across the bed on her stomach. But Roberta did none of those teenage things and was back in the living room within a minute, plopping onto the couch and tucking her legs beneath her.

"Depending on how things go and how you feel," Gertrude went on, "you can stay here until you graduate, until you turn eighteen, or longer."

"Why are you doing this?" she asked, resonating her earlier confusion from when they had escaped her house. But before Gertrude could compose an answer, she guessed, "Because of your dead sister?"

It was her greatest fear realized, that she was so transparent people would know she had lost her mind, but she didn't shy away. "Doris had scars on her legs. She had kept them hidden. She had been harming herself. In her mind she had reason to, it made sense to her."

"It's just a distraction," she said quietly, her gaze falling to her lap.

"A distraction from what?"

"Everything."

"What were you looking for when you were digging around your house?"

"I'm not your dead sister, okay?"

"Yes, I know that," she quickly offered. "I only want to help."

"Help who?"

"I don't want to scare you," she said, fishing her cell phone from her pocket, "but I need to ask if you know who did this?"

Gertrude pulled up the photo she had taken of the deer in the field behind the Kings' house. The image was disturbingly sharp, but she angled it for Roberta to see.

Looking at it, Roberta's gaze went slack and she clenched her jaw, darkening in a way that didn't translate as fearful, but rather agitated. Then Gertrude thought she caught the clever wheels turning inside Roberta's fast-working mind. A chilled grin came through her expression.

"Looks like Weird Wanda escaped the institution," she surmised, meeting Gertrude's gaze.

"Weird Wanda didn't attack those men who were found with their faces eaten off," she countered, retrieving her cell and placing it on the coffee table. "What about the symbol?" she pressed. "Do you recognize it? Have you seen it before?"

"No," she said over Gertrude.

"Roberta," she started, trying not to gape in astonishment that the girl was making it difficult to protect her. "I know you know what's going on at that house. I know you have an idea of whatever rituals are taking place in the field out there. If you're afraid of them, whoever they are, you need to tell me. This can all be over."

Staring at her, the grin slid off her face and her gaze went so soft that she looked suddenly vacant, darkness hollowing her out as if she could beckon the cold hand of death to take her. Then, like her mother and like Peter, she argued, "You think that has anything to do with Maude?"

"Yes. I do. How could it not?"

"Or do you think it has to do with Doris?" she asked, "You can't tell us apart, can you?"

"Of course I can. It was a slip of the tongue, I told you that. I muddle my words sometimes."

"I don't think you're muddling your words," she countered. "I think your brain has been destroyed."

Gertrude felt a hot flush break out across her cheeks, but she wasn't offended or angry or shocked, only deeply saddened. Nothing hurt like the truth.

"I want to help you," she said, her voice a thread she barely recognized.

Then Roberta leaned forward, surging into herself so starkly that Gertrude found herself drawing away.

"You don't even know how close you are," she said, searching her eyes as if she could see the distance between what Gertrude knew and what she had yet to discover. "But you don't want to close the gap and remember," she warned, relaxing into the arm of the couch. "Trust me."

Gertrude startled when her cell vibrated on the coffee table. After grabbing it, she checked the screen and saw Jake's name and number flashing so she accepted the call, rising off the couch and pacing away into the hall.

"Hey," she said softly.

"Where are you?"

He sounded rattled, but sensed his ease when she said, "At home."

"I had my contact run the blood from the book I took," he began, his tone tensed then he paused, breathing. "You're not going to believe this. It was a match for the cop who fell off payroll July 5th."

"What?"

"Kevin Robinson. He had to have been the one who made up that homicide report. Anyone who knows or suspects anything is getting plucked off the face of the earth. I would like to come over. Is that okay?"

"I have Roberta here."

His sudden silence set her teeth on edge.

"I filed for custody," she said, nervous to admit it.

"Gerty, we found prints on the candles. They belong to Roberta. She was in your house. She had something to do with that satanic scene. You aren't safe with her there."

A sixth sense told her she wasn't alone. She turned around. Roberta was standing in the mouth of the hallway, her eyes fierce and searching. Jake's voice sounded tinny through the receiver—*Gerty, what's happening? Are you okay?* But she had lowered her cell phone from her ear, suddenly certain that she had made a terrible mistake.

"Who are you talking to?"

CHAPTER SEVENTEEN

SPYING THROUGH THE window, which caused him to trip over his bicycle, sending the tire spinning from where it lay on its side, Quinton neared the glass pane, stepping into a stark reflection of sunlight that momentarily blinded him. He thought he heard voices murmuring inside the cabin, but he couldn't detect Roberta's distinct timber—high and melodic no matter how harsh her words.

The sun was roasting him. His back felt slick with sweat, which caused his black tee shirt to cling uncomfortably, but when he fit the length of himself against the rounded logs, pressing his nose to the glass, it was just shady enough to afford him an ounce of relief.

Coming here greatly deviated from her instructions, but when she had told him the address over the phone, he couldn't help it. He had to make sure she was okay. He hadn't seen her since the night at Jake Livingston's house. It had been three terror filled days, waiting for the verdict on the photos he had taken, a verdict that had yet to be delivered.

In her absence, Quinton had feared the worst, visions of Roberta being tortured in the field plaguing his thoughts—Roberta strapped down to a stone slab, whipped and beaten, sliced to the tune of their harrowing chanting, made to watch deer being skinned alive, forced to drink blood, and humiliated—heinous acts he had never witnessed but imagined were likely, given the instruments he had stumbled upon in the Kings' basement.

Quinton realized he was peering into a living room. The wooden edge of a coffee table jutting into his sightlines, a bookshelf and wall to its right formed some semblance of a common area. From the far corner of the room came the social worker looking rigid, her cockeyed hat threatening to slip off the side of her head. Roberta followed after and he deduced that they had entered from a hallway. He nearly did a double take seeing her. She was dressed like a normal person and her hair was fluffed clean.

Their body language was strangely intimate. Both looked closed off, yet testing the other with brief glances that reminded him of the fallout after a fight.

When the social worker turned towards the window, he ducked, heart galloping zero-to-sixty before his knees hit the grass. She hadn't seen him. He had been too quick, but it would be best to get out of there before he got caught. He didn't particularly want to deal with the brain-damaged woman who he feared would make things worse for Roberta, but at least Gertrude didn't induce his panic like Roberta did. Disobeying her had never gone well for him in the past.

He scrambled for his bicycle, hunching and dragging it low to the ground until he felt certain he wouldn't be seen should either of them glance out the window. The spokes and pedals tore grass up as he went, but when he righted the bicycle, he tapped the sod free then swung his leg over the seat, hopping on and peeling out.

Cutting through the woods and bouncing with the Huffy's high-tech suspension that was completely unlike his previous bike, he veered between trees and loose rocks until the tires hit the smooth asphalt of Opechee Street. The leafy Maple treetops cast shadowy patterns across the road as he rode along the bay. He wished that by the time he got to where he was going, it would be nighttime. Darkness would give him a fighting chance of pulling this off.

He hadn't had enough time on the phone. Roberta had been sharp and demanding, brushing over the glaring upheaval of her life. Quinton, desperate to understand why she was with the social worker, had listened hard, scrambling to do the math—*Living there? She moved? She's not coming back?* As reality sunk in, ratcheting up his anxiety, chest clamping like a giant fist tightening around it, Quinton leaned right, angling the bicycle onto the shoulder just shy of the Kings' driveway, and as he stumbled off it, jogging and dropping the bike, he slammed against the thick trunk of a Maple.

He spied Zhana on the porch, but she wasn't alone.

Draped on the railing, legs crossed long with a womanly point at the knee, martini glass in hand, stem between her long fingers, Zhana gazed up at Peter, who looked like a drill sergeant lying his way into the heart of his weakest cadet. There was a pleading quality to his eyes and posture, however.

Taking quick stock of his options, Quinton swept his gaze along the tree line then the yard, noting the shadows he might hide in and the trees that were thick enough to skulk behind. If he was stealthy, he could dart to the corner of the house, whip into the bushes, dig hard and fast and get what he needed then dash off again for his bicycle.

But though Quinton took great risks diving into his mission, scurrying from one tree to the next in plain view, and working his way closer and closer to the porch—all guts for what glory might come as a result—a terrible instinct rattled his bones, which told him he wouldn't succeed until Zhana and Peter were gone.

Spying them from where he had hidden himself behind an old tree stump eight yards off from where he needed to be, Quinton watched for his moment. Zhana had her back to him, but until Peter turned away, he would be able to spot him if Quinton darted any closer.

"You're focused on the wrong thing," said Peter, berating Zhana for something Quinton hadn't heard.

"My hair is falling out, Peter," she barked, distressed and pulling her silken handkerchief from her head to exhibit the evidence. "My hair. The plants. We're all getting sick."

"I told you I'm working on it," he snapped. "It's not a priority until we find them."

As if disgusted with the bald patches on her scalp, Peter paced away from Zhana, leaving Quinton the opportunity he needed. Ducking low and punching his sneakers into the grass, he sprinted to the side of the porch then slid soundlessly into the yellowing vegetation.

The second he landed he held his breath, checking himself at every angle to be sure he was concealed. Pressing his back into the lattice, he sensed there were a good six inches from the top of his head to the porch landing.

He peered up and saw the gnarly fingers of dying branches overhead. Through them, he spied the length of Zhana's back, her hands knotting the handkerchief into place behind her head.

"You said you found your camera?" Peter asked, his boots stomping hard against the wooden slats with each step. "No film inside?"

"I'm sure she had it developed," she said, warily. "They're probably around here somewhere."

"*Probably* and *somewhere* aren't good enough. Do you have any idea how damning that article was, and Jake is just itching to print another. I can smell it."

"What do you want me to do?" she asked, though her tone betrayed her with a curt edge of resignation. "Dig in the dirt? Knowing Roberta, she buried it somewhere. Christ." She snorted a tired laugh. "She's made so many deposits over the years. I would get sidetracked, trying to fathom the nonsense she's hidden in the ground."

"How can I impress upon you the gravity of the situation, Zhana?" He was yelling now, irate to get through to her, but Quinton only heard her gulping her martini, unfazed.

"I thought you said she knows what to do," she challenged after setting her glass on the railing with a click.

"I don't trust her," he clarified. "When she's within my control, when she's *here*, it's a different matter. I wouldn't have permitted her to go to Inman's cabin if I had known she had taken the photos."

"So modify the plan."

"I have no leverage, don't you get that? Getting rid of Livingston is the only card worth playing."

Silence fell between them and it set Quinton's heart pounding. Had they sensed him? Were they mouthing to each other a plot to ambush him? It was too quiet to dig for the photos. His fingers stilled in the soil, every inch of him freezing. He dared not breathe.

"You need to clean up that snotty attitude," he told her, breaking the lull.

Another snort of nervous laughter from Zhana, and Quinton could feel the tension rising between the adults. "Maude should be alive."

"I agree."

"Yet you're harboring Charlie," she pointed out in a snide tone.

"Charlie's not right in the head, you know that."

Quinton heard Peter's boots pounding across the porch then Zhana asked, "Where are you going?"

"To fix this the only way I know how."

"Don't hurt her!"

No response.

It wasn't until Quinton peered through the tangle of bent branches and saw Peter stalking towards his truck that he permitted himself to breathe. The engine fired up. Peter backed the truck around, then he tore off down the driveway.

Above him, Zhana sighed, "Damn," pushing off from the railing and padding a few paces. Quinton heard the screen door whine open then thwack shut, bouncing against the frame.

Then it was quiet. Only the breezy trills of nature all around him and the faint taps of Zhana's sandals deep within the house could be heard. Quinton hopped on his knees, clawing frantically into the dirt as though a ticking bomb would detonate if he didn't find the photos fast enough. Soon his nails scratched paper—the flap of the pocket containing the photos—and in his thrill he lost all sense of his surroundings, deaf to the whine of the screen door easing open.

With the photos in his grasp, he listened but heard nothing, then edged his way out from the brush.

The second he stood up, he realized he had made a grave error.

"What have you got there?" Zhana asked in a singsong tone that made the hairs on the back of his neck stiffen. "Quinton?"

He didn't want to turn around. Discreetly, though he felt like a bad magician, he shoved the stack of photos down the front of his pants—their crisp corners scraping his skin, dirt-cooled paper zinging his underbelly.

He turned, facing her.

"I asked you a question," she sneered through a mean smile.

Deflecting, he asked, "Is Roberta around? No? Oh, okay, sorry to bother you-"

"Hang on." She stomped down the steps and rounded the yard, advancing on him.

He was screaming at himself to bolt, but caught in the spotlight of her emerald glare as she towered over him, Quinton didn't have a prayer of forming a believable lie, much less dashing to his bicycle.

"Why were you hiding in my bushes?"

Her gaze fell to his pants, defeating him, and when she snapped her eyes up, meeting his, her mouth curled with a sly smile that he didn't trust. "You like helping Roberta, don't you? You like watching her mess around with men. Isn't that right?"

The insinuation turned his stomach.

"You would like to keep those photos for yourself, I'm sure." Leaning over so that the delicate end of her nose hovered so near his face that he could smell her lavender breath, Zhana cocked a single eyebrow, whispering, "Have you missed me?"

Bowels loosening, a hot rush of nerves flooded through him at the reference. He had spent every day since Maude's bizarre funeral party trying to forget all that had transpired between them. "Mrs. King, I really need to go."

She yanked his tee shirt up and shoved her hand down the front of his pants until she had the thick stack of sleeved photos in her grasp.

Her eyes brightened, as she cooed, "What have we here?"

"Mrs. King," he squealed, turning and shuffling away from her, but she grasped hold of his collar, forcing him back around.

As she tucked the stack of photos into her back pocket, she whispered, "Why don't you give me a hug? You know my husband hasn't been around and I found you so comforting that night."

He recoiled, but didn't flee. His entire body felt like hardening cement.

Straightening up, she took on a severe tone. "It's my hair, isn't it?" She touched her handkerchief self-consciously. "It's obvious." When she leaned over again, she grabbed his chin, making him look at her. "Do you have any idea how hard I've worked to keep the cult away from you and your family? You have no concept, do you? And this is how you thank me? By cringing? By not having the decency to look me in the eye?"

He willed himself not to shudder. Her fingers were tendrils of ice wrapped around his chin, but he made himself meet her gaze, all the while scheming in the back of his mind.

He needed the photos.

He couldn't leave without them. As Roberta had explained over the phone, spewing out curt commands in breathy whispers he hadn't grasped until after she had hung up, she was done being their slave. Everything would change now that she was with Gertrude. But if Peter got his hands on the photos, Roberta's last line of defense would be shot to hell. *He wants me here, he thinks I'll take her out, kill her, he thinks I'm still one of them,* she had said, voice urgently euphoric, as she had detailed her good fortune, *Everything we need to shut them down is buried at the damn house, don't you see? Once Gerty gets all the pieces, I'll be free!*

Quinton had to do it. He had to tear the photos out of Zhana's khakis, sprint as fast as his legs would go, but when Zhana pulled him in, angling her mouth to his, he was already running.

Tangled thoughts clouded his understanding of what had just happened.

As though he was watching himself from six feet above, he yanked the bicycle up, jumped on, and began pedaling.

It wasn't until he hooked around the Opechee Bay that the magnitude of his failure came crashing down, shattering all hope of Roberta truly loving him.

CHAPTER EIGHTEEN

REELING WITH disturbed guesses about how the slippery vixen, Roberta, had wormed her way into Gertrude's home, Jake pounded on the cabin door, wrestling down a lump of tension in his throat and listening hard for commotion inside that wasn't there.

If the circumstances had been any different—if Roberta hadn't exposed herself to Jake the other night, having coiled around him like a viper in a misguided attempt to seduce him…

… if she hadn't succeeded using the same tactics with five other men…

… if she hadn't been raised as one of the Kings and if she hadn't been warped into the same perverted shape…

…then discovering Roberta's fingerprints on the satanic candles wouldn't have induced the kind of anxiety that was splitting through Jake's stomach. He would have brushed over the detail as an unfortunate coincidence as though it was no cause for concern.

But Roberta *had* entrapped men. She *was* warped, and she seemed to delight in the art of destroying lives.

Why had Gertrude taken her in?

How long had he been standing out here? It felt like an eternity had passed since he had knocked on the door.

The porch light buzzing overhead grated on his nerves. His urgency was mounting, so he continued pounding on the door.

When the door finally sprung inward, Roberta was standing on the other side.

Jake blurted out, "What have you done with Gerty?"

"I haven't done anything."

She leaned against the door frame in a leisurely posture, looking like a 1956 cigarette ad—*Blow in her face and she'll follow you anywhere!*

Jake pushed past her, barrelling inside.

Gertrude was seated cross-legged on the couch.

The first thing Jake noticed was that she wasn't wearing her beret hat. One side of her hair was braided, but the scarred side of her head looked buzzed. He could see a track of staple-stitches on her scalp around her ear.

She was focused on laying a thin sheet of plastic over the cracked screen of her cell phone.

She glanced up and they locked eyes.

"Jake?"

Gertrude placed her cell phone on the coffee table and rose to her feet with a dancer's fluidity.

Jake caught a glint of apprehension flicker behind her eyes, as Roberta joined them.

He turned to Roberta and asked, "You're staying here?"

"If you're asking if you'll be seeing a lot more of me..." the girl finished the statement by smirking at him.

Jake didn't trust her.

And he couldn't fathom why Gertrude did.

As if she was as innocent as apple pie, Roberta asked, "So, you guys are friends?"

He let Gertrude answer.

"We're old friends," she lied before saying, "Excuse us."

Gertrude joined Jake and invited him to speak privately with her in the bedroom.

As he followed Gerty into the bedroom, he felt Roberta's penetrating gaze and realized that he preferred the girl unwashed with greasy hair and wearing an old, tattered dress. Freshly bathed and wearing clean clothes, as she was, she now seemed oddly potent, as though her filth hadn't enhanced her power before but had bogged it down.

Once they reached the bedroom, he shut the door behind him.

"What were you thinking, bringing Roberta here?" he asked in an angry whisper. "I told her, her fingerprints were on the candles."

"She couldn't have had anything to do with all that," she countered, but her eyes were pleading for him to agree. "There have to be a million reasons why her prints were on the candles."

"But Gerty." He stopped himself before implied that he thought Roberta being here at all was wildly inappropriate. He didn't want to offend Gertrude or alienate her. "Do you really think she's in danger?"

"I know she is. DCYF got the go-ahead from the court to remove her from Charlie's house," she explained.

"You couldn't have set her up with a foster family?"

Clamming up, she folded her arms and drew in a carefully measured breath. Her eyes darkened with worry, and her lips stiffened in a way he found impossible not to stare at. A sudden impulse to hold her clouded whatever point he was mentally preparing to make, and instead of speaking, he attempted to understand the situation from her perspective.

But it was impossible.

"You really think she came to my cabin and used Kevin Robinson's blood to paint a satanic star on my wall? You really think Roberta did all that?" she questioned, trying to wrap her mind around the idea, but fighting her suspicions at the same time.

"As a matter of fact, yes, I do. Granted, she may only be a pawn, but yes I believe she has been in on it from the start. I don't know how responsible that makes her," he added, softening his stance. "I don't know if she acted alone. I don't know if she's being brainwashed or groomed, and you probably did the right thing removing her from that house, but taking her in like this, into *your* home, could be dangerous. She lures people. She sets people up."

"She didn't lure me into this. She didn't even ask to be here. This was totally my idea."

"You're not giving her enough credit."

The need to convince her was tearing his mind apart, and if she were a man, he wouldn't hesitate to disclose his own experiences with Roberta, and explain the long history of Roberta's bizarre attempts to force him into having sex with her. But he didn't want Gertrude to find out about any of that.

"If there's a silver lining in terms of her staying here with you," he continued, hoping to high heaven that something positive might come out of this, "maybe you can get her to open up. Maybe she'll tell you about what's going on in terms of the cult and how the cult connects to Maude's murder."

Mustering up some semblance of control to correct a potentially grave error she had made by deciding to foster Roberta, she said, "Okay, yeah, I can do that."

Gertrude fell into deep thought. She seemed to be grappling with the possibility that a weakness she hadn't recognized she possessed could very well end up being her downfall.

For some reason, this compelled Jake to kiss her.

It was a rash move and poorly thought out, if it had been thought out at all. And yet, kissing Gerty was exactly what he wanted.

She must have wanted to kiss him, as well, because she was reciprocating.

Her smooth lips pressed against his, her nose softly brushing his cheek and her fingertips lightly touching his waist.

Jake wrapped her close, feeling her against him.

When she urged him back, he whispered, "Sorry."

"Let's not complicate things."

"No, we shouldn't complicate things."

But her lips met his again with a gentle peck, which was entirely her doing, and he felt her hands drape gently over his shoulders.

In-between kisses, she said, "It would be a bad idea."

"I think so, too."

Neither could stop.

"We should stop kissing."

Unless she did, he wouldn't, but he uttered, "Mm-hm," in agreement.

Finally, she stepped back. Her fingertips were pressed against her mouth and she was too shy to look at him.

She sat down on the edge of the bed and, looking up at him, she asked, "You're sure it was Kevin Robinson's blood?"

"My suspicion started as a hunch, but I confirmed it. I had my contact in Grafton County test the blood. He's a guy named Ed Cohen, who works as a floating M.E. out of Dartmouth-Hitchcock. I had to pull a few strings to get *him* to pull a few strings, but Robinson had undergone a paternity test years back, and Ed was able to get his hands on the DNA record on file. The blood on the book was a DNA match. It was Robinson's."

"But Robinson stopped working for the police department over a month ago."

"Which means the cult either went after him-"

"Or never let him leave in the first place," she supplied. "Do you think they were holding him hostage or something?"

"That's what I would like to know. If he left, and the cult tracked him down, that would mean that Robinson was traceable based on his whereabouts. But using all of my resources at the Daily Sun and my contacts in a number of precincts, I couldn't find any record of his whereabouts since July 5th whatsoever. This leads me to believe that the cult could have abducted him."

"Where were they keeping him, then?" she asked, confused.

"Where *are* they keeping him?"

She froze, horrified at the implication, and asked, "How could they have possibly gotten so much of his blood and kept him alive? Jake, there had to have been a gallon of blood all over my living room. Why are they doing this?"

He didn't have any answers.

"What are they hiding? Why are they killing people to keep their secrets safe? Why did they have to kill Maude? Roberta is still alive, so why have they killed one girl but not the other?"

"Some kids are strong willed. Maybe they weren't able to control Maude. As seemingly strong-willed as Roberta may appear, it's far more likely that she's completely obedient and subservient to the cult."

Jake fished a scrap of paper out of the front pocket of his jeans.

"I filed a Missing Person report for Robinson in Grafton County to get the ball rolling. I can't even think about what he's going through if he's still alive out there in whatever makeshift prison they've got him in..." He trailed off, reading over his own messy handwriting on the piece of paper. "Ed had an idea about testing the blood for heavy metals, thinking it might shed light on where they might be keeping Robinson."

He touched eyes with her, and it was clear that she was keeping up with him, so he went on, "He didn't find any, but he did find high concentrations of radon."

"We had radon in our basement," she said suddenly as though her mouth had remembered before her brain did. "Growing up, my dad was always replacing the radon detectors and taking Doris and me to the hospital for blood tests."

"It's not unheard of around here. Dig a deep enough foundation and the uranium levels increase, or so Ed tells me."

Gertrude's gaze softened and a faraway look filled her eyes.

"It tells us that whatever crap they're up to," he continued, "they're doing it underground, like the walls around them are just dirt." After an excited pause, he said, "And we tested the homeless men who had turned up in Opechee. Same toxicity. Radon. It ties their murders to the Kings, but it doesn't hold water. Not yet."

From out of nowhere, Gertrude spoke in a whisper, asking herself, "Dad was a doctor?"

"Gerty?"

"Hm?" She was released from the recollection, but didn't share it with Jake.

He touched her leg to help her focus, but then he suddenly became distracted. "Do you hear that?"

She listened out. "No."

"Wait." His ears pricked up, but the sound wasn't there. "It sounded like the window was opening."

On his feet, Jake listened at the door and thought he caught wind of voices murmuring deep in the living room. When he glanced over his shoulder at Gertrude, she had fallen back into deep thought on the bed.

He eased the door open, keen to overhear Roberta, but it wasn't until he crept up the hallway, leaving Gertrude in the bedroom, that he thought he heard a boy speaking in hushed tones, too.

Peering around the corner, he spied Roberta kneeling on the couch and angling her head out the window.

In the shadows, a kid was standing outside, staring up at her with a desperately apologetic look on his teenage face.

The second the boy saw Jake, he dashed off, his feet punching over leaves and grass outside.

Roberta whipped around, she was so surprised. For a moment, the girl was stripped of her cunning, but the moment was fleeting.

She locked eyes with Jake and slid down on the couch and crossed her legs, as if she was mildly amused to have his company.

"Hey," she grinned. "What's going on?"

Gertrude finally emerged from the bedroom. She crossed the living room and rounded into the kitchen. As she went, she shot Roberta an easy smile and asked, "What do you feel like? I've got a frozen pizza, but we would have to thaw it."

Roberta was staring at him and her coy grin drooped, her gaze drifting downward, as though something massive was hitting her.

"Pizza sounds good," Jake answered even though Roberta should have. He eyed the girl and asked, "You okay?"

Roberta looked like she might come clean and say something helpful, but there came a knock at the front door. Whoever was out there was persistent.

Slumping into the couch, she sighed, "Damn."

Gertrude padded to the front of the cabin to see who was there.

Roberta winced as if she knew exactly who had come to the door and exactly what would happen next.

"I didn't want to," she whined.

"You didn't want to do what, Roberta?" Jake demanded.

From the doorway, Peter King asked Gerty, "Is Jake Livingston here?"

Peter didn't wait for a reply. He barged into the cabin with two police officers in tow.

"Livingston!" he said, as the officers took Jake by the arms.

Gertrude exclaimed, "What are you doing?"

The incomprehensible surrealism of being arrested rendered Jake utterly inept.

And what followed unfolded like a bad avant-garde film—Peter sneering with satisfaction, the police officers wrestling Jake to the floor, Roberta smirking, Gertrude gaping in horror as the officers used terms like *arrest* and *statutory rape* and *right to remain silent.*

As if Jake had any rights…

The reality of being hauled out of the cabin with his hands cuffed behind his back was as shocking as ice water in his veins.

One of the officers threw Jake into the back of the police cruiser.

It wasn't until the cops had locked him in the back of their car that Jake regained his faculties enough to shout, "I didn't touch her!"

Gertrude looked on in abject horror, while Roberta glared at him with a blood-curdling mix of intrigue and remorse.

Then the cops drove off with Jake, following a black sedan that Jake assumed Peter was driving.

An eternity passed before they reached the Laconia Police Station—Jake shifting uncomfortably in his seat, catching glimpses of his reflection in the side window, jarred by the sight of his haggard eyes, his ill grimace, and the face of a stranger he didn't recognize staring back at him. He managed to gaze out at the dark forest, but it soon disappeared, the dull lights of Laconia, its gas stations and fast food joints wilting in a summer sweat, taking its place.

When they arrived at the precinct, a depressed one-story brick building that looked more like a weathered cardboard box than it did adequate law enforcement quarters, Peter opened the cruiser door and jerked Jake to his feet, thrusting him towards the entrance with a sense of victory.

Beating them to it, one of the officers held the door open, while the other brought up the rear, shoving Jake from behind as though doing so was at all necessary.

After roughly depositing him in a chair, closing the interrogation room door, and switching the surveillance camera off for (in his words) *a chat*, Peter flipped open a manila folder and began demonstratively placing photos across the table as if it would provoke Jake into explaining.

"I want to call my lawyer," he said, refusing to look at the photos.

"You don't need one," Peter said, acting friendly in a way that set his teeth on edge. "This conversation's off the record."

"I've been arrested. Everything's on the record."

"I don't like how you handled my granddaughter," he stated, invading Jake's personal space, as he sat on the table and pressed his thick forefinger against a photo of Roberta.

In the photo, Roberta was naked as sin and tangled in Jake's arms. There was a distinct look of distress in her wide eyes, and Jake looked strangely aroused. Jake remembered the moment that the photo had been taken and despised the story it told, because the story that the photo told was a damn lie.

Jake wished he hadn't glanced at it.

Staring up at Peter was no better. Old as he was, he looked strong as an ox and the way he was holding his mouth taut, gaze lingering on Roberta's splayed breasts in the glossy print, gave Jake the worst intuition. Peter wasn't disgusted with the encounter. He was interested in it.

"Do you think it's okay to treat women like this?" he pressed, leaning in, his sour breath blowing in Jake's ear. "Roberta told me what you did to her."

"You know I didn't do anything to her. This is a joke."

"Oh, you think this is funny?"

"You seriously believe the courts aren't going to catch onto your conspiracy? Eventually, you're going to get caught. Locking up innocent men year after year who were trapped in identical scenarios with Roberta is going to come crashing down on you sooner or later."

Working his way around the table until he settled into the chair across from him, Peter said, "Evidence doesn't lie. Those men weren't innocent."

He nodded at the prints. "You call that evidence?"

"What would you call it?"

"She threw herself at me."

Laughter erupted out of Peter and he said, "You think I'm bad. Wait until I tell the feminists around here. They'll skin you alive."

"I want my lawyer."

"You'll get your phone call. Settle down. I have a right to question you."

Pondering the sewage Peter had to have poured into his brain that would cause him to believe his statement would even remotely resemble police procedure was enough to make Jake's head spin.

Going on the offensive, Jake asked, "Why did you do it?"

He just stared at him, lilting his head back with an edge of curiosity.

"You killed her, you're granddaughter," he pushed. "Why?"

"No one killed Maude, but Maude. And it's a damn shame. It's a tragedy I thought I would never see."

"And brainwashing Roberta isn't tragic?" he countered. "Using her. Making her seduce and entrap adult men isn't tragic? Terrorizing her under the guise of your cult isn't tragic? Really?"

"Cult?"

He had meant to turn the tables and imply Jake was out of his mind, but a glimmer of worry leapt through his expression.

"Did you make her dig up Gerty's dead dog? Are you that sick?"

"Now you listen here," he said, turning to stone as he angled across the table, his dark eyes sharp and ugly. "This can all go away." He was referring to the photos. "I can let you walk out of here. If you *leave*."

"Leave? Leave Laconia?"

"Leave New Hampshire."

"Did you trick Kevin Robinson with the same kind of deal? I keep my mouth shut. You let me ride off into the sunset, except that I won't get far, will I? Where are you keeping Robinson? Where's your underground lair? And what the hell are you doing down there that you have to kill men and children to keep them silent?"

Peter leaned back in his chair, studying Jake, his eyes glazing over in the effort, until eventually he asked, "What happened to us, Jake? You, me, and Weird Wanda, those were some good times, I thought."

CHAPTER NINETEEN

"STATUTORY RAPE?" She kept her tone even, tempering the outrage that was building within her on a cellular level, as she studied Roberta.

The girl was leafing through a bloodstained book she had plucked off the shelf, as if Gertrude's anger would blow over. When it didn't, Roberta returned a glance, but it was short-lived.

"He came onto me," she said with a shrug.

"He came onto you?" she questioned. "Or he slept with you? An older man attempting to flirt isn't 'statutory rape,' but Jake was arrested for statutory rape."

Roberta frowned.

"Why does your grandfather think that Jake raped you?" she pushed.

Growing defensive, Roberta slammed the book on the coffee table and said, "I told you how it works. I practically spelled it out for you when we were at my parents' house. Whoever Peter wants in prison, goes to prison. It isn't hard to get men to incriminate themselves."

Gertrude couldn't deny that Roberta had mentioned all of this to her, but Gertrude had been naive enough, apparently, to assume that Roberta would never try something like this with Jake.

"So, you gave a statement to the police?" she asked in disbelief.

Roberta stiffened, her gaze falling to the floor where her toes were clutching at the wood.

"You can recant," Gertrude suggested.

"There are photos," she said in an ashamed voice then quickly added, "for the record I didn't give the photos to Peter. Quinton messed up. The second I got here, I told myself no more mistakes. I'm on your side, Gertrude. I'm not going to mess this up."

"Things are so messed up right now, Roberta, I can't even..." Trailing off with no words to frame what was going through her head, Gertrude was vaguely aware the phrasing made her sound more teen-aged than the temptress on her couch. "You seduced him?"

She didn't actually want to know the answer or whether or not Jake had succumbed to the girl's seduction, but the question had flown out of her mouth, and Roberta was already formulating a response.

"If he went to prison," Roberta began, speaking frankly in a way that was jarring, "it would make sense."

"Did he rape you?"

"No."

"Did you have intercourse?" She couldn't believe she was going there, but the larger part of her needed to know.

"No, not at all."

"Well, what, then? Tell me what happened. Were you two involved?"

Roberta smirked weirdly at her and asked, "Are you jealous?"

Taken aback, Gertrude realized with sobering clarity that Roberta could be scheming even now. It suddenly dawned on her that Jake could have been right about the girl.

"No," she answered in delayed reaction, while in the deepest recess of her mind, she analyzed the possible motives for why Roberta might want her to think the worst of Jake.

"You have a thing for him," Roberta determined. "I would nip it in the bud if I were you. Jake is no good."

"You don't know what you're talking about."

"Don't I?" she challenged.

"Why do you want me to think badly of Jake?"

"Because of what happened to Wanda Trentwell."

Gertrude asked, "The homeless woman?"

"Jake is doing the same thing to you that he did to Weird Wanda, you know. Or maybe you can't see it."

"What did he do to Weird Wanda?"

"You don't remember?" She smirked. "You'll remember if you try."

"Stop messing around, Roberta."

"The real truth would have made headlines if Jake hadn't been controlling the newspaper and the story, and *everything*."

Gertrude was getting fed up. "What are you talking about?"

"He set her up," she said. "Jake is the reason that Weird Wanda ended up in that mental institution."

Internally, Gertrude felt like she was crumbling into pieces, but she didn't let it show.

"Wanda was turning tricks out in the park," she went on. "She didn't even want cash, she just wanted drugs. Cut out the middleman. Peter knew that Weird Wanda would do anything to get high. *Anything.* She did a few jobs for Peter, but it wasn't long before she wanted out."

Evidently, disclosing this kind of information required no encumbrances, because Roberta unfastened her bra, and after a juggling act beneath her shirt, she worked the lacy garment free through her left sleeve and tossed it on the floor.

"The next thing Wanda knew, Jake was moving in on her, which I bet she loved. Jake was acting like he was interested in her," she went on. "He got her cleaned up, and invited her to move in with him. They were boyfriend and girlfriend. Meanwhile, there's a reason everyone calls her *weird* Wanda. She's out of her mind, psychotic. And of course, she was still doing things for Peter because she still needed crack or whatever her deal was. And then when Wanda *finally* tried to cut ties with Peter for good, because she thought she'd *finally* turned her life around and won't need his drugs, Peter asked her to do one last job for him and promised to leave her alone after that as long as she agreed to do the job."

"Okay?" Gertrude said, even though she wasn't sure that she wanted to know.

"And she agreed. She did one last job, and Jake was *there*," she went on, as a grin spread across her face. "That's when I knew Jake was working for him."

Gertrude thought she might throw up, but she asked anyway, "Working for Peter?"

"Next day, Jake drops Wanda off at Opechee and she's arrested." Roberta let that hang for a beat, then drew the conclusion in case Gertrude had missed it. "Without Jake, Wanda wouldn't have gotten locked up."

As gradually as oil rising through water, Gertrude slowly recalled why she had turned Jake down when he had asked her on a date at the farmer's market last year. She had known about Weird Wanda and the circulating rumors. She had heard about Jake's strange relationship with the homeless woman, his sordid involvement, and the shameful result. Gertrude had heard about his tarnished reputation that had followed. When he had introduced himself at the farmer's market, she hadn't trusted those cornflower blue eyes of his. The endless gossip had shrouded him, colored her perception of him, and she hadn't been able to get away from him fast enough that day. At the time, she hadn't known for sure whether or not the rumors were true, but she had believed every word anyway.

But last year, Gertrude *hadn't* yet experienced first-hand how rumors could be wrong. As a result of having driven her car into the lake, however, she had learned the hard way that people in this town had a knack for drawing the wrong conclusions.

Did that mean she should give Jake the benefit of the doubt?

Or should she keep her distance?

Gertrude asked, "If Jake was working with Peter, what was he doing?"

"Look," she said, turning flippant. "I only know so much, and it's not like Peter tells me everything. I just happen to be close to the situation."

"So, you don't know for sure?"

"Gerty," she snorted a laugh. "If you trust Jake, you're more brain damaged than I thought."

"What did Peter want with Wanda? What were those jobs all about?"

Darkening, Roberta told her, "Wanda was getting rid of the bodies."

Gertrude felt hot bile sting the back of her throat, but she swallowed and focused all of her attention on steadying her racing mind.

Then she asked the girl:

"What is the purpose of the cult? Is it really satanic, or is it an organized criminal enterprise?"

"It's just sex."

"Involving underage girls," she supplied.

When Roberta met her gaze, her eyes darkened.

Gertrude asked, "Maude wouldn't go along with what the cult wanted her to do?"

"No, she wouldn't," Roberta admitted. "But I'll be straight with you. I don't have a damn clue who killed Maude. If the cult took her out, they didn't kill her in the same way they have been killing everyone else."

CHAPTER TWENTY

ROBERTA'S ACCOUNT that Jake had willingly been in cahoots with Peter King to protect the cult was mind-bending. Wanda Trentwell had been exiled to a life in a padded room, and Roberta was convinced that Gertrude would suffer the same fate if she trusted Jake.

Fathoming this was more than enough to keep Gertrude up all night, lifting in and out of fitful dreams where the lines between her own life and Wanda's blurred, where the differences between Roberta and her own sister failed to exist, where Jake's face interchanged with Peter's so seamlessly that her skin broke out with a cold sweat in response, as she shifted and tossed on the hard living room couch.

Roberta's harrowing point was inescapable. Why had Maude been shot in the head when the others had been held, tortured, and dumped, dead and faceless, in Opechee Park?

By the time the dawning sun—tangerine sharp and blazing—pierced through the living room,

Gertrude was resigned to her exhaustion. Today would not be an easy one to get through.

As she rose from the couch, the fact of Jake's arrest hit her like a sandbag to her chest. He was the sixth man to go to jail. In Charlie's absence, Peter was mastering the strategy of taking out anyone who got in the cult's way. Had Jake really been one of them, but ended up turning on them? Was that the reason behind setting him up?

Drinking coffee was futile. After two cups she felt no more awake. The eerie sickness that had plagued her sister growing up, the hospital visits and blood tests her father had performed in the secluded corners of his private practice across the street from Laconia Mercy, filled Gertrude's thoughts with nightmarish logic. In the waking hours, it didn't make sense. It couldn't. But in dreams the connections were ironclad.

And underscoring the swirling fragments that wouldn't fit except insanely was her bizarre longing for Jake. It wasn't simply that an innocent man shouldn't have been arrested. If that were the case, she might be able to function with a sense of practical determination. It was that he meant something to her now. Their kiss, those fleeting five minutes alone with him, had elevated her feelings into the realm of undeniable attraction. He thrilled her and she wanted him.

In the bedroom, Roberta was a murmuring lump embedded under a heap of blankets when Gertrude stepped soundlessly towards her closet. It irked her to leave the girl unsupervised for the day, but there was no getting around it. Aspects of Roberta's disclosure had been honest during their panicked conversation, but Gertrude had also seen red flags.

Was Roberta right about Jake or was Gertrude being conned?

It was the dilemma stemming from this that compelled her to make the short drive over to Lakes Region Mental Health as soon as she had dressed and slipped out the front door.

Wanda Trentwell had been admitted last year on the grounds that she was mentally unfit to be tried for the murders of Thomas Black, Jordan Holloway, and Miles Tanner, who each had brief, messy rap sheets laced with misdemeanors of a sexual nature according to what Gertrude had been able to pull up last night in her worst hours of insomnia, logging into the DCYF database where it intersected with police records. It had been Roberta's nonchalant response—*Just sex*—which had given her the idea to check.

If the cult had killed the men, then they had to have either seen something or played a role in it in the first place. And if Wanda had been arrested and had faced the possibility of a trial prior to the court determining that she wasn't mentally sound, then Wanda had to have gleaned the particulars of the case built against her.

But more than anything, Gertrude needed to hear from Wanda whether or not Jake had in fact worked with Peter to destroy her life.

A three-story brick structure with dormers overlooking the lake, the facility looked more like an asylum from the 1940s than a government regulated institution funded and monitored by state officials. Originally, the building had been used as a school for feeble-minded children—an antiquated term for the mentally disabled—as a place for children with Down Syndrome and other genetic disorders affecting mental health, to be raised and cared for, forgotten by parents who couldn't afford the crippling stigma that came with not rearing a normal child.

Dismal though it looked, the staff appeared to be doting, as an orderly walked Gertrude into one of the common rooms where he believed Wanda was *doing some of her art.*

"She hasn't had a visitor," he explained, pausing at the edge of the room to point her out.

"Ever?"

He confirmed with a frown then added, "This isn't where she belongs, but considering the alternative, she's probably better off here."

Gertrude wondered if he thought Wanda had manipulated the system.

"There's nothing in her chart, no behavioral evidence that I've seen, that would lead me to believe she was capable of anything that she was accused of," he added grimly. "Which is to say you shouldn't feel intimidated, but if you are, I'll be right over here."

Hesitating, Gertrude studied the woman who had been the center of so much controversy last year. Wanda's mousy brown hair was a touch greasy at the roots and tucked behind her ears, which gave Gertrude a clear view of her profile. She had sad-looking eyes with heavy lids, a long scooping nose, and a narrow mouth. Her skin was ruddy and her overall demeanor seemed masculine—her shoulders rounding into a hunch over her sketchpad, her elbows planted on the table. She looked like a vulture protecting scraps. Whereas the other patients rocked and hummed and cast sideways glances, looking at but not quite seeing each other, Wanda functioned with a distinct sense of clarity as though she knew where she was and why she was here. There didn't seem to be a shred of insanity behind her sharp hazel eyes.

When she leaned back in her chair, glimpsing through the window at the lake to rest her eyes, Gertrude started for her, passing patients who were muttering and rocking in their chairs.

She came to Wanda's table, which was barely long enough to contain her sketchbook.

"Hi Wanda, I'm Gertrude."

With clear eyes, she glanced up at her, taking stock of the visitor she didn't recognize.

"You're here to see me?" she asked, interested.

"I am. Can I sit?"

Pulling her sketchbook into her lap, Wanda stared at her with unblinking eyes and a curious smile formed at the corners of her mouth.

"What's this about?"

"Your name came up a few times in a case I'm working on. I'm with Child Protective Services."

"Okay?"

"I have been assigned to investigate the home of the Kings," she stated and watched as the name washed over Wanda like a bucket of ice water. "Do you know Charlie and Zhana King, or Charlie's father, Peter King?"

"Did something happen to those girls?" Her face became anguished. "I knew those girls wouldn't be safe."

"Maude was killed."

Wanda sighed, but hardly looked surprised. She must have seen this coming from a million miles away.

Hanging her head, Wanda took a long moment to think, and in the interlude, Gertrude saw how easily she herself could wind up in a place like this. Wanda was cognizant and lucid, and yet, somehow, Peter King had gotten her institutionalized.

"I was hoping you could tell me what you know," she went on when she had Wanda's attention.

"It won't hold up in court," she said.

"That's not something I'm worried about right now. I heard you were involved with Peter King and also with Jake Livingston, and I would like to know about those relationships."

"I didn't kill those men," she stated.

Keeping her tone very quiet and stripped of all judgment, Gertrude asked, "Did Peter pay you to get rid of those bodies?"

"He didn't pay me anything, not after the first time he rolled through the park, and that was only for some time with me in the cab of his truck. Normal stuff. Nothing I ever thought would've led in the direction it did."

"So, he was blackmailing you into helping him?"

"If you want to call it that."

Gertrude knew the bodies had been found poorly buried at the park so she didn't ask about the details of Wanda's role in that aspect.

"Did you interact with the girls at all? Did Peter ever bring you to Charlie King's house?"

Wanda nodded. "When I didn't want anything to do with it anymore."

"Can you tell me what happened?"

She winced as though she was trying not to taste something bitter in her mouth.

"You wouldn't believe it," she said finally once the memory had left her.

"I promise you I will." When after saying as much, Wanda still looked reluctant, she leaned in, explaining, "They got into my house. It looked like they had performed a satanic ritual in my living room. All because I've been assigned to make sure Roberta King is safe. Maude King's death was chalked up to a suicide. The more I know, the more likely I'll be able to stop them."

Interrupting, she corrected Gertrude. "There's no *stopping* them. All that satanism stuff is fake. It's a smokescreen. They're not trying to conjure the devil, or perform black magic, or live by a dark code."

"But there have been accounts-"

"That's what he wants people to think. Peter wants whoever knows or finds out, to actually believe that group of losers is into that stuff, because it's outlandish. You go off to some other county, some other police station that isn't knotted up in Peter's corruption, and you tell them there's a satanic cult in Laconia, they'll look at you like you've got two heads and then they'll throw you in here with me."

"What is it a smokescreen for?"

Rather than come out with it, Wanda led into a lengthy explanation that at first had Gertrude entirely thrown in terms of what in the hell Wanda was talking about and how in the hell it tied into Maude's murder.

"The human mind has these built in preservation mechanisms that safeguard you for survival. If something's too traumatic, if something's so horrific it threatens to shatter your psyche, your mind will block it off, and bury it. You won't remember. Like a car accident. People don't remember the impact. They don't remember the aftermath. Children are particularly susceptible to this phenomenon. If you take an eight-year-old and strangle them within an inch of their life and they truly believe they're going to die, they won't remember it afterwards, especially if it's their parents doing the strangling. Those rituals are just their way of getting those kids to forget."

"Forget what?"

"They're not a cult of satanists. They're a cult of pedophiles. And they've found a way to get away with it, because they know how to get the kids to forget what's happening to them *as it's happening*."

Shocked, Gertrude asked, "How do you know this?"

"I saw it with my own eyes. Peter dragged me down there. Out in that field, there's a trap door that leads down into an underground room. I tell you, in my whole life I've never been so scared like I was down there. I didn't do a thing except stand there trembling, but my biggest mistake was that I had believed Peter's threat. He took photos of me there. Told me I would go down for every act they had ever committed. So I did what he wanted." She rubbed her eyes with the heels of her hands, saying, "The things they did to that girl." When she returned her gaze to Gertrude, she added with an edge of delirium, "Those men rip Roberta apart in that underground room, and then her mother puts her back together like Betty-friggin-Crocker baking an apple pie."

Gertrude felt sick, but pushed herself to collect every last answer she had come for.

"How does Jake fit into this?"

"Jake was my second biggest mistake. I believed him, too."

Wanda turned lax and a faraway look clouded her sharp eyes, her face drawing long and slack until she swallowed hard, tensing. As removed as she appeared, her words came clearly.

"I thought he loved me. He swooped into my life and cleaned me up. I felt like I was his wife. It felt like things were going in that direction. Then we got together with Peter. Jake used me. I never would've guessed he was one of them, but then he went with me to Peter, and had me act like we wanted *in* on their sick operation, like Jake's into it, anything to get down into that room, that's when I knew he was one of them the whole time."

Gertrude couldn't bear to hear another word.

She jumped up from the table and ran.

Tearing through the common room, she knocked into empty chairs and clipped her hips on tables, desperate to get the hell out of there as fast as she could.

Running away from Wanda and her insights hadn't been a conscious decision.

As soon as she fell into the driver's seat, having thrust her car door open, nearly dislodging it from its hinges, she screamed and clawed index cards off the steering wheel and dashboard in a guttural outpouring of sickened rage.

Wanda was crazy, she told herself. Wanda would say anything. Wanda used to be a prostitute and a drug addict and couldn't possibly remember the past with even a fraction of clarity.

But Gertrude believed her.

And the torment that resulted was ripping her mind and heart apart like they were as fragile as paper.

Peeling out in Reverse, her Audi stalled and died. She twisted the key in the ignition, pumping the gas and the engine turned, causing the vehicle to buck forward, but then the stick popped out of gear and the car died again.

She jammed the gear shift, yanking it down into Reverse, popping and pressing the clutch and gas, forcing the thing to life and when it caught, she swung fast around and gunned it out of the parking lot, swerving around parked cars and orderlies who were making their lazy way to the entrance.

The second she merged onto Route 12, she slipped into dark remembrance, and it wasn't until she jerked off the exit, barreling towards the Brain Injury Rehabilitation Center that she came back into herself.

She cut into the parking lot then as soon as she angled into a spot, she jumped out and ran at a sprinter's pace.

"I need to see Dr. Hagstaff," she yelled breathlessly when she reached his assistant's desk, her eyes glued to his door, which was shut.

"I'm sorry, he's with a patient-"

She was already pushing the door open, his assistant objected and started after her.

The wilted man on Dr. Hagstaff's couch cowered at the intrusion as though a bomb had gone off.

"I need to talk to you," she blurted out then yelled, "out!" at the stunned man on the couch.

"Gertrude, if only you called ahead," he said, quickly getting to his feet as if he planned to usher her out at once.

But she began explaining the emergency, and Hagstaff knew it would be easier to ask his current patient to come back later than it would be to get Gertrude out of his office.

"Can I find you in an hour?" he asked the man, who had collected himself into the assistant's care in the doorway.

When the man indicated he could, Hagstaff eased the door closed.

"That was uncalled for. You've missed several appointments, Gerty, and you could've easily rescheduled."

"I know. I'm sorry. I think I'm having a panic attack."

He helped her to the couch then he sat in a nearby chair, crossing his legs and settling into a calm repose of breathing in a slow and steady rhythm meant to inspire her to do the same.

"*Are* you having a panic attack?" he asked in his sharply nasal tone that she realized she missed.

She wasn't hyperventilating. The room wasn't spinning and the walls weren't closing in.

"No, but I'm remembering things, crazy things that couldn't have happened except that I know they did. I can feel it. It's making me want to tear my skin off."

Dr. Hagstaff pushed his horned rim glasses up the bridge of his nose and laced his fingers together, observing her, his mouth curling with concern.

When she didn't dive in, her thoughts scattering like spilled marbles and her mind meshing people and places from her past into the case at hand so darkly she couldn't trust it and couldn't trust her impressions or conclusions, he filled the gap, asking:

"Have you been taking your anti-anxiety medication?"

"Why haven't I remembered my upbringing? It doesn't make sense that the car accident wiped out *all* of my memories."

Taking a carefully measured breath to calm the irritation that had been building, Dr. Hagstaff reminded her that they had been over this. "You have to give it time."

"Albert was a doctor."

"Your father?" he asked.

"Yes, he's a doctor. And Doris was sick a lot. Bedridden. We were tested all the time for radon poisoning, but that wasn't it. That wasn't why we were sick. It had something to do with a *rash*, but I can't remember."

Furrowing his brow, he refrained from questioning the significance, but his very expression made her feel immense pressure to start making sense.

"I can remember having these moments growing up where I was baffled that I couldn't remember anything. I knew I had these giant holes in my memory. I don't think the accident caused me to forget. I don't think I was remembering things properly in the first place."

"Remembering what?"

"Remembering that Albert and Marsha were abusing her. Albert was abusing her and Zhana was putting her back together."

"Whoa now, hang on. Who's Zhana?"

"Roberta's mother."

"Roberta?"

"My case."

"Gerty, I think you're confusing your own life with someone else's. This is a girl whose case you're dealing with? Has work become overwhelming?"

He took a prescription pad from the inner pocket of his corduroy jacket and started writing.

"I don't want any drugs," she blurted out. "I'm not losing it. I'm onto something. This woman, this mother I met, she *pretends* to be oblivious to what's been happening to her daughter and it reminded me of *Marsha*, of my *mom*."

"But you also voiced concern that the things you were remembering might be crazy," he pointed out, which wasn't how she recalled putting it.

"I don't think Doris was sick. Being bedridden, I don't think my mom was keeping her ill. I think she was putting her back together after... I don't know, I can't remember. And Doris hated herself so much for it. She used to cut herself. Just like Roberta has been doing. Whatever is happening to Roberta was happening to Doris. And I just learned what was happening to Roberta. I'm so scared..." She trailed off, asking herself, "Rashes? All over our skin..."

"Gerty, I want you to take a deep breath. I want you to center yourself." After she did him the courtesy of leaning back into the couch and drawing air into her lungs with grand, heaving breaths, he asserted, "I think this case of yours is too much. I think you're making connections that in reality don't exist. It was too soon for you to go back to work."

"No, that's not it. I'm not making this up. There's a connection."

She pitched forward on the edge of the couch, desperate for him to see it as clearly as she could, and in response, he jutted a flat palm at her, coaxing her to calm, but it only riled her up.

"I would like you to get this prescription filled at the pharmacy in the lobby. I would like to walk you over and help. And I'd like to watch you take it."

"I'm not wrong about this."

"Please-"

"I need to talk. There's more and I can't handle it. There's this man, Jake, and I don't know if I can trust him-"

"Gertrude," he said sternly. "We *will* talk. We *will*. We can talk for the rest of the hour, but only if you take this prescription. I don't want to scare you, but you're exhibiting signs of psychosis-"

Jumping to her feet, she shrieked, "What?"

"You're still functioning, Gertrude," he went on, his tone soft as a smile. "That's the good news, but I can't let you slip away. This is very important."

She sat down again and dug her heels in.

"Do you suppose speaking with your parents might expel some of your fears?"

"I can't talk to them," she said sharply, though the knee-jerk reaction didn't seem anchored in history, but rather in a mist that coated every cell in her body. Then an outpouring followed. "I won't go near them. I tried. We tried. We practiced. It didn't go as planned. It was a disaster. We were laughed at."

"What are you talking about?"

She didn't know. She only sensed it was true. And that it had led to her drinking in the bar that night, the frantic drive home, the swerving, the lake—the figure of a person in the road.

"The case I'm working. A ten year-old girl shot herself in the head, but it was a cover up. I heard the shot. July 2nd. Doris and I heard it while we were driving home the night of July 2nd. Moments later, I had to swerve the car because the shadowy figure of someone had stepped into the road. What if the figure that night was the killer? What if Maude's

257

death wasn't an accident? It's too perfect to be a coincidence. It happened right after Doris and I confronted our parents and I still don't remember that confrontation, but Roberta is so similar to Doris that I can't help but use one to answer the other. It's too identical to ignore."

"And your supervisor assigned the case to you... why?"

"I'm not paranoid," she stated when his tone had implied she was.

"But you're suggesting that there is a conspiracy."

"Because it is." She held her tongue before divulging information about the cult.

Slipping into deep thought, she racked her brain for the best way to tie Peter King and his cult to Kevin Robinson's disappearance and subsequent bloodletting or murder as the case might soon be. Radon in his blood wouldn't be enough to link it even if she could get a soil sample. As Jake had explained, radon was common in these parts. So what would connect the dots and incriminate the Kings? What could she do other than sit around reeling with maddening intuitions?

Suddenly, Dr. Hagstaff was holding her by the upper arm and urging her to her feet. "Come now, before the pharmacy closes."

Dazed with strategies she knew wouldn't amount to much should she execute them, Gertrude pondered relentlessly as she zombie-walked beside her doctor through the lobby where the pharmacy counter was tucked beyond the nurses' station.

"Cup of water?" he said to the pharmacist, as he tapped two purple pills into Gertrude's palm. She hadn't even noticed him taking her hand. When the pharmacist placed a little cup of water on the counter, he told Gertrude *chop-chop*. "This medication will smooth the whole matter over and you'll be able to see it for what it really is."

His encouragement was soothing. Her hand floated up and she brought the pills to her mouth, as her other hand wrapped the cup, preparing to knock back the medication.

But she snapped out of her relaxed fog and she flung the pills away…

…and the next thing she knew, she was jogging towards the exit as Dr. Hagstaff yelled after her, "I'm very worried about you, Gertrude!"

So was she.

More worried than she had ever been.

After jumping in her car, Gertrude drove with fever-pitch intensity through Laconia, gunning it and slamming on the brakes in manic alternation with the ebb and flow of traffic until the roads cleared, rounding Lake Winnipesaukee. In a blur, her Audi spilled through the thickening forest, nearing the Kings' house.

Zhana was flitting about on the porch when Gertrude pulled onto the grassy shoulder, spying her in the distance beyond the trees. A number of dead bushes, uprooted and on their sides, lay strewn across the front yard, and Gertrude caught sight of dirt encrusted clothes bundled in their midst.

Next, the woman descended the steps with purpose. She held a canister of accelerant in her hand. As she circled the bushes, kicking them into a heaped pile, she squirted the accelerant, holding one hand over her nose and mouth. Then, dropping the can, she produced a matchbook and struck one, watching the tiny flame.

As soon as she let it slip from her fingers, the flame flickered in a downward twirl, the fumes ignited, and the pile went up in a bonfire of smoke. Zhana seemed to stare at the blazing fire vacantly, easing back and fanning tendrils of smoke from her eyes. Soon a pillar of black smoke rose up to the sky and Gertrude, stepping cautiously out of her car, could smell the faint mix of chemicals and burning brush.

She kept hidden behind a tree at the edge of the driveway and observed Zhana hike up her waistband, while rounding back to the porch where she collected materials Gertrude couldn't identify.

Then after one last glance at the steady fire, Zhana started off towards the back of the house, touching her thinning hair gently as she went.

The crackling fire masked the sounds of Zhana's footfall, but Gertrude sensed wherever she was going she wouldn't return for a while, so Gertrude started for the fire in a swift jog, her beret jostling off-kilter atop her head.

As she neared the fire, molten heat wafted at her, causing her to break out in a hot sweat, but she jogged onward, easing along the side of the house.

Cool air rushed at her from the lake, as she slipped into the shade.

Beyond the crisp divide where the backyard turned into the field, Zhana stomped through the tall grass, taking the very same route Gertrude had ventured days ago when she had discovered the massacred deer.

Following her, Gertrude trekked into the tall grass, keeping her distance without losing sight of the woman who reminded her so much of her own mother that it scrambled her brain.

It wasn't until Zhana bent over, momentarily vanishing from view to lift a steel door vertically into the air, that Gertrude was suddenly struck with the importance of Charlie King's absence. She had never gotten a hold of Charlie. Zhana had indicated he wasn't around so much anymore, and at the time Gertrude had pitied her, assuming her husband had abandoned the family. But now it seemed he hadn't disappeared at all.

Was he hiding out underground?

If he was, there was no greater evidence of his guilt. Maybe the gun used to kill Maude was also tucked deep within those earthen walls where radon saturated the air.

From where Gertrude paused, watching Zhana through the wavering stems of grass, it seemed the woman was talking to someone below. Then she huffed, pivoting and easing down into the hole in a manner that led Gertrude to believe a ladder was the only way in or out.

Suddenly, the door fell flush against the ground.

Feeling pressed for time and thinking fast, Gertrude deduced that going after her would only put her in danger. Zhana had set those bushes aflame for a reason. She had needed to burn those clothes, and as Gertrude jogged back towards the house, she only hoped whatever evidence the clothes contained wouldn't be charred beyond recognition.

Thick smoke billowed up from the fire and as Gertrude rounded it, looking for the clothing she had seen Zhana kick towards the pile, she caught sight of a boy spying her from the road. Then the fire spat embers, stealing her attention, and when she gazed back at where the boy had been standing, he was gone.

Angling her foot into the base of the fire where underwear was burning, she managed to hook the tip of her shoe and sweep them free. Quickly, she wriggled her blazer off and used it to thwack the flames away until the garment was only searing. In the same manner she freed a tee shirt, another pair of underpants, and a journal that was buckled up with something tucked in its spine. She kicked at the journal, rolling it awkwardly until the flames extinguished, and when she kneeled down to see what was causing the wedge, she found her DCYF identification card concealed between the pages.

Not wanting to linger, she placed the garments and the journal onto her blazer then wrapped the items tightly into a bundle. Once it seemed secure enough to carry, she pulled her shoe off then her sock and rushed to the planters lining the porch where she grabbed fistful after fistful of dirt, shoving it into her sock with panicked thrusts, all the while checking over her shoulder that Zhana wasn't coming back.

When she got to her car, she glanced up the road then down it, scanning for the boy. She had seen him before on the night she had left the Kings' house—his tight, mousy face ever burned into her memory. But he was nowhere, so she set her blazer full of burnt items and dirt-swollen sock on the floor in front of the passenger seat and started off, but where specifically she didn't yet know.

CHAPTER TWENTY-ONE

A FULL WEEK elapsed. Days spent dodging Harold McNeil and hiding behind Wendy at work became commonplace. Evenings with Roberta were a routine in keeping a level head—*What would you like to eat?* and the girl's blunt reply, *Anything, I'll eat anything, when will it be ready?*

The long, dark nights of tossing and turning on the couch with Jake at the forefront of her mind started to feel familiar.

She hadn't seen him, hadn't heard from him, and didn't dare ask Roberta for her take on the matter of his arrest or whether he would make bail, even though those kinds of questions were spreading through her thoughts like a virus.

She made efforts to be proactive. She drove to Grafton County and barged into Ed Cohen's office at Dartmouth-Hitchcock like a maniac, waving underpants and soiled clothes in the air. She thwacked her dirt-filled sock on Ed's desk, shocking the man. *You tested Kevin Robinson's blood? Can you pull DNA from these soiled, burnt items?*

I'm sorry, who are you? he replied.

I'm Jake Livingston's... she trailed off, unsure of what to say. Was she Jake's friend? His associate? His almost-girlfriend?

We stopped seeing each other when he was arrested for statutory rape! she blurted out, sounding so mentally ill that Ed was unsure of what to do with her other than appease her. He promised to test the items and sent Gertrude on her way.

The result of succeeding with Ed left her in a state of paralyzing dread.

What if Jake's DNA was found on those articles of clothing, like the underwear? What if Roberta was right, and Jake deserved to be incarcerated? What if the man she had built up in her head didn't match the reality of him? What if her perception of reality was so warped that she didn't have a prayer of reconnecting to what was real even if she discovered the truth?

Dr. Hagstaff's extreme concern for her bothered Gertrude. She didn't feel psychotic, but what if she was? Had she merged Roberta and Doris so tightly that she couldn't distinguish one girl from the other? Was there no correlation at all between the girls, except for Gerty's distorted view of reality? Or was her instinct correct? Was Roberta a roadmap of all that Doris had survived? Did Roberta hold the key to Gertrude's own past? And if she set that key in the lock and twisted, would the whole truth be revealed to her?

Would she learn the reason she had taken Doris in, the reason they had driven to their parents house that night, the reason it had all gone south so hard and fast that she hadn't been able to drink herself out of it? What was the ultimate reason she had crashed into the lake that night?

Who did the shadowy figure belong to? If it had been Maude's killer, why had that person stepped in front of her vehicle?

It was all connected, but the lines were so translucent that she couldn't trace them from one point to the next.

After another visit to Ed Cohen's that he hardly appreciated, she arranged to have the body of her dead sister exhumed, having given Ed the full authority to perform the necessary autopsy tests that might shed light on her suspicions and help draw evidence-based correlations. She requested the same tests to be run on Maude King's remains, the paperwork of which she compulsively forged, compelled by a terrible intuition that the two dead girls had suffered the same fate.

In the evenings after Roberta had gone to sleep in the bedroom that Gertrude had once shared with her fidgeting sister—the blankets always too hot or too cold, Doris unable to get comfortable, tossing mercilessly in fits of irritation that had been designed to provoke Gertrude, *Would you go to sleep already?* and Doris' snappish response, *How old is this mattress? It's completely sunken in!* and Gerty's teasing reply, *You're worse than The Princess and the Pea!*—Gertrude read through the journal she had recovered from Zhana's bonfire.

The pages contained accounts in Roberta's own hand. The journal entries were detailed to the point of grotesque and included her sexual conquests and exploitations. All information had been written with an air of comical detachment as though the girl had zero awareness that she was being used. Most entries also included disturbing references to her father, Charlie King, who had beaten her even when she had done what she'd been told—*I'm only doing what he says so they don't take Maude down there and start hurting her, too.*

Reading Roberta's journal gave Gertrude the impression that Roberta had been protecting Maude from the abuse. Roberta lived in a constant state of horrified anticipation that one day soon the cult would begin to abuse and sexually torture her sister instead of her.

To Gertrude, this meant that Maude hadn't been abused yet.

The journal entries were dated right up until the first day that Gertrude had arrived at the Kings' house, so unless Charlie and Peter had managed to snatch Maude for their cultish rituals without Roberta knowing, the journal was evidence that the youngest King girl had gone unscathed.

So why then had she been killed?

If they killed her, she didn't die like the rest.

And she hadn't. Maude had been shot in the head. The others had undergone torturous disfigurement. Their faces had been torn off. Their blood had been saturated with radon, indicating that they had been held weeks or months underground.

As far as Gertrude could fathom, the men who had been killed, had been members of the cult. Abusers. Pedophiles. And they were probably men who Charlie and Peter feared would expose the cult, perhaps by reporting the cult's activities to a police station in another county where Peter couldn't control the investigations and bury the reports.

In fact, those that had been killed were strictly those men who had perpetrated the actual abuse. As

Roberta had hinted and Wanda had corroborated, the cult members were pedophiles who functioned *under the guise of* satanism.

Maude had been killed, but Gertrude had found no evidence that other children had been killed, which only made Maude's murder all the more puzzling.

As the days passed, Gertrude catered to Roberta's needs, but was often reminded of her dead sister whenever a strange argument unfolded. Sometimes, their arguments were so similar to the ones that Gertrude used to have with Doris that Gertrude accidentally called Roberta the wrong name.

I don't have time to debate with you, Doris, I have to get to work!

I'M NOT DORIS!

When Gertrude got to the DCYF on Monday morning, she felt horrendously knotted up with anxiety.

Outwardly, she was determined to keep her head down and act normal, but inwardly, she was being mentally assaulted by an onslaught of images that Roberta's bizarrely misplaced sexual behavior had put into her head—memories of Roberta stalking into the kitchen where Gertrude was pouring iced tea, Gertrude startling to find the girl buck-naked and creeping up behind her, Roberta coiling strangely around her little boyfriend, Quinton, who kept sneaking in through the bedroom window, Gertrude gasping at the sexual sight of them and scrambling to break them apart.

Harry barked her name as soon as she ducked into her cubicle, having poured herself a mug of coffee.

"Can it wait? I have a lot of paperwork."

"Now, Gerty."

As soon as he disappeared into his office, leaving the door wide open for her, she felt the incredible weight of the stress she was under.

Wendy peered down at her over the top of the cubicle wall they shared. Her friend's eyes looked wide and scared for Gertrude.

She whispered to Wendy, "Do you think he found out I have Roberta?"

"I'm afraid he did, Gerty."

Gertrude collected her notepad and a pen, and then padded into her boss' office, cowering every step of the way.

"Sit," he said, but quickly added, "close the door first."

She did as he had asked, after which she sat on the chair in front of his desk.

"I didn't realize that you filed to have temporary custody of Roberta King," he began.

She froze and wondered if now was the time to explain herself, or if Harry had more to say to her.

"So, Roberta is living with you?"

"She's doing very well."

"So I've learned from reading *your* reports," he said and she felt embarrassed.

"The reports are still accurate," she maintained, "even though I wrote them."

"This is unorthodox, but not unheard of," he allowed. "But that's not why I asked you in here." He grimaced at her as though he wasn't quite sure what he would do with her. "Eli Hagstaff gave me a call."

Harry studied her reaction as the information seeped into Gertrude's brain like acid.

Her smile turned to stone.

Perhaps to alleviate her worry, he told her, "Your position is not in jeopardy. But Hagstaff voiced some concerns that I would be remiss to ignore."

"I'm fit to work," she insisted. "And Roberta can't stay at the Kings. I'm a fit foster parent"

"Gerty-"

Her tone went shrill, as she asserted, "I've taken her in, and that's final."

"Your doctor explained to me that you refused some medication," he went on, setting the stage for his justification.

"I'll sue," she blurted out. "My God, he has violated doctor-patient confidentiality! He shouldn't have told you that! I'll sue his pants off!"

"If a patient proves to be a danger to herself or others, then the doctor has the legal right to break confidentiality," he pointed out, but doing so only infuriated Gertrude.

"I haven't tried to kill myself! I would never harm Roberta!"

Harry tried but failed to choose his words carefully, "Psychosis is a serious, a *very* serious diagnosis-"

"I'm not psychotic!"

"People with untreated mental health issues cannot be foster guardians, Gertrude, we have strict rules against it."

"But I don't have mental health issues-"

"Stop!"

His voice slammed through her.

"Look," he went on as she recovered from her outburst. "I'm going to take over the King case. I'm going to reassign Roberta to a competent foster family, and in the interim, Roberta will have to return to the Kings."

"That's a huge mistake-"

"Stop," he cut in, this time quietly, but with no less effect. "It was obviously too soon to expect you back at work. You're hereby temporarily suspended. I'll write it up as an extended medical leave. I highly encourage you to return to the inpatient program and continue therapy with Dr. Hagstaff."

"I've drained my savings and you know it."

"You'll find a way around it. Apply for financial aid with the hospital, I'll help you. But you aren't to set foot in this office. And you won't be overseeing the King case. No contact."

"You're playing right into his hand. This is what he wants. I'm the only one who has uncovered what's really going on over there."

"You struggle to differentiate between Roberta King and Doris," he pointed out, shocking her. "It was a very long phone call I had with Hagstaff."

"So, I'm just supposed to leave? Keep my mouth shut and return to the Brain Injury Center, what? Indefinitely?"

"I've arranged for your leave not to exceed two months-"

"Two months? That's a death sentence!"

"After which point you'll be reinstated, and I promise none of this will tarnish your work history or reputation with the DCYF. That's the best I can do."

If she had thought this would be an uphill battle, she would have kept fighting Harry.

But it was a losing battle, one that she had already lost.

"I'll be at your cabin in a half hour to collect Roberta."

"To drive her to the Kings?" She snorted, appalled that this was his answer to the horrors unfolding in the Kings' corner of the lake.

"Yes," he stated matter-of-factly.

Resigned, she rose from her chair and tried not to glare at him.

"You're-"

"Making a huge mistake?" he guessed. "What about you? What about your mistakes?"

When she got to her cubicle and began collecting her things, Wendy popped up and stared expectantly at her over the dividing wall.

Without looking at her, Gertrude asked, "You knew?"

"Harry told me five minutes before you got into the office," she explained to divert all blame. "I told him there would be detrimental repercussions."

What could she say to that? Wendy wasn't at fault. And yet the way that Wendy was looking at her with pity in her eyes made the situation inescapably worse.

In a hollow tone, Gertrude told her friend, "See you in two months," then she tore through the office with her laptop satchel in hand.

When she got outside to her parked Audi, the sweltering summer sun was beating down on her so hard, she thought she might faint. But the sun wasn't causing the feeling. She had just suffered the most humiliating moment of her entire career as a social worker and it was making her dizzy.

Roberta was wrapped around Quinton like a barnacle when Gertrude stepped through the cabin door. Nestled on the couch, the girl's long legs were coiled around the boy's waist as he lay splayed over her. Roberta made no attempt to correct the scandalous pose for Gertrude's sake, though Quinton sprang up with a healthy degree of shame.

"You're back from work already?" she asked, surprised.

"Bad news," she began. She would like to have a shred of tact, but riding the sting of having been more-or-less fired, Gertrude knew that *tact* was beyond her capabilities. "I lost temporary custody of you. You're going back to your mother's."

"What the hell?" She bolted upright then, while Quinton scrambled to grasp the magnitude of what was happening, she advanced on Gertrude with outrage. "I can't go back there. I don't want to! What the hell is going on? How did this happen?" But before Gertrude could delve into the harrowing nuts-and-bolts of her presumed psychosis, Roberta came up with her own plan. "We can say that you're my friend or something, and that I'm going to stay with you, can't we? Won't that work? Can't we get away with it?"

"I'm afraid you have to pack your things."

"You mean Doris' things," she pointed out, her snide tone slicing through what calm Gertrude had managed. "This is your fault, isn't it? You let on that you're losing your mind."

When Gertrude shook her head, Roberta lunged at her, but Quinton acted quickly.

He captured Roberta and pulled her into a tight hug, and to Gertrude's surprise, the girl didn't try to shove Quinton off. Instead, she clung to him for dear life.

"You're getting back at me!" she yelled from the shield of Quinton's embrace. "Because that douche-bag, Jake, got arrested, this is how you're getting back at me?"

"I'm not getting back at you, Roberta. This is killing me. I had nothing to do with this decision and I'll be fighting it, I promise you."

"How are you going to fight? Your brain doesn't work!"

Furious, Roberta jerked away from Quinton's grasp and stomped her way into the bedroom where the sounds of clattering followed.

It wasn't long before she returned with her belongings in a mesh laundry bag slung over her shoulder. She looked Gertrude dead in the eye and said:

"They're going to kill me. You know that, right? And when they do, it'll be your fault."

"Roberta-"

Gertrude rushed to her and took hold of Roberta's shoulders, forcing her to make eye contact, though the embrace made Roberta cringe and glance away.

Gertrude demanded, "Tell me what those men have been doing to you. Tell me everything, now. Before they come. Please. Give me something. Anything. And I'll get you out of there. We can go to the police-"

"The police! Peter *is* the police!"

"I know there's an underground... What, is it a *lair*? Where the rituals take place. I know that the cult members have killed dissenters. I believe you."

"So what?" Her gaze flattened and her eyes went dead. "You think Peter is going to fairly and objectively investigate the crime scene that he created?"

The girl's horrific point was undeniable.

There came a knock at the front door, and Roberta started off, resigned to her inescapable fate.

Watching her, every inch of Gertrude felt like it was vibrating with dread, but she trailed after and when Roberta reached the door, she touched her shoulder. Roberta turned, but didn't give her a chance to express her heartbreak.

"I'm glad she's dead."

The words sliced through her heart and Gertrude studied her face, memorizing its every angle, the sharp curves of her cheeks, the stark line of her jaw, her muddy eyes that seemed to hold a world of sorrow.

She whispered, "Why are you glad she's dead?"

"Because it means they can't get to her."

Harry knocked on the door again and when Gertrude opened it, he met her gaze with a crestfallen smile. Roberta padded out towards his Chrysler.

No words were exchanged during the long moment that Harry and Gertrude looked at one other—Harry regretful, Gertrude ill with premonitions of an inevitable murder on the horizon, neither brave or bold or cruel enough to press their argument further than it had gone in his office earlier.

When finally Harry started for his car, Roberta was already getting situated in the backseat.

Gertrude watched them drive away until the Chrysler disappeared beyond the trees.

"I can keep an eye on her."

Turning, she found Quinton standing in the foyer. His brow was knit nervously together.

"I live up the street," he added. "I won't let them kill her."

She realized that she had never spent a minute alone with him, never had him one-on-one, and never had the opportunity to probe him for what he might know about the dark family on the west side of the lake.

"She trusts you."

Nodding in agreement, he said, "There's nothing I wouldn't do for Roberta."

"Did you feel the same way about Maude?"

A breathy snort escaped his nose as he said, "Roberta couldn't stand her."

"Why not?"

His mouth twisted, perhaps second-guessing his statement. "Sometimes I read memoirs written by war veterans," he said thoughtfully. "And they say how the things they survived were nothing compared to knowing what their comrades had to go through. Like it's knowing they couldn't stop their friends' torture or death that eats them alive, even years after returning home. I think that's how Roberta felt about Maude. She knew the torture was coming. Everything she had suffered and survived would soon hit Maude, and knowing that, knowing she couldn't stop it or save her, made her hate her."

"*Hate* her?" she questioned.

"Yeah," he confirmed.

"What are you telling me?"

The boy fell silent as though she was misunderstanding him.

"I need to get going," he said.

As though it wasn't strange at all, instead of simply walking out the front door, Quinton rounded through the living room and climbed out the open window. His bicycle was out there on the lawn, and once he hopped on, he rode off around the cabin and into the woods.

When she heard a vehicle growling up her driveway, Harry came to mind. Had he returned to apologize? Or maybe haul her off into Dr. Hagstaff's care himself?

She returned to the front door and threw it open, expecting to find Harry's Chrystler.

But a familiar Dodge Ram pickup truck came to a rolling stop in her driveway.

Jake climbed out of the truck and, with a nervous glint in his eyes, he began approaching her.

She felt afraid. Was he a member of the cult, or the man she thought she had gotten to know? Maybe he was a stranger.

"They released me," he said, pointing out the obvious.

"I can see that."

"Can we talk?"

She stepped outside and closed the door behind her, drawing a clear boundary in terms of where she would permit him—outside, and not into her heart.

"I'm out on bail," he explained.

"So, the charges are sticking?"

"Unfortunately. I have a good attorney, though."

"What makes you think your lawyer will be any better than the ones that Mike Waters, Jimmy Smythe, or even Wanda Trentwell used?"

"I didn't do it," he said sharply. "Do you believe me?"

She hesitated to answer him directly, but asked, "What evidence do they have against you that proves you slept with Roberta?"

"Gerty," he said, stepping so near her that her defenses were at risk of crumbling. "I want what we started to have a chance."

"Don't do that, please."

"No, I have to. I don't want to pretend it didn't happen. You've been on my mind since I first met you and I didn't forget about you when you were in the hospital. I never stopped wondering about you and praying for you."

She told herself that he was lying, and that his talk sounded cheap, but Jake seemed more than sincere. He seemed tormented.

"I just need to know you believe me and that you're on my side."

"It boils down to *sides*?"

He looked as though the last thing in the world that he wanted to do was tell her about the evidence against him.

"It's not good," he admitted.

His cornflower-blue eyes darkened as though he couldn't believe the week he had just survived.

"Roberta came to my house," he went on. "She took her clothes off. Someone took pictures."

"I heard."

"Nothing illegal happened, and what *did* happen wasn't my doing. But the photos tell a different story. It looks like I roughed her up. Look," he exclaimed when she recoiled. "You matter to me. I don't know how else to say it. I've been framed and I need you to believe me. I need you, Gerty."

"I spoke with Wanda. Yeah, that's right. So forgive me if I feel like a lot of what you're saying sounds familiar. You did the same thing to Weird Wanda. You acted like you wanted her and needed her, and now look at her. You think I want to get institutionalized as a consequence of getting involved with you?"

"Wanda and all that shouldn't have happened."

"What *did* happen?" she challenged, and he immediately sighed in defeat, his shoulders rolling forward and his gaze falling. "You were working with Peter?" she accused. "You were in that cult?"

"No! Is that what you think?"

"That's what Wanda thinks."

"No, no, no," he muttered, plowing all ten fingers through his hair as though he were coming undone. "I've suspected that Peter, Charlie, and others were running a cult for a while now. I had a hunch that Wanda had somehow gotten involved with Peter, so I had to get close to her. Maybe it was wrong of me to start a relationship with her just to investigate Peter. And yes, she was institutionalized. That was awful," he admitted with remorse. Regaining his composure, he explained, "Peter had gotten Wanda to dispose of the bodies in exchange for drugs."

"He was blackmailing her."

"Fine. She was still guilty of doing it. The fact that she wound up at Lakes Region Mental Health and not a federal prison was a pretty good deal in my opinion."

"Why didn't you go to a police station that Peter didn't have sway with to report the bodies?"

"I was trying to get information about the cult. I was trying to break a huge story for the newspaper and win awards. I was blinded by my own ambition. I didn't want to give the glory away to some police department in another county."

"How selfish are you? Do you realize that if you had gone to the police, Maude might still be alive today? Kevin Robinson might not be missing?

Charlie and Peter King might have gone to prison by now? Roberta might be safe?"

"Yeah, I know! Do you realize how much I hate myself right now?"

She didn't know whether to feel sorry for him or slap him across the face.

"I wasn't in the cult," he insisted.

"I believe you," she said, but immediately stopped him when he looked relieved. "But you used Wanda. I'm not going to let you use me, too."

"I'm not using you. Please, Gerty, you know I'm not using you."

She searched his eyes, but said nothing, as a ray of hope took hold.

"I was set up," he insisted. "These charges are serious. We're up against something monstrous. I can't fight this if I don't have you."

"Yes, you can."

"I don't want to. God! I'm sick of chasing a story! I want to chase something meaningful for once and catch it! Like you!"

Before she could say another word, Jake kissed her.

She couldn't resist him. His kiss was her undoing.

She opened the door, and they spilled across the threshold.

Clamoring towards the bedroom, they stripped each other's clothes off as they went.

A quiet voice in the back of Gertrude's mind screamed that this was a bad idea, but she ignored it, as they fell onto her bed.

Being with him felt so good that she hoped this would never end.

In the afterglow, when Jake cradled her in his arms and Gertrude began drifting into sleep, she heard the faint buzzing sound of her cell phone vibrating on the nightstand.

"Hmm?" he groaned, as she grabbed her cell.

"Someone's calling," she said with a raspy voice.

The LCD flashed a number she didn't recognize except for its 603 area code. She swiped the screen, answering.

"This is Ed Cohen," the caller said. "I have the test results you ordered, if now is a good time."

"Yes, yes of course." Shifting up so that she was resting against the headboard prompted Jake to do the same.

He trained his attention on her and on Ed's voice that was coming through the line.

"In terms of the radon levels, there was none that I could detect in Maude King's tissues," he began, speaking clinically. "However, Doris Inman had high levels. But that's not why I'm calling." After pausing to shuffle paperwork, he continued. "I found a rash on Doris' back. I thought about retesting her blood and found a complex array of enzymes."

"Meaning what?" Jake asked.

"Well, the rash appeared to be a hemoglobin, a symptom of hemolysis-"

"Meaning what exactly?" Gertrude asked impatiently.

"Meaning, she had been bitten, several times in fact, by a venomous spider. Now, I illegally acquired both Roberta and Zhana King's medical files—don't ask me how—and they were both treated on several occasions for spider bites. They were put on a steroid treatment, as well as other medications to neutralize the toxicity."

Suddenly, Gertrude's mind was filled with memories of her dark upbringing with Doris. Spending hours in their father's doctor's office. Seeing countless other specialists to treat the rash that Doris had all over her body. Doris had gone again and again. She had received shot after shot. Had those treatments also been for spider bites?

But though Gertrude tried to convince herself that those visits to the hospital all those years ago could've been innocent, she was blinded by the glaring possibility that Doris had been down in the Kings' underground chamber.

"Spiders are everywhere, Ed," said Jake.

"There are too many correlations, Jake, they can't be ignored," he countered. "The bites, the uranium levels in Inman's lung tissue," he went on, "were staggering, as though she had been breathing toxic air during the months or days leading up to her death."

Impossible. Doris had been living with Gertrude, and yet she asked, "Could this type of venom cause hair loss? Could an infestation of spiders kill a crop of plants?"

It sounded like Ed was reading through paperwork and mumbling to himself. Then he said, "Hair loss is a symptom, yes. Regarding the crop, it would depend on the specific plant and the extent of the infestation." He waited for her response, but when it didn't come, he asked, "Are you there?"

"Yes, yes, I'm listening."

"Interestingly, I found someone's DNA on Inman that matched the DNA I found on one of the soiled pairs of underpants."

She was too afraid to ask, but Jake tipped the phone to his ear and asked for her.

"Yeah, what DNA?"

"The underpants contained Peter King's DNA, semen I found dried to the fabric that also matched samples from inside Doris Inman."

"*In* her?" asked Jake.

Gertrude sprang from the bed, abandoning the call and scrambling for her clothes.

She didn't hear that Peter's DNA had been found in her sister's vagina. She didn't undergo the same, gut-clenching shock that was now gripping Jake. She was focused on getting the hell out of there.

She would find Roberta, kidnap her if need be, anything to save the girl from suffering the same mind-splitting abuse that Doris had endured.

"Hang on, Ed? Yeah, hang on," said Jake, lowering the cell. "Where are you going?"

Though she pulled her shirt over her head, she could still hear Ed's voice coming tinny and faint through the receiver:

"There was urine as well. Hello?"

"Harry all but fired me," she told him. "He returned Roberta to the house. I can't leave her there. I don't care about the consequences."

"Would you wait a minute?" Scrambling, he told Ed, "Will you be in the office? I can head over." Then to Gertrude, he pleaded, "I say we both head over to Ed's."

"You go," she said, calling out over her shoulder as she tore up the hallway. "I'll meet you there once I have Roberta!"

Moulton Street was bathed in haunting shadows—black trees and faded asphalt so buckled that the road seemed ashamed—as Gertrude angled her Audi onto the shoulder where she had parked a million times before.

Not one light was on in the Kings' house, but the darkness hardly settled her nerves.

Memories tangling with pitch-black fears clawed through her mind so distractingly that she couldn't think straight.

Why would Doris have had Peter King's DNA on her and *in* her *right after* Gertrude and Doris had confronted their parents that night?

Had it been a confrontation? Or had something much darker transpired with Marsha and Albert Inman that night?

Pushing the horrifying notion from her mind, she sprang from her car and stalked up the driveway, feeling terrified and yet bizarrely murderous.

She was prepared to do *anything* to get Roberta out of that house.

When she reached the front porch, she noticed that the plants, flowering bushes, and vegetation in the planters looked healthy.

As she touched a leaf, she heard voices through the forest.

She listened out and realized that the voices weren't coming from the field far behind the house, but rather people were talking up the road.

When she turned towards the sound, she saw faint amber lights glowing beyond the trees.

Was that a shed?

Padding quietly, snapping twigs and crunching pinecones underfoot, the sounds of which threatened to give her away, she came upon a weathered shed that belonged to one of the neighbors.

The shed wasn't too far from a modest Colonial house where a family was having dinner inside, the lights along the second floor illuminated a well-manicured lawn.

Gertrude returned her attention to the shed.

She recognized the voices she heard.

Inside the shed, Roberta and Quinton were arguing.

"You have to do what they say!" said Roberta, sounding scared out of her wits. "They'll kill me if you don't do what they tell you to do, Quinton! I only have to do it again this one time! Then I can leave!"

The boy's response sounded equally tormented:

"That's what they said to Doris!"

CHAPTER TWENTY-TWO

EAVESDROPPING, Gertrude neared the door and pressed her ear against its peeling paint, but Roberta and Quinton had hushed, speaking in clipped whispers. One of them shifted their weight, and the floorboards creaked underfoot, which told Gertrude that they sensed she was out here.

No sooner than Gertrude tiptoed away from the door, Roberta threw the shed door open and their eyes locked.

Roberta looked far from startled. Gertrude couldn't read her poker face. But Quinton was already cowering. Bathed in shadows, the boy looked like he would crack easily if she pressed him.

"'That's what they said to Doris'?" she questioned, quoting him. "What did they say to my sister?"

Roberta's tone came out so steady it didn't sound human. "Quinton doesn't know what he's talking about."

"How do you know Doris?" she demanded.

"We know her from school like I told you before when you asked."

"No. You're lying." Barreling inside, she cornered Quinton in the poorly lit shed. "The cult didn't kill Doris! My sister died in a car accident."

Trembling, he shuffled backwards until he knocked into a table, jostling tools that clattered to the wooden floor.

"He's not going to talk if he's scared," Roberta warned her, as if Quinton was a dog she had trained.

"One of you is going to tell me what's going on!" Gertrude barked as she shifted her gaze between the teenagers.

When neither responded, she stated:

"Doris was with me when I crashed my car into that lake on July 2nd. We had just heard a gunshot that I now know was the shot that killed Maude. Someone stepped in front of my car that night and if I hadn't swerved to miss the person, my sister would be alive right now. Do either of you know who that person is? Was it intentional?"

"I don't know anything about your car accident," said Roberta, folding her arms.

"But *you* do," said Gerttrude, locking her sights on the boy.

Again she advanced on Quinton. His mouse-face pinched into a grimace that to Gertrude looked an awful lot like guilt.

"Tell me what you know."

Swallowing hard and mustering his voice, he said, "Spiders."

"Quinton, don't," said Roberta in a cutting tone.

"They're rock spiders," he said as though that would clear it up.

Glibly, Roberta stated, "I already told her that."

Had she? Gertrude had no recollection, but even if she had, the term *rock spiders* meant nothing to her.

Roberta raised her eyebrows and said, "The men."

"If this is your way of speaking in code, I don't appreciate it. What does this have to do with my sister?"

"We were friends with Doris," said Quinton, but Roberta immediately cut him off. Regardless, he kept going, abandoning the reference to rock spiders in favor of offering some semblance of logic. "Before Doris moved in with you, she used to come here to hang out. Sometimes she would just sit and stare like she wasn't even in her body anymore, like she was in some far away place. When she moved in with you, we knew they would find a way to get to her and they did."

Sharply, Roberta said, "Gertrude doesn't remember any of that, Quinton."

"Then help me remember-"

"No." Roberta angled her feline eyes up at her and a glimmer of compassion shined through. "I won't. You're lucky you don't remember. It means it worked."

"What worked?"

She didn't answer, but Wanda Trentwell's theory about the nature of satanic ritual abuse sprang to mind—*if it's traumatic enough, the child won't remember.*

Had the cult abused *Gertrude*, too?

Was that why Gertrude couldn't remember anything?

She pushed the dark thought from her mind and demanded, "Why did they have to kill Maude?"

No response.

"Where's the gun that killed her?"

Quinton was trembling and looking at the floor. When he spoke, his voice was a thread. "You can't be here."

"He's right," said Roberta in a resigned tone. "You should go home."

"I came here for you. To get you," she said, remembering why she had risked driving to the Kings in the first place and jogging through the woods to find the girl. "There's evidence of the abuse now. It's with Grafton County. It's not safe here. You have to come with me."

"I can't go with you," she said. Her tone sounded unemotional, but her expression looked pained.

"Why not?"

Roberta exchanged a heavy glance with Quinton and a silent conversation ensued.

"Why not?" she demanded, repeating herself.

"I don't know how they did it," she began in a hollow voice, "but they got to your sister, because she left. I can't go."

She was making excuses and Gertrude got the sense that in the hour that had elapsed after Roberta had left her cabin, Peter had threatened her somehow.

Without thinking, she grabbed the girl by the arms and thrusted her towards the door.

Roberta grimaced, digging her heels in, and she tried to wriggle free. But Gertrude clutched the girl tightly and begged Roberta to come with her, yelling with intensity that matched the desperation she had felt trying and failing to save her sister's life.

All the while, Quinton stood alarmed, and watched them tangle.

Roberta twined her spindly fingers around Gertrude's hair and pulled hard. Then she shoved her off to free herself, which worked.

Gertrude stumbled backwards and slammed into the door at a bad angle that caused her head to smack against wood, as her ankle twisted.

"Why won't you let me help you?" she cried, her thoughts scrambling under the weight of memories that were interlaced with nightmarish imaginings so disturbing that it felt like her brain was tearing apart.

Mortified, Gertrude didn't wait for an answer.

She fled, running through the woods with no recollection of having thrown the shed door open, no memory of Roberta's anguished statements that she hadn't heard but were now echoing through her mind—*I'm sorry! You're a good person! I can't be saved!*

Driving home was a blur that seemed to happen without her, her hands clamping the wheel in a white-knuckle grip, her eyes scanning the road, the woods, and the darkness beyond the shock of headlights that bounced off the rising fog that billowed over the windshield of her car.

It means it worked.

What worked?

Fragments of their argument swirled through her mind, but were anchored to nothing. She had asked *what had worked*, hadn't she? What had Roberta said? Nothing. It wasn't there. But it had been, hadn't it? She sensed it had, but some protective aspect of her psyche had already buried the pieces deep down.

She had hoped to find Jake's truck in front of her cabin, but there were only tread marks left in the dirt. He had gone somewhere, but tracing through the events of the night she couldn't place it, as she angled her Audi towards her cabin and killed the engine.

When she crossed the deck and reached her front door, it wasn't locked. Instantly, she recalled that she had left Jake here. She had stormed off to get Roberta, leaving him here in the wake of their impulsive lovemaking.

The phone call.

She suddenly remembered it, as she eased the door open and stepped soundlessly into the dark living room. Ed Cohen had called from Grafton County to deliver harrowing details that connected both Roberta and Doris to the cult—rock spiders.

What did the term mean?

Countless times her father had taken Doris and her to the hospital, because their skin had bubbled up in a rash.

The rash had been from spider bites, hadn't it?

Fears of Doris and Gertrude going into anaphylactic shock had been Albert's main concern, as well as their mother's.

The last thing we need is a couple of dead kids on our hands, Albert!

You think I don't know that, Marsha?

Their parents' so-called concern had never been genuine, but rather self-serving.

This fact floated to the forefront of Gertrude's mind then vanished when she saw a body on her living room floor.

Her heart jutted up her throat at the sight and she scanned the walls, the bookshelf, the floor for satanic paraphernalia, but there was none.

As she neared the body, she realized the dead man was lying on his side and facing the couch, away from her. His arm was sprawled out, his legs twisted.

Terror crushed Gertrude's windpipe like a tightening fist, blocking the air from her lungs.

She knew exactly who it was—Kevin Robinson.

Using her foot, she rolled him onto his back and gasped when she saw what had happened to his face.

It had been torn off.

"No," she whispered, backing away, as the room began spinning all around her. Shadows cloyed at her. Her vision blurred with dizzying surrealism, as an onslaught of dark conclusions crashed over her—they needed a scapegoat, Jake had destroyed Wanda, the homeless woman had let him into her life, Roberta refused to come back, it was happening all over again, and Gertrude had to get out.

Strategies of rushing to Grafton County formed in the forefront of her mind, but as soon as she turned for the door, Peter King stepped inside her cabin and she screamed.

"Got a call about screams coming from this cabin," he said with a grin on his face.

Suddenly, police lights began flashing through the windows, brightening the living room with a chaotic mix of red and blue, as tires crunched over gravel outside.

"This doesn't look good for you, Gertrude," he sneered when he saw the dead body.

Pressing her mouth into a sickened line, she glared at him, as two officers passed through the front door, making slow work of assessing the scene.

Peter took strong, confident strides towards her, eager to share his clever police work.

"I've kept my eye on you, you know. Your little visit to Wanda Trentwell at the institution gave me a hunch."

He shot one of the officers a sly glance and the man, whose wiry posture and sharp-toothed grin made him look like a gargoyle, chuckled menacingly.

"Made me wonder if we caught the right woman last year. Maybe we didn't. Maybe you killed all those men." He eyed what was left of Robinson and frowned, then his attention locked on Gertrude. "I'm rarely wrong in my hunches."

"Like you would release Wanda from the institution," she said.

"Oh no, we can't release her. She is being cared for where she is, and it's not my place to disrupt that," he said easily, his tone dripping with conceit, which turned sharp when he said, "step away from the body."

She backed away as instructed and the officers motioned for her to come forward, while Peter stalked over to the body and squatted, taking careful note of Robinson's skinned face.

When the officers took hold of her upper arms and began cuffing her hands behind her back, she yelled at them to let her go.

The officers then yanked her out the door, as Gertrude tried and failed to jerk free.

"You won't get away with this! Grafton County has evidence against you!" she yelled. "Against all of you! It won't matter your reach, Peter! It won't matter who you've threatened into keeping your secrets!"

The cops tossed her into the back of their police cruiser and slammed the door.

"Robinson was one of you," she went on, shouting at the back of the officers' heads, as they drove, heading down Opechee Street. "Kevin Robinson was a police officer, and his only mistake was that he correctly reported the murder of a little girl! For that, Peter killed him! He'll do the same to both of you!" she insisted, astounded that they could ignore her so easily. "You know I'm innocent!"

She wasn't even close to the brink of running out of steam, but when they turned off Opechee, pulling along Moulton and the forest grew thick all around them, Gertrude knew they weren't taking her to the precinct.

Suddenly, she felt like she couldn't breathe.

Again, the officer behind the wheel angled the cruiser around another turn, but she didn't recognize where they were, and as the vehicle bounded over rough terrain, she understood that the driver had gone off-road.

She demanded, "Where are you taking me?" but was met with heavy silence that landed like a fist to her chest.

Pressing her nose to the window, she watched as the trees thinned out.

Up ahead was a field.

In the distance, where the tall grass cleared, torchlight faintly illuminated the scene.

Then the chanting began. Low and guttural, it emanated through the vast expanse, punctuated only by the sounds of a beating drum.

"You can't do this," she said in a small voice, as they pulled her out of the backseat, having parked to the wayside.

Dragging her through the tall grass, the officers didn't acknowledge her and weren't challenged when she tried to fight to free herself, kicking and jerking and yelling.

As they neared the cult—men dressed in black cloaks, their faces masked in hoods, all but their mouths concealed—the satanic circle parted and the officers threw her in the center of the chanting cult members.

Gertrude stumbled and fell. Her palms struck against matted grass, her chest slamming against the earth and her head bouncing hard against a metal plate on the ground that she hadn't realized was there.

But before she could connect that the metal plate was the trap door that she had seen Zhana lift earlier, Gertrude's world suddenly went black.

CHAPTER TWENTY-THREE

REGAINING CONSCIOUSNESS was a slow climb. Several times during each attempt to ascend, she thought she had opened her eyes, reached consciousness, and understood where she was—hooded men, mouths with shadowed faces surrounding her, torchlight lapping them from behind, casting them in dark silhouettes, as they closed in on her, chanting and beginning the ritual, the air thickly scented with soil like the underground walls were breathing.

But soon the nightmarish scene disappeared, as she fell into darkness again; rising and falling, two steps forward, one step back.

The side of her head was throbbing and it sent a painful slice behind her eyes with every pulse.

She must have hit her head on the metal plate, she thought, opening her eyes. The impact had to have been inches above the arching scar around her left ear.

Gradually her vision focused. She smelled the rich soil all around her, but the room wasn't full of men. She couldn't see anyone, but sensed that she wasn't alone, as she watched the flame of a single torch burning bright, crackling and illuminating the room just as it had been in her nightmarish dreams moments ago.

She was on the ground, lying on her side, her shoulder crooked against the hard earth, her head pitted against soil, the back of her hands resting on dirt.

Her hands.

They were in front of her, not cuffed behind her back as they had been in the police cruiser.

Pushing up, she muscled her way into a seated position, but the effort sent her brain pounding hard against her skull. That's when she smelled it—rancid, rotting flesh, and the sharp tang of iron.

She looked around, gaze darting from one corner of the room to the next, terrified to confirm she had been dumped here alone with a dead body. Kevin Robinson's? Had they moved him? Or was it Charlie, the man who no one could seem to find?

But there wasn't a body.

She sensed movement behind her then heard the distinct thud of a boot striking dirt and startled, turning and skittering back like a crab, as she met eyes with Peter King.

"You hit your head pretty bad," he commented as if reading a bedtime story. "Do you know why I brought you down here?"

She was afraid to imagine, so she stopped herself, and that feat was enough to prevent her from answering.

"You've got all these ideas in your head about what we are and what we do and you're so close, aren't you? At least that's what you think, that you've almost got it nailed down."

"You killed Charlie, didn't you? You left him down here. That's what I'm smelling, isn't it?"

She felt the earthen wall at her back and pressing against it, made her way to her feet, though doing so sent her head reeling. To steady herself, she dug her fingers into the packed soil of the wall, forcing the air in and out of her lungs, though it was so rank it nauseated her.

"What are you smelling?" he prodded.

"Death."

"How would you know what death smells like?" he countered as if anticipating her response piqued his interest.

She was quick to point out, "You exhumed and left my dead dog in my living room," but her tone—wobbly and thin—didn't deliver the blow she had intended. "Robinson's dead body had a definite smell to him as well."

Her conviction broke when she felt the spindly tickle of something skittering over the back of her hand, which made her squeal, flicking her wrist to get it off. The second she had, she realized she had been bitten. Her hand was stinging and when she rubbed it to work the prick away, she felt a lump forming on her skin.

"You'll want to keep away from the walls," he said. "The place is crawling with spiders."

Horrified, she stepped away from the wall, staring at it over her shoulder with wide eyes. She saw a spider tucked in a crack. And the longer she scanned the wall, the more she spotted spiders skirting from one crack to the next. The back of her hand was growing numb and when she looked at it she noticed a rash forming.

Advancing on her so fast it caused a surge of adrenaline to shoot through her veins, Peter reached around her, leaning around and pinching a spider off the wall.

When he eased back he was too close for comfort, examining the twitching arachnid with such intrigue that he didn't object or even look up as she took cautious side steps away from him.

She kept her eyes on him, studying how Peter handled the thin, brown spider, and it occurred to her that he was admiring it.

"They have a bad reputation, you know," he said, offhandedly. "Rock spiders. Have you heard the expression?"

Only once, she thought, and it hadn't made any sense.

"Like these creatures, the term migrated here, adapted to the environment. Prison jargon," he went on, ruminating explanations that seemed to have little context. "It's what they call child molesters. You know..." He trailed off, smiling at her in a way that made the hairs on the back of her neck stand up, "because they're always getting into small cracks."

"I would like to go now."

"Go? No, Gertrude, this is simply a detour on our route to the station. You've been arrested. Nothing's changed, except that I'm hoping you'll remember a thing or two. They say the smell of a place can bring memories back. Is it?"

What kind of sick game was this?

And why was he winning? The very notion that she might be able to remember the past by simply being down here was mind-bending and soon she couldn't think straight.

"How's your hand?"

When she glanced down, at the eerie power of his suggestion, having compelled her to do so as though she were an impressionable child, she discovered the rash was spreading down her fingers and up her forearm.

"Most people are allergic," he mentioned with fascination. "But there's a shot that can clear it up within a few hours."

A shot?

Suddenly, her many visits to the doctor growing up, Doris feverish and lying in bed, the incredible guilt that had plagued her having left her sister behind with those monsters, bubbled up from her subconscious bringing with it more details—firearms going off in the house, gunshots resonating through the forest where no one was around to hear them, her father raging, waving his weapon, dragging Doris out the back door, her mother cooing as though Doris was merely in the throes of a childish tantrum, Gertrude holding her head as she cowered in a hunch between the couch and the wall, praying this would be over, but knowing if it had happened a thousand times, it would continue a thousand times more.

Peter flicked the spider to the ground then brushed his hand against his slacks, angling his dark eyes on her and stirring up the blackest dread in her gut, as she slowly backed around, circling away from him, terror heightening, panic ratcheting up her spine, though she was certain not to make any sudden movements.

Pivoting as he watched her, he explained, "The rash is the most mild symptom. Makes a person ill. An infestation can kill a crop of plants. Some people lose their hair. It starts falling out in chunks. It's because their saliva is poisonous. But I've never had a problem."

The image of Zhana's hair was a starburst in her mind's-eye, but the woman's plastic grin morphed into her mother's face—Marsha combing her brown hair, clumps of it pulling out with the comb's teeth, her mother grimacing, horrified to find another bald patch. Marsha would wrap her hair in a silken handkerchief and pour herself another drink, immune to Doris' tormented cries that sounded muffled through the wall.

"But you had a problem, didn't you Gertrude? And your sister did too. She was sick a lot, wasn't she?"

She whispered, "No."

"Yes, she was."

"Stop it," she said, her voice light as air.

"It'll never stop, Gertrude. It never has. Not after you moved. Not after you went back for Doris. Not after you drove back to your parents' house like a damned fool. You can't stop this and you can't escape it, not unless you choose between prison and death."

"No," but the word came as faint exhaling. "You killed Maude," she said in a desperate attempt to anchor herself before the memories pulled her under. "We have enough evidence. You'll be locked up. You'll be a rock spider behind bars. The inmates will tear you apart."

"You know, I've always felt bad for you, Gertrude. You know why?"

She was shaking her head, her vision having gone soft. She was slipping away.

"Because," he said, leaning in close. She could smell his sour breath invading her face, "you were the most willing. You thought you could save the others by volunteering yourself. Roberta's the same way. But Doris never was. You're glad she's dead, aren't you? It gives you relief, doesn't it? Because you know she can't get hurt anymore where she is. Because you know you don't have to keep being a martyr."

She tried to deny it, to scream *no*, but nothing came out except tears that stung her eyes and dampened her cheeks.

"Let go, Gertrude," he instructed with such a soothing tone she found herself trusting him. "Shatter. And you won't have to go to prison. You can join Wanda and make art all day in a drugged, peaceful haze. It can all be over."

She was slipping away.

And then she was gone.

Just like that.

Floating deep beneath the surface of reality, the night and the confrontation and the car accident came rushing back.

She remembered all that she had forgotten.

Every. Last. Detail.

She had found Doris in the bathroom. It had been early evening and the stark, orange sun was slicing sideways through the window, setting Doris in fiery light where she sat on the tiles, one arm draped over the edge of the tub, her other hand red with blood.

It had taken too long for Gertrude to process the injury, the razor blade on the floor, and the streaks of blood beading up along the fresh cuts on her sister's thigh. Doris wore nothing but underpants and an old sports bra. Her forehead was dewy with sweat. Pearls of it rolled down her cheek.

She had seen a face peering in from the window. Cat eyes and hollow cheeks and dirty blond hair, comprising a teenaged girl she didn't know, but did—*Roberta*—somehow, somewhere deep in her mind déjà vu had been erupting. She had chosen to forget, hadn't she?

"What have you done to yourself?" she had asked, dropping to her knees beside her sister, clamoring across the tiles to the cabinet beneath the sink, riffling through in a panic, grabbing rubbing alcohol and cotton balls and a first aid kit that was dusty, its supplies nearly depleted.

"I had to," Doris had said, her voice raw and raspy, Gertrude craving a hard drink just hearing her. "We never talk about it."

"Talk about what?" she had demanded, impatiently.

"About them."

Gertrude had saturated a wad of cotton balls with alcohol and managed to dab them over Doris' cuts and though the girl winced, sucking air through her teeth in rapid gasps, the sting seemed to calm her strangely.

"That feels good," she had said.

It had chilled her.

"They're going to come back for me."

Quickly silencing her, Gertrude had said, "No, they aren't."

"Roberta said they were coming. We have to get to Mom and Dad. We have to threaten them. We have to make them believe we'll go to the police and get them locked up. If we put pressure on them, they'll get the cult to back off, you know they will. You know they're scared, too."

"They're not scared," she had said, dismissing the notion, because it would be giving Marsha and Albert far too much credit. "And they're not coming here."

Doris had locked eyes with her, studying her sister's lashes rimmed in black liner and her intense gaze. Doris had been pleading a silent case in favor of both their lives, and Gertrude, under the force of those eyes, had agreed.

"We'll go tonight," she had said. "After we get you cleaned up."

They had practiced in the living room. They had recited variations on what they might say to their parents, crafting the threats they would make, revising the wording and phrasing. They had sparred to test their speeches, taking turns playing devil's advocate, role playing so that they would be well prepared for their parents' responses, which could range from volatile to denial to attempted murder. Doris had proposed they record the confrontation on her cell phone *just in case.*

Doris and she had driven around the lake, tension rising between them, terror weaving through Gertrude's chest like a spider's web.

After arriving and they entered inside the house, pleasantries had elapsed briefly, while Marsha had attempted to plow the girls with alcohol. Gertrude had accepted to calm her shaking hands, but its effects weren't felt, not with Doris' eyes, moonlit from where she sat in front of the window, glaring at her.

Their parents hadn't denied it.

But though they had admitted all they had done and Doris' cell phone, hidden deep within her purse, was recording every word, Albert had a dark request.

It had been a bargain—one that Gertrude had begged her sister not to make. But Doris had gone with him anyway, trekking out across the field, while Gertrude waited, cringing from her mother's slippery assurances—*You girls turned out just fine.*

As jarringly as the memory had sucked her in, Gertrude sprang out of it, returning to the earthen underground room, her vision clearing, eyes focusing on Peter and his sickening smirk.

How could she have forgotten all that? How could she have buried it as easily as Roberta covering shirts and underpants in the dirt outside her house?

And what she and Doris had done afterwards was unfathomable.

She had driven Doris to a bar like they had weathered nothing stormier than a typical holiday at home, like they were normal kids from a normal family with normal issues deserving of a stiff drink or two?

Peter assessed her state then told her how they would proceed.

"I'm not going to cuff you. You're going to come willingly. We'll get you checked into Lakes Region Mental Health. You're going to sign all the forms." He paused expectantly as though he needed confirmation and when she didn't give it, he clarified. "Prison or death, Gertrude. I'm giving you a chance at a nicer prison. They have arts and crafts at the institution, for God's sake."

Peter shifted his weight in such a way that the gun holstered at his hip reflected torchlight into Gertrude's eyes like a premonition.

With an air of authority, he waved her over to a ladder, which was angled up at a metal plate on the ceiling.

As soon as she stepped forward, he turned his back to ascend the ladder and it was then, without any thought, just her wild determination, that she lunged for his gun, clawing it out of the holster, gritting her teeth through the pain of his blows, his fists punching awkwardly at her neck, the side of her head, and her shoulder.

She wrestled the weapon free, overcoming her aversion to the gun or the memories it stirred up, though such revelations threatened to cripple her.

She had it in her grasp, cold metal, slick with the faintest oil, but Peter was smothering her like a bear.

She screamed, fighting and jabbing and kicking as hard as she could, and in her struggle, she realized that this was the beginning of the end of her life.

CHAPTER TWENTY-FOUR

QUINTON SAT NERVOUSLY on the edge of Roberta's bed, as Zhana walked her fingertips along a desk, strolling lazily and offering him sly glances. Whether she was taking stock of her daughter's bedroom or him, he couldn't decide, but she was giving him the impression that she had more than a few ideas of how they might spend their unexpected time alone.

It made his stomach twist with knots.

He jolted when he heard a faint *POW* coming from the field and his thoughts of Roberta narrowed into a razor's edge.

Zhana didn't appear to have heard the gunshot. She was going on about her mother and how she had been a wonderful woman, as she pivoted, facing him. She leaned back, resting on the desk.

"Why does Roberta hate me so much?" she asked innocently as if she were a victim, as if she had suffered great hardships and didn't deserve her daughter's nasty attitude, as if Quinton might care, sympathize, and give her what she wanted, the same thing she had taken from him the night of Maude's funeral.

But he wasn't paying attention. His eyes were glued to the dark field beyond the window. His shoulders were shaking. Had the shot killed Roberta? Why had it been so faint, muffled as if underground? Who else was out there?

Mysteries shrouded in a nightscape too dark to see into was the story of the field.

"I won her back, you know. That woman is unfit. A child needs her mother no matter what, that's the cold, hard, truth, Quinton. No matter what."

"Hmm," was all he could manage to say, acknowledging her and hoping she would slip into the next monologue without waiting for his input.

And she did, this time about a baby, some toddler named Bennie, who Quinton had no interest in, grisly fantasies of what might be happening to Roberta at this very moment attacking his foremost thoughts.

He knew he should be with her now. Every cell in his body was screaming for her to come back, vibrating with panic because they had been separated, and quaking from intuition—tonight was the beginning of the end.

Roberta had been stripped of all hope the second Gertrude had left. She had hardened and he thought he caught her dying inside when the odd social worker's footfall had disappeared beyond the shed. They had listened to her car drive off in the distance, and the incredible silence that followed sent Roberta into a fit of despair.

He shouldn't have told Gertrude that he had known Doris; that they both had. He shouldn't have implied their lives had been woven so tightly it was impossible to distinguish where Doris ended and Roberta began. But it was also impossible to please Roberta. One minute she was desperate for a new life, punching him into helping Gertrude and preventing Jake's downfall. And the next, she was bullying him into going along with the cult, frantic it would be the only way to save her life.

He couldn't win.

He had known about Kevin Robinson, the set up. He had watched Gertrude through the cabin window. He had given the word when Jake had left quickly after Gertrude.

They had expected Quinton to be in two places at once, and when he had finally made it to Roberta at their usual rendezvous point, the shed, and saw her tearing it apart, furious at what they wanted her to do next, he knew he had been too late.

And though Gertrude had shown up moments later, she had been too late as well.

He had kept at her heels as she started for the road, Roberta turning and shoving him off, Quinton begging her not to go—*I have to be there*, and his plea *You were right, she can help*, and her abrupt reply, *She can't, don't you get that, she's gone now, it's over*, and his warning, *They'll kill you*, and hers, *If I'm not there by the time Peter takes her to the institution, then yes, they'll kill me.*

Quinton had stopped in his tracks, though she had been walking away, and with conviction he had stated, "I have what she needs to help us." But Roberta didn't turn. She didn't pause or miss a step.

That's why he had come here.

He needed to get it. But his timing had been terrible and as soon as he scurried across the front yard, nearing the planters, keeping low to the ground as he skirted along the row of newly planted bushes, Zhana had spied him through the window, stepped through the screen door, and made a performance out of crossing the porch and discovering him.

"You know, I've always wanted a son. But Bennie was unruly. Not at all like you." She eased onto the bed, sitting so close that the weight of her caused Quinton to lean, which he corrected, angling away from her and feeling awkward that he wanted to inch away, but couldn't. "Why do all my children do that?"

"Hmm?"

"Kill themselves, Quinton. Where are you?"

Startled by her bluntness, he stammered nonsense.

"Roberta is fine," she said, patting his leg then giving him a slight squeeze. "Roberta is how she is and you can't stop her."

The statement, her ignorance, had him gaping. But rather than challenge her as to why Roberta would go along with any of this—she was perpetually terrified and lived in a constant frenzy to stay alive—he asked, "Who else besides Maude killed themselves?"

A motherly smile spread across her face. "Bennie, who I've been telling you about. I used to model. Did you know that?" She didn't wait for a response, but launched into a woeful tale. "I had a promising career. I had only just started. I had barely scratched the surface when Bennie came along."

Her smile suddenly went slack and the stark contrast gave him chills.

"The baby ruined everything for me. He took something from me that wasn't his to take. My body. My life. And he was ungrateful. I could see it in his eyes. Roberta has the same look in her eyes, the look of resentment, even though I didn't ruin her life. We were on vacation, Charlie, Bennie, and me."

She paused only to touch the silken handkerchief around her head, smoothing her palm over it, feeling for bald patches along her scalp that might have become exposed.

"Why we had to bring a three-year-old on our vacation I'll never understand, but we went to the beach and Bennie wouldn't stop throwing sand at the seagulls. I was reaching the limit with him, I'll admit. And Charlie had wandered off to do God knows what. He left me alone with the baby. Charlie knew what I would do."

Again, she fell silent and Quinton's heart began punching through his chest, longing to escape, dying to run through the woods, through the field, find Roberta, and discover her alive.

"Bennie knew how I felt about him and he must have known I was angry. I don't know why he listened to me when I told him to go on out in the water. He shouldn't have listened to me."

Her gaze softened as though she was drifting away, no longer seated beside him in Roberta's bedroom where the suggestive grins of band members leered at him from fading posters, their corners curling off the wall, but back on that beach, back on vacation all those years ago in a life before Roberta.

"He went out in the water, Quinton, splashing and glancing back at me. The smile on his face was a grimace. He looked evil. And then he was snatched. The undertow got him."

Gradually, her vision focused as she returned to her senses. She locked eyes with him and asked, not rhetorically, but as if she genuinely needed an answer, "What's wrong with my children that they do that sort of thing?"

In a voice that sounded as small as he felt, he murmured, "I don't know."

He needed to get out of there, get to the plants, remember where he put it, get it to Jake despite the detriment that would shatter life as he knew it, but Zhana was angling in on him, leaning near, her gaze softening, a prelude to another dark exchange.

"Things will be different," she whispered, "now that Charlie's out of the picture."

Voice hitching up in his throat, he croaked, "He is?"

In his ear, she breathed the words, "He's dead," then studied his reaction—his widening eyes and a mouth that wouldn't close, though he kept his head down, staring at his Converse sneakers, the only safe place to look.

"You're surprised? Of course he's dead. Everyone thinks he killed Maude and Peter wouldn't allow this family to get a bad reputation." Then from out of nowhere, she bolted upright, launching to her feet and exclaiming, "Roberta!"

Quinton hadn't heard her come home, pad up the stairs, or tear through the hallway, until the bathroom door slammed shut.

Zhana was rushing after her, Quinton at her heels. She pleaded through the door, "You're all right, aren't you? Please don't shut me out! We never talk, Roberta and I know, I just know in my bones you would be fine if only you would let me help you."

Pulling her away from the door and surprising himself because of it, Quinton said, "It's me. Can you let me in?"

But Zhana peeled him off, taking his place at the door. "I've been thinking, Roberta. I've been thinking we should go on a little vacation, just you and me, to the beach maybe. Would you like that?"

Horrified, he struggled to overcome the implication—did Zhana think she could get Roberta to drown in the ocean like Bennie?—but managed to tell Zhana, "I can get her out," the intensity of his eyes adding, *If you leave.*

After a long moment sizing him up, her emerald green gaze slicing him down his center, she lifted her angular brows like a warning and eased back.

"I'll be downstairs."

"Why don't you go into your room?" he said.

The suggestion was far too bold and her expression turned questioning, but after a carefully measured breath, she agreed, pacing off up the hall and rounding into her bedroom.

Quinton rapped his knuckles softly on the door.

"It's just me. Can I come in?"

It was quiet on the other side of the door, too quiet.

"Please, Roberta, I love you."

It had slipped out and there was no way to catch the words that had escaped him.

To mask his mistake, he quickly added, "I know where it is." He wasn't whispering so he corrected his tone before explaining, "The gun, Roberta; the gun that killed Maude. I know where it is."

The door popped open, startling him, Roberta on the other side, the red dress hanging off the curves of her body.

"You what?"

"I know where it is."

"And you didn't tell me?" She demanded. "I've been looking for it. I've been digging in the dirt like a Goddamn dog all month looking for it and you've known?"

He mouthed, "Come with me," insisting they speak in whispers or not at all, as he took hold of her hand, leading her out of the bathroom and up the hallway, rounding the landing and descending the stairs with quick steps, crossing the porch and hooking around into the planters where a plague of spiders had once devoured the vegetation.

Before he endeavored to locate it, he grabbed her shoulders like he had never before dared and stared up at her, terror like a firestorm in his eyes.

"You can't go on vacation with her. She'll kill you."

But Roberta's eyes flattened and her arms went stiff in his grasp.

"How do you know where the gun is?"

Deflecting, he said, "Did you hear the gunshot earlier tonight? I thought it was you. I thought they shot you."

Cocking her head as if he had her thrown, she asked, "Gunshot? I didn't hear any shots."

"Coming from the field."

"Where they took Gertrude?" she asked, alarmed.

He could feel her trembling in his grasp, but she shoved him off then fell to her knees, her shoulders rounding in a hunch of despair.

Kneeling beside her and forcing her to look at him, he was about to offer any semblance of hope that he could, but she was already crying out, "She was one of us. I thought she could do it, Quinton. I thought she could help."

"Let me help. I can help." Reassurances kept tumbling out of him, but weren't reaching her, until finally he scrambled to the spot and started digging. "It's here. I buried it here," he explained. "It has his prints on it. It was Peter's gun. It's all we need, Roberta. We can end this."

"You buried it?" She was standing over him, enraptured by the location, staring at him, at it, mind-boggled that she had never come across it in all her attempts. "How did you get it in the first place?"

Turning the weapon over in his palm, his fingers flexed back so he wouldn't get his own fingerprints on it, he faced her.

But she only shook her head, backing away.

"We have no one," she said. "There's no one we can go to with the gun. It's all over."

"Don't give up."

"Why didn't you bring this to me sooner when we had a chance?"

He glanced down at the weapon in his hands, desperate to formulate a response that wouldn't drive her away, but none came.

"I couldn't," he said finally and then noticed a rash developing down the side of her neck, down her left arm, and across her chest on the same side. "What happened to you?"

"I found him," she said in a dead tone and when Quinton furrowed his brow questioningly, she added, "My dad. His body."

Overhead a cloud crept across the moon and her face fell into shadow then brightened as it passed, but though the faintest glow once again bathed her, the glint of life in her eyes had gone out.

"He was covered in them. Spiders. They leapt on me. I couldn't swat them off fast enough." After falling silent, focusing purely on ridding the memory, she said, "I don't know what that gun will mean, but my dad's body is evidence enough to get Peter locked up for a very long time."

"Where was he?"

Quickly countering, she asked, "How did you get the gun, Quinton?"

He swallowed hard. He had never been a good liar.

"I saw them."

"Who killed Maude?"

"Look, I can tell you everything, but not until we get out of here. Let's take the gun to..." he stammered through their resources, of which they had virtually no one. "Who will help us?"

"Who killed Maude?" she repeated.

But Gertrude stole their attention.

Gertrude was stalking towards them, carrying herself with exhausted steps.

Her eyes, black and hollow, looked as dead as Roberta's. Her beret was no longer on her head, making the bristles of her sheared hair all too apparent. The longer side swayed with her staggering gait, and when Quinton looked down the length of her, he saw that she was covered in blood.

She looked like death walking.

He didn't want Gertrude to see the gun in his hand.

He tucked the gun down the back of his pants, shuffled behind the plants, and hoped like hell that the end drawing near wouldn't be his own.

CHAPTER TWENTY-FIVE

ROBERTA WAS BACK to wearing that dress. In the low light, covered in shadows but for the moon outlining her silhouette, only her eyes popped through the darkness as she stared at Gertrude.

Quinton stood nearby, but he wasn't Gertrude's concern.

The girl was a stranger and yet so completely familiar, an eerie clone of her sister, maybe a clone of herself, that Gertrude couldn't fathom what to do next.

The sheer sight of her, that red dress, the memories that twisted and tangled because of it, had Gertrude bogged in confusion.

"You warned Doris and me," she said, staring at the girl, whose eyes narrowed as if to indicate they were in danger.

Shifting her gaze in a quick flash to Quinton then back to Gertrude, Roberta seemed to stiffen. Her hands balled into fists.

Gertrude had to push her point through. She needed to know that she wasn't crazy.

"You were outside the bathroom window the night Doris died. The night she cut herself. You told Doris they were coming. But they weren't."

In a panicked whisper, Quinton said, "Zhana is right inside the house. We have to get out of here."

"Get out of here and go where?" Gertrude snapped, angling her eyes on the boy until he shrank. "To my cabin? To another body so I can be arrested again?"

Advancing on Roberta, Gertrude pressed her point:

"Doris was scared. You terrified her. She convinced me to drive that night. We went to our parents' house. We would've never gone there if it hadn't been for you."

"And then what happened?" Roberta coaxed as if the girl needed Gertrude to remember.

"You tell me," she begged.

Again, Quinton tried to get them to leave. He started blathering and yanking Roberta's arm, but she shoved him off and he fell to the bushes.

Gertrude reached for Peter's gun, which she had tucked down the back of her jeans, but didn't draw the weapon or threaten Quinton.

Her hand was ballooning with spider bites. Her fingers felt numb, but even if they weren't, there would be no point in threatening a child with a weapon.

"You're glad Doris and I went to my parents' house that night?"

Roberta's sharp eyes softened.

"You were there that night, weren't you?"

She said nothing.

"Albert took Doris out to the field, and I stayed in the house with my mother. They were gone for hours. You know what happened to her that night, don't you?"

Her voice was trembling and almost too faint to hear, as she said, "Maude."

Insistently, Quinton rushed at her again, pitting himself between them and saying, "None of this matters. We have to get out of here, don't you understand?"

Before Gertrude could shut him up, Roberta grabbed Quinton and tossed him into the plants in one scrambling, ugly movement.

After landing badly, he rubbed his elbow and tucked his knees to his chin like a wounded animal.

"That night, the cult said that Maude was old enough," Roberta said. "They made us..." She trailed off then clarified, "They made *Doris and me* take Maude out into the field. But it didn't go as planned. I didn't want to hurt her. But Doris... the hatred in her eyes... She didn't care about Maude. She had no sympathy. I begged Doris that we should run off into the woods. The men hadn't seen us. They were chanting in their circle around the trap door. They were so far off in the distance. We could have run away. We could've escaped to Jake's house or Quinton's parents' place. There were so many options."

Her dark eyes misted over with tears and she had to bite her lower lip to stop from sobbing.

"But Doris wouldn't. I could see it in her eyes. She had turned all her pain into rage. She thought Maude would replace her. That sacrificing my sister would free her."

From the bushes, Quinton got to his feet and peered through the living room window as if he expected trouble to peer back at him from inside the house.

"I hated Doris for it," she went on. "I tried to fight her. Maude was confused and I kept yelling at her to run, but she wouldn't. I could sense they would hear us. I could feel them glance over their shoulders at us. I knew they would come for us. They would take matters into their own hands so I punched Doris in the leg, right where she liked to cut herself. The pain incapacitated her, and she doubled over, falling into the grass, and I grabbed Maude and ran like hell."

"Please," said Quinton urgently, but both Gertrude and Roberta were deaf to him.

"I brought Maude to the shed, to our safe place, and told her to wait for Quinton, because I knew they would come after me. I couldn't wait with her. I went back and the rest of the night was routine except that my dad told me I was dead for not bringing Maude." She quieted then turned to Quinton and demanded, "Where were you that night?"

"She wasn't there," he insisted. "I told you that. I told you when I got to the shed, Maude wasn't there." Quick to assert his point now that he had their attention, he begged, "We have to leave now."

But Gertrude barked, "No, Quinton."

As cutting as her tone was, it only infuriated him.

In the blink of an eye, he whipped his hands forward and the movement was so fast that it took Gertrude a moment to mentally process the fact that he had drawn a gun on her.

Her reflexes took hold, and she drew her weapon as well and there was a standoff.

They both held steady, breathing hard and silently daring the other to shoot.

Roberta froze on the sidelines.

Tears streamed down Quinton's face and his hands began shaking, rattling the gun.

"Maude was in that shed," guessed Gertrude, piecing the sequence of events together. "Everyone was out in the field. They never went back to the house that night, did they? After the ritual, after Doris returned and she and I went to a bar, the Kings searched for Maude in the field and in the woods. But you brought her into the house, didn't you, Quinton?"

"I didn't mean for anything to happen," he said, crying.

Roberta's face went slack, staring at him.

"But something *did* happen," Gertrude pressed. "You killed her."

"She wouldn't stay quiet," he said, pleading, desperate to be understood. "I just wanted her to keep quiet."

"No," said Gertrude, reading the anger that was building behind his eyes. "No, it wasn't an accident. You were with Roberta before she left for the field that night. You had never seen her in a panic like the one she was in because Maude had never before been in danger."

Finally, the dam broke and a torrential flood tumbled out of him.

"It would've killed you," he said to Roberta. "You knew you couldn't stop it. Even if you saved her that night, there would always be another night, another chance for them to take her. So I shot her. I brought her back to the house and held her down in her bedroom and killed her. Charlie should've been arrested. Zhana should've been arrested. It should have all been over."

Roberta lunged at him, but he stiffened his grip, aiming the gun at her with precision, his eyes darkening with such determination that Gertrude feared he might actually pull the trigger.

"I love you," he said. "I did it because I love you. But then I couldn't find you. I biked as fast as I could, heading towards Gertrude's cabin that night, thinking that you might be there with Doris, hoping I could catch you and explain and show you how killing Maude was for the best. Then I saw her car," he said, flicking his eyes at Gertrude. "I thought you were in the car with Gertrude and Doris. I biked down the hill to get to you, Roberta!" His voice went shrill, wailing, but he calmed himself enough to go on. "But I hit a rock and wiped out just as the car was driving over the bridge. I ran the rest of the way and darted out into the road, in front of the car and it swerved."

A storm cloud rolled through Roberta's eyes and she turned wild.

She lunged at Quinton again, swinging her fists and clobbering him to the ground, screaming and tussling, as Quinton shrieked between blows.

As Roberta tangled around him, delivering one blow to his head then the next, Quinton kept trying to aim his gun at the girl.

Gertrude pointed her own gun at Quinton and yelled, "Stop!"

But he wouldn't.

Suddenly, the porch light popped on and Zhana stepped out and gasped at the sight of Gertrude poised with a gun clutched between her hands.

Instinctively, Gertrude aimed her gun at Zhana, and the second she did, the woman's face began distorting and transforming into Marsha's.

Gertrude shook her head, but she couldn't see straight. She felt like her mind was being scrambled with insane hallucinations that she couldn't escape or control.

Zhana was eerily calm. "They're coming," she said coolly, her gaze locked on Gertrude so fiercely that Gertrude felt her heart shudder. "You should've gone to the institution. You won't be offered an opportunity like that again."

That's when she heard them—the cult.

Chanting behind the house grew louder and stronger.

Torchlight brightened the grass.

Gertrude's blood ran cold—*the cult was here!*

Zhana's mouth twisted into the shape of a smile, but then without warning, someone fired their weapon at Zhana over and over again.

Zhana bucked and jutted as bullets pelted through her, her blouse turning red with blood

Stunned, Gertrude felt suddenly beyond her body. She didn't know if she had shot Zhana or if someone else had.

She couldn't feel her fingers, which were numb and betraying her, spider venom spreading across her skin.

But when Zhana collapsed to the porch and the cult began swarming around the house, Gertrude saw a thin stream of smoke wafting into the night air.

It was coming from Quinton's gun, which he kept aimed at Zhana even though she was dead.

The cult closed in on Gertrude, Roberta, and Quinton who didn't have any bullets left to ward off the cloaked men.

Gertrude did, but she was paralyzed, an old reaction to the cult whenever those men put their hands on her.

She couldn't think straight. She could barely process that they were capturing Roberta and wrestling Quinton to the ground.

The cult began dragging all three of them towards the field where a sea of men chanted in torchlight—stark as the flames of hell.

Gertrude fought, twisting and writhing in their grip, jumping and digging her heels into the soft earth, screaming and hissing.

Her mind split open, fragmenting into a million splinters, each slice an image reflecting horrors she had survived long ago.

But just as the men were about to toss her down into the earthen chamber all over again, bullets started zinging every which way and the chanting men began dropping dead.

The cult was being attacked.

The next thing Gertrude knew, she was on the ground, her cheek to the grass. She was frantic to assess whether or not she had been hit, though she didn't move a muscle to find out.

Then strong hands wrapped around her arms. Someone hoisted her up to her feet and began rushing her through the field.

Confused, she managed only to get a sense of what was happening. She saw a helmet, a man's profile, his bulletproof vest, military boots punching the earth in quick strides.

Turning her head, she saw Roberta being rushed off in the same manner and behind her was Quinton being escorted by another member of the SWAT Team.

When they reached the front of the house, flashing ambulance lights momentarily blinded Gertrude, and she sensed more than saw a team of medics rolling Zhana's dead body on a gurney towards the back of the vehicle, while others ran to Roberta and the boy, wasting no time to investigate their injuries, as they helped the kids into the back of a second ambulance.

"Gerty!"

In the chaos, she whipped around and found Jake jogging towards her, his blue eyes catching the light, his expression conveying a world of relief and also anguish for not making it there sooner.

"God," she said. Her voice was a mere breathe, as he wrapped his arms around her, needing to feel her against him in order to believe that she was alive. "They killed Kevin Robinson."

"I know," he said, urging her back so he could study her face. He searched her eyes. "We found Charlie. He's dead. We'll capture Peter. We don't have enough to pin Maude's death on the cult, but we have enough to get King locked up."

"I know who killed Maude," she said, stepping back.

"Peter?"

"No."

The SWAT Team was stationed at the tree line in the front yard and Gertrude's attention was stolen when she heard one of their men assert, "Peter King is dead!" The man pressed his fingers to his earpiece and listened to more information. "Shot in the chest. They're pulling him out of the hole now."

"My God," said Jake, returning his gaze to her. "If Peter hadn't killed Maude, then who did?"

"Quinton Avery, Roberta's friend. He has the gun—the murder weapon."

Gradually, Jake began nodding to show her that he understood, and then pulled her in for another hug.

"Thank God, you're alright," he whispered, kissing the top of her head.

But was she?

After all she had just learned, would she ever be alright?

EPILOGUE

GERTRUDE SAT IN her Audi, surrounded by index cards, their motivational advice calling to her—*Always do your best, what you plant now, you'll harvest later,* and *Life is 10% what happens to you and 90% how you react to it,* and *You've come this far, don't give up!*

She stared at the house she grew up in.

Blue and stately, the two-story Colonial house set against a backdrop of Lake Winnipesaukee, wrapped in a white picket fence, and bathed in the late-summer sun didn't at all convey the dark history that had unfolded all those years ago within its walls.

Climbing out of her car was an exercise in overcoming every instinct she had to run. But she couldn't turn back. For Gertrude this wasn't over.

It was a very long walk to the front door and when she reached it, lifting her knuckles to its white surface and willing herself to be brave, she accepted the fact that nothing could have prepared her for this moment, not the week she had spent meeting with Dr. Hagstaff, not the hours she had given to the Grafton County Police, and not the long nights she had shared with Jake going over every last shred of evidence to help the District Attorney build an airtight case against all individuals involved in the conspiracy.

A cult hiding in plain sight was a hell of a beast to take down. And though the authorities had incarcerated nearly every member, there were two left who had eluded the police.

Marsha and Albert Inman.

And Gertrude would be damned if she let them get away with it.

With conviction, she pounded on the door, but the second she stepped back to wait, her hands began trembling and she lost sense of the ground beneath her feet.

She startled when the door popped inward, revealing her mother's elegant face, which was so like Zhana's that it made her reel—vibrant eyes rimmed black with precision, a taut mouth stretched thin into a brittle smile, an overall manicured presentation though her head was wrapped in a silken handkerchief, hiding thinning hair.

"Gertrude," she said in a carefully measured tone that revealed the slightest hint of apprehension. "What brings you here unannounced?"

"I have to talk to you. Is Dad home?"

"He's tinkering in his study. Model trains," she said with a casual eye roll as though her husband was as whimsical as Santa Clause and not the monster Gertrude had come to realize. "Come in, please."

Clutching her purse, Gertrude glanced over her shoulder, one last look at safety before she stepped inside.

Marsha closed the door and though the living room was bathed in daylight, to Gertrude the house looked dark and threatening.

"You're looking well," she said, indicating she could have a seat on the couch while she rounded into the kitchen where a long-stem martini glass sat waiting for her to return. After plucking it off the counter she circled back, perched on the edge of a lounge chair across from her daughter, who she began studying, her gaze traveling the short side of Gertrude's hair then down at her attire—a loose blouse and black jeans, Keds ill-matched with navy blue socks, an eclectic outfit her mother seemed to disapprove of. "We're told your memory hasn't been restored, but Albert and I feel it's a blessing."

"Hmm," she said, trying not to tune out, fighting the urge to slip into the dissociative state she used to live in during her years home alone with Marsha, with Doris struggling for life upstairs, with Albert raging in the background. To anchor herself, she buried her hand in her purse and gripped Doris' cell phone, reminding herself this would all be over soon. "Yes, my memory," she echoed. "I was in the hospital for a very long time."

"Oh where are my manners?" she asked, springing to her feet.

"I don't need a drink, Mom," she said impatiently, but it didn't stop her mother from proceeding into the kitchen and busying herself with cocktails as a means of avoiding wherever this conversation was leading.

Then, in a tone like ice, she said, "Shame about Zhana King," and the way Marsha kept her steely eyes on Gertrude made it clear that the comment was in fact a warning.

Finding her voice, she said, "It would've been nice if you visited me," even though it was a lie. Though she had felt that way while struggling to regain her faculties during her long four weeks at the Brain Rehabilitation Center, ultimately she was glad they had abandoned her. "It might have jarred my memory if you came."

"Again, Gertrude, I think it best you take it as a blessing. You're back at work now. You're managing. There's no need to dredge up the past."

"But we both know that's exactly what I've done, don't we, Mother?"

To punctuate the implication, she set Doris' cell phone on the coffee table and watched Marsha's reaction to it, though the woman had none, other than to sip her martini in a manner that was so like Zhana's that Gertrude felt momentarily dislocated from reality.

She snapped back when Albert Inman stalked in from up the hallway. His gaze, dark and beady, locked onto her like a heat-seeking missile the instant he stepped into the room, and the veneer over his hardening expression told her he was holding himself back from ripping her apart, as he said, "I didn't realize you were planning on dropping by."

"Albert, dear, don't be testy," Marsha ordered then quickly reminded him their daughter was still recovering. "She still doesn't remember a thing," she stated as though it would prevent him from boiling over. "Have a drink."

Judging by his posture—the broad shoulders framing a barrel chest, his thick arms and legs—Albert was built for combat more so than treating children in his private pediatric practice. But it was the glint in his eye, the flat-darkness she couldn't escape, that called to mind Peter King and all that went down underground.

She had killed him.

As Marsha returned to her perch on the edge of the lounge chair, and Albert settled into an adjacent one, Gertrude forced the ugly memory from her mind—Peter tangling around her, Gertrude squeezing the trigger, the gun jamming, her panicking, him laughing as he spun her around, spiders fleeing every which way, Peter glaring at her as he choked her without realizing she was lifting the weapon, pulling the trigger, the gun barrel to his chest, *POW*.

Focusing on her father, she crawled out of the memory just as she had that night from the ground, and lifted Doris' cell phone off the coffee table.

"I remember that night," she said. "I remember everything you said. You didn't deny the abuse. Doris recorded it on this phone. Every word."

Albert's expression went slack and he turned white, while Marsha launched into nervous laughter.

Gertrude knew she could kill them. She wouldn't need a weapon. After everything she had been through, she could probably rip their throats out with her teeth. But they were already dead—Peter in the bottom of a hellhole that he helped create, Zhana sprawled across a porch.

She cued the cell to play and as it did, she set it on the coffee table and watched her parents' web of secrets unravel.

"Turn it off!" said Marsha in a shrill tone as though she couldn't stand hearing the sound of her own voice smugly offering up an indignant confession. "What does this matter?" Desperately, she turned to her husband. "Tell her this doesn't matter. The cult is finished! It's over with! There's no sense in crucifying us!"

Albert lunged out of his chair and Gertrude knew what would come next, but in the same breath, she was on her feet, yelling at him.

"The Grafton Police have that recording! I'm here because I wanted to see your faces. I will never forget those looks," she yelled, pointing to each of them and memorizing every detail of their long, stunned expressions. "I will never forget your shock at the fact I exposed you."

She started for the door then turned on her heel.

"Doris might have died in that car accident, but you killed her. And for that, you'll pay."

As she spilled down the walkway, vaguely aware of the police cruisers pulling into the driveway, sirens blaring and officers jumping out, eager to arrest the Inmans, Gertrude focused on her breathing then trained her attention on steadying her hands from shaking.

By the time she parked in front of the DCYF and angled her beret onto her head, the brief moments spent at her parents' house felt like a distant dream, haunting but completely unreal.

Wendy met her in the entryway and wasted no time holding blazer after blazer up to Gertrude's chin, eyeballing which option would work best, while up the hall a photographer explained his vision to Harry McNeil as if there would be anything artistic about capturing Gertrude's image for her award.

As Wendy talked her through the pros and cons of each look, beaming with a wide and excited smile, Gertrude drifted into the mind-bending facts that had been unearthed in the weeks leading up to this moment.

Two decades-worth of children who had been reported missing throughout the Tri-State area had been found buried in the field behind the Kings' house. The cult had stretched far and wide, and had used children like Roberta, like Doris, and like Gertrude to execute their dark operation without killing them. Ed Cohen's work linked countless members to the grisly goings-on in that dark neck of the woods, and Jake had written an award-winning article exposing the cult on a national level.

As heartbreaking as it was, Quinton had been arrested for the murder of Maude King and sent to the Sununu Juvenile Detention center where he was sentenced to stay until his eighteenth birthday at which point a review board would determine whether he would be released or transferred into the state penitentiary.

Harry hurried Gertrude over to the photographer, as Wendy trailed behind, blazers swinging from hangers that she carried, in rhythm to her proud strides.

Maneuvering her into the bright lights, the photographer asked her to smile on his count and reminded her to *look alive*. The photo would forever live on the wall amongst achievement placards and the various awards in social services the DCYF had accumulated throughout the years.

Alive, she was.

SMILE!

And she did. It was radiant and victorious and most of all real.

CLICK.

When she turned from the photographer, who thanked her while Wendy bragged to the other social workers how she had always known that Gertrude was something special—*My best friend, the hero!*—Gertrude spotted Roberta lingering just beyond the glass door, as Jake strode up to the girl.

Approaching the door, Gertrude waved them in.

"Don't be shy. The photo took two seconds," she explained, brushing over her accomplishment as they stepped inside.

"I'm hungry," said Roberta, who had put on a few pounds in Gertrude's care, but could use a few more. "And I want to help build my room."

Jake shot Gertrude a sly grin. "Which means she wants more clothes."

"Of course, I need more clothes," she argued with dark affection, ever laced with a flirtatious air. "I need work clothes, and clothes for school, and clothes I can get messy. What?"

"Ha, ha," said Jake, handing Roberta his keys. "Get in the truck and we'll see." When she padded off through the parking lot, he asked, "You sure you can handle her?"

She was, more than anything, she was sure.

THE END

ALSO BY MIRA GIBSON

Thomas from the Sea

Who Killed Leeanne?

The Kensington Killers: The Complete Series
Lunatic (The Kensington Killers, Book One)
Crank (The Kensington Killers, Book Two)
Maniac (The Kensington Killers, Book Three)

The New Hampshire Mysteries: The Complete Series
Daddy Soda (A New Hampshire Mystery, Book One)
Rock Spider (A New Hampshire Mystery, Book Two)
Tar Heart (A New Hampshire Mystery, Book Three)

ABOUT THE AUTHOR

I write mystery novels, detective novels, sleuth mysteries, and psychological literary fiction! You can find me most days working on my computer in the sunshine of beautiful Long Beach, NY where I dream up small town characters and write dark mysteries that are filled with unsuspecting tenderness.

Find me on Facebook! **/MiraGibsonAuthor**

Visit MysteryRoyalty.com to learn more.

www.ingramcontent.com/pod-product-compliance
Lightning Source LLC
Chambersburg PA
CBHW021445240626
47153CB00001B/303